IN
THE
RED

IN
THE
RED

Mark Tavener

HUTCHINSON
London Sydney Auckland Johannesburg

This edition first published in 1990 by Hutchinson

Century Hutchinson Ltd, Brookmount House,
20 Vauxhall Bridge Road, London SW1V 2SA

Century Hutchinson Australia (Pty) Ltd
20 Alfred Street, Milsons Point
Sydney NSW 2061, Australia

Century Hutchinson New Zealand Limited
PO Box 40–086, Glenfield, Auckland 10, New Zealand

Century Hutchinson South Africa (Pty) Ltd
PO Box 337, Bergvlei, 2012 South Africa

British Library Cataloguing in Publication Data

Tavener, Mark
In the red.
I. Title
823'.914 [F]

ISBN 0–09–174356–7

Set in Baskerville by 🅰 Tek Art Ltd. Croydon, Surrey
Printed and bound in Great Britain by
Guernsey Press Co Ltd, Guernsey, Channel Islands

IN
THE
RED

PROLOGUE

25 May 1986

Dear Mr James
            ACCOUNT NO: 08661862
I thought you would wish to know that, according to our records, your current account is overdrawn £657.

Yours sincerely

M J Carson
(*Manager*)

8 June 1986

Dear Mr James
            ACCOUNT NO: 08661862
I am writing to inform you that the overdraft on your current account is £993. There is no arrangement for this and I shall be grateful if you will let me know what steps you propose to take to rectify the position.

Yours sincerely

M J Carson
(*Manager*)

20 June 1986

Dear Mr James

ACCOUNT NO: 08661862

I have today passed cheques, presented under the protection of your cheque card, which bring your overdraft to £1064. In spite of my previous letters, you have not made the necessary budgetary adjustments and I must ask you to contact me at your earliest convenience. In the meantime, no further cheques should be presented.

Yours sincerely

M J Carson
(*Manager*)

---

25 June 1986

Dear Mr James

ACCOUNT NO: 08661862

In spite of my previous letters, which you have not answered, you have continued to write cheques under the protection of your cheque card. Your overdraft now stands at £2445 and I must therefore demand the return of your cheque card, as I am no longer able to extend this facility. Your cheque card should be returned to me, immediately, cut in two for security purposes.

Yours sincerely

M J Carson
(*Manager*)

27 June 1986

Dear Mr James
                    ACCOUNT NO: 08661862
I am writing to inform you that any further use of your
cheque card will constitute an offence under the 1968
Fraud Act and will be treated accordingly.

                    Yours sincerely

                    M J Carson
                    (*Manager*)

---

28 June 1986 (a.m.)

Dear Mr James
                    ACCOUNT NO: 08661862
I am writing to inform you that any further use of your
cheque book will constitute an offence under the 1968
Fraud Act and will be treated accordingly.

                    Yours sincerely

                    M J Carson
                    (*Manager*)

28 June 1986 (p.m.)

Dear Mr James
ACCOUNT NO: 08661862
We are no longer prepared to act as your bankers.

Yours sincerely

M J Carson
(*Manager*)

---

30 June 1986

Dear Mr James
ACCOUNT NO: 08661862
I am writing on behalf of the bank's legal department to advise you that you must contact this office immediately to make arrangements to repay the outstanding balance on the above account, which has been closed. Failure to do so will leave the bank no option but to make an application for bankruptcy.

Yours sincerely

H C Shoebury
(*Assistant Head, Legal Department*)

Mr Andrew James of Mysore Road, Battersea, London SW11, placed the collection of letters from his bank manager on the fire. He had been intending to publish them as an appendix to his memoirs. But as the rental company removing his television set collided with the debt collectors from the credit card company, he had a better idea. He looked out of the window of his humiliatingly stripped bedsitter and muttered softly, 'There's only one answer for people like you, my friend.'

CHAPTER
1

George Cragge was a worried man. Partly, he was worried about money. Partly he was worried about his job. But mostly he was worried because he had just thrown up over his dentist. George had made one of life's cardinal errors; he had arrived at the dentist's torture chamber with a raging hangover.

No one enjoys visiting the dentist but normally George managed to treat the ordeal the way he treated everything, as a joke. He would seat himself in the huge black chair, make a grab for the dentist's groin and declare playfully, 'Now we're not going to hurt each other, are we?'

Not today. Today, he sat thinking of that dreadful crunching sound that accompanies the extraction.

'Oh, shit!'

He thought of being told afterwards to have 'a nice big gargle,' with that appalling pink stuff. *Pink stuff*? On top of eight pints of Guinness, six double whiskies and an ill-digested vindaloo? In consequence, George had somewhat overreacted to the instruction, 'Open wide.'

First his mouth had opened wide. Then his stomach had opened wide. Shortly thereafter, the door had opened wide and George had found himself looking for a new dentist.

In the usual course of things, this wouldn't have mattered much. It would have been 'just old George being old George'. At this stage of his career, however, George could not afford news of such escapades to reach his employers, with whom he was in trouble enough already. George was an experiment, a prototype. He was the first full-time crime correspondent BBC Radio had ever taken on to its staff, and after its experience of him he might well turn out to be the last. He was a damn good journalist; he was very bright, despite his lack of formal education; he had a journalist's nose and not just because it was red and bulbous and stood out even on his ruddy features. He would talk happily to anyone and everyone. If a crime were committed at the Palace, George would winkle facts out of all the interested parties, from Her Majesty to the lowest footman. He knew all the country's top policemen and most of its top criminals.

But George was out of sympathy with the times. That, in his view, was the real reason he was, that afternoon, to face a disciplinary interview. He was, in his own words, a hairy-arsed old pro in a profession rapidly being taken over by grey and boring young men and even greyer and more boring young women, straight from the universities. Young people who had not cut their teeth – reporting garden parties, weddings and balls as George put it – on the smaller provincial papers. They, he told himself with righteous indignation, had never 'got their macs wet'. Admittedly, his own was at that moment bone-dry on a peg in The George just round the corner from the BBC, but then if a large Scotch or two were not justified by a traumatic visit to the dentist, when were they?

Suitably refreshed, he returned to the newsroom on the third floor of Broadcasting House. As usual the nerve centre of Radio News (and of the universe, according to its inmates) looked a tip. Where there were not empty coffee cups, there were full ashtrays. Where there were not full ashtrays, there was paper. Oodles of the stuff. This was the agency tape which was the raw material of BBC Radio News. White bits from the Press Association, green bits from Reuters, the basic facts waiting to be turned into crisp radio prose by the sub-editors.

There were three long desks in the newsroom. One, the General News Service Desk, served the broad function of exchanging information with the other BBC newsrooms at the Television Centre, at Bush House and in the local stations. At another, the Summaries Desk, were prepared the shorter news broadcasts, particularly those for Radios 1 and 2. George approached the third desk, Bulletins, which was responsible for the longer transmissions on Radio 4. The next bulletin was at one o'clock and it was now only 11.20, so that the sub-editors were in states ranging from comatose to clinically dead, a sight which aroused George's further contempt. They didn't know they were born, some of these young sub-editors. As far as George was concerned, he was always working, even when he was in the pub. He would tell them so at the interview that afternoon.

At the end of the Bulletins Desk was a rubber plant looking decidedly sorry for itself. It had looked that way since the day George had returned from lunch, resolved that it needed watering, and proceeded to water it in a fashion that testified more to the nature of his lunch than to his grasp of horticulture. Beside this unfortunate specimen was the Assistant Editor, the man in charge. Because he was past fifty and had not been to university, George was prepared to regard him as 'not a bad journalist on his day' and to treat him with the respect due to his position.

'Hello, you red-faced old dosser.'

'Morning, George.'

'Anything for me?'

'Well, yes.' The Ass Ed picked up a piece of paper marked Press Association.

'There's been another one,' he said informatively.

'Another what?'

'You know that bank manager who was murdered in Battersea? Carstairs, or Carson or something. Well, another one's copped his lot.'

George looked at the agency tape.

'Well, well, well,' he mused. 'Sounds like we've got a nutter on our hands. OK, I'll look into it.'

He ambled round to his office to prepare his piece for the One, a two-minute report for the one o'clock news. A minute later he was on the phone.

'I'm afraid we have nothing to add to our official statement,' said the Scotland Yard Press Office.

'Don't give me that,' George told him.

Press officers were even worse than sub-editors in George's view. They were the lowest form of journalistic masturbator.

'Who, after all,' he asked himself disgustedly as he put the phone down, 'would become a press officer if he could be a proper journalist?' POs would talk about nose and instinct and about good copy, and then devote their professional lives to saying 'No comment.' George turned wearily back to the PA report. It contained few details, however. A Mr Addison, manager of a small branch of Barclays in Tooting, had been found dead that morning in his office, buried under a mountain of one-pound coins. Nothing about his personal life, no suggestion of likely suspects.

In desperation George rang Scotland Yard again, but this time asked for the Commissioner's office. The Commissioner, unlike the Press Officer, greeted him warmly.

'George, how nice to hear from you again.'

'And you.' George came straight to the point. 'Why are you lot being so reticent about these bank manager murders?'

'On the record or off?' The Commissioner was not the Commissioner for nothing.

'Off for the time being – if there's a reason for it.'

'All right.' The Commissioner knew he could trust George. 'The fact is, old boy, we think we've got a maniac on our hands. The latest murder is exactly like the one in Battersea. Whoever did them leaves notes.'

'Saying what?'

'Well, listen.' The Commissioner rustled through his papers. 'He left this on the body in Battersea: "Dear Bank Manager, I am writing to inform you that, according to my records, it is high time you had your account closed. Malthus lives – which is more than can

4

be said for you." And this is the one we found this morning: "Dear Bank Manager, I am writing to inform you that I am foreclosing on you. It gives me great pleasure to welcome you to the Bank of St Peter."'

'Bugger me,' said George.

'Exactly. And we don't want that getting out because . . .'

'Because it'll spark off a load of imitations and you won't know where you are,' George finished for him. It was standard practice, when you were dealing with a headbanger, not to release the details.

'All right,' he told the Commissioner, 'I'll keep that to myself. Thanks for your help.'

It was frustrating because it meant there was precious little George could say on the one o'clock news, but at least he now knew the reasons behind the official silence. He made his way to the studio, sentences and, indeed, whole paragraphs writing themselves in his head as he went. The knack on these occasions was to appear to be saying a great deal when actually you were saying nothing.

It was only 12.15 when he reached the studio, but there seemed little point in hanging around.

'We might as well record this,' he said to the s-m, the studio manager, responsible for pushing the buttons, twiddling the knobs, winding the tapes and, most importantly, making sure George sounded sober. At this hour of the morning that was not a problem and they got a satisfactory recording first time:

'Mr Addison was the second London bank manager to be found murdered in the last month. He was discovered by his secretary at ten o'clock this morning submerged in one-pound coins. The causes of death were multiple fractures of the skull. Officers in charge of the case say they have no clue as to motive although there are some similarities between this and a previous murder which took place in Battersea. They haven't given further details. All the major banks are reviewing their security, and bank managers are advised to be on their guard.'

5

'It doesn't say much,' grumbled the Assistant Editor as he listened to the tape.

'That's because there isn't much to say,' George replied. He was not about to reveal confidential information to the desk.

'Oh, all right. I suppose we'll have to make it the lead story.'

'Of course it's the lead story.'

George headed for the bar, a good, albeit slightly frustrating morning's work done. A man with a disciplinary interview to face must be well prepared.

Mr Andrew James, of Mysore Road, Battersea, London SW11, took the Northern Line from Tooting to Embankment feeling well pleased with himself. He, too, thought he had earned a drink.

CHAPTER
2

'You know Reform Government Works.' Well, you don't actually – not unless you can remember 1903. That is the last time Reform Government was given the chance to work before the party was consigned to a much deserved and apparently permanent electoral oblivion. But that was what the yellowing and tattered sign said. It hung on a door, on the first floor of a dingy and dubious house in Berwick Street in the heart of Soho, where the Reform Party now had its headquarters. On the ground floor an up-and-coming – or so they said – rock band practised their distinctive contribution to contemporary culture. They called themselves Razzmatazz ('I'm Razz, he's Tazz and this is Ma') and their rehearsals generally consisted of attempts to drown their words with their music, a course which any independent critic of their illiterate lyrics would have felt bound to approve.

On the top floor there was, if you believed the postcard over the doorbell, a model. If you didn't and climbed the stairs, you would find a sign on the door declaring 'Madam Sin Invites Lonely and Submissive Males to Climb the Walls of Ecstasy'.

The Reform Party was sandwiched between these two, rather appropriately in view of its political position which was all too often exactly midway between those of the two major parties. Once upon a time, there had been several hundred Reform MPs. Today there were ten, claiming to exercise a moderating influence on the affairs of the nation, the manifest fact that they exercised no influence at all being understandably inadmissible to those concerned.

That morning, Party HQ was blessed with a visit from

the Leader. If you had asked Geoffrey Crichton-Potter, MP, precisely why he was Geoffrey Crichton-Potter, MP, he would have given you no very satisfactory answer. He might perhaps have pointed to the fact that the Crichton-Potters had been Reformers for generations. He might have told you of the long tradition of public service in fine old families such as his own. He might even, at least after a couple of bottles of the Chateau Margaux on which he virtually lived, have admitted that the total absence of anything resembling a brain cell had something to do with it. The simple truth was that he had become Geoffrey Crichton-Potter, MP, by accident, his constituents having taken both pity on him and complete leave of their senses.

A man so patently unemployable anywhere outside Westminster has various ways of masking his intellectual deficiencies once he gets there. Crichton-Potter resorted to the practice, common nowadays amongst politicians, of using a speechwriter. His was called Henry, and Crichton-Potter made a point of never saying anything that Henry hadn't written for him; of reading out precisely what Henry did write for him and of altering not a comma.

The recruitment of Henry had been just as much of an accident as Crichton-Potter's election. There was no doubt that Henry was clever. Unfortunately he was the kind of swot who was totally unable to open a sardine tin. Indeed, when challenged to do so by a resentful father who had hoped to breed a Wimbledon champion and had bred Henry instead, he had repaired to a supermarket, inadvertently purchased a tin of boot polish and then been unable to open that anyway.

Yes, there was no doubt that Henry was clever. He looked clever, which is after all, half the battle. Well actually, he looked a complete mess. He was short and thin, with a head several sizes too big for his shoulders and spectacles several sizes too big for his nose. His black curly hair resisted every attempt to comb it; the correct way to tie a tie would be a mystery to him for ever, and his early attempts at ironing his shirts had been so calamitous that he had now desisted from the practice entirely. No one in his right mind would have recruited Henry, which is probably why he applied to the Reform Party. Even there he might not have been successful, had not the several pints of Dutch courage he had consumed before his interview begun, in the middle of it, to refresh those parts which all beers are bound to reach sooner or later. The desire to relieve himself imposed more and more on his consciousness. Consequently, when invited to comment on the fact that the party's support had dwindled to a trickle, Henry declared that it was liable to become a bloody great stream at any moment. He declared it with such conviction that he was engaged on the spot, his new employers marvelling at his enthusiasm for the Reform Party's cause.

Henry was, in short, a shambles. He was hopeless in every area, save one: he could write extremely good speeches. Thus was born what was, in Reform Party terms, one of the great partnerships, Henry the brain and Crichton-Potter the mouth.

Even Crichton-Potter's mouth, however, was having some difficulty that morning. Upstairs, the sounds of swishing noises and the howls of torment suggested that some poor unfortunate was finding the walls of ecstasy hard going. Downstairs, Razzmatazz were rehearsing their next single, whose lyrics were, roughly, these:

> I never promised you happiness,
> I never held out hope,
> What made you think I'd give up the drink?
> And even lay off the dope?

'I said dope!' Razz would add for good measure. 'I'm talkin' 'bout dope!' Tazz would contribute, lest anyone took him to be talking about the Hegelian dialectic.

In the midst of this cacophony, a high-level political discussion was in progress.

'Wot?'

'I said bank managers.'

'I can't hear a bloody word you're saying!'

'I said we might make something out of this bank manager thing!'

'What bank manager thing?' Crichton-Potter never read the papers – after all, what did they pay Henry for?

A brief lull in the appalling din enabled Henry to make his point.

'Look,' he explained, 'two London bank managers have been murdered in the past month. The police think the crimes were connected. I reckon it could be an important political phenomenon.'

'Oh God, could it?'

Important political phenomena were not Crichton-Potter's strong point.

'Well, look, how does this grab you?' Henry read out a portion of the speech he hoped to persuade his leader to make:

'"Those bank managers were murdered not as individuals but as unwitting agents of the Government's monetarist policies. It was not their fault; they were the hapless, but most direct and visible symbols of an oppressive and callous capitalism now so tragically out of hand."

'Now how does that grab you?'

It grabbed him. Crichton-Potter was not quick on the uptake but even he could recognize a political knife when he saw one.

'That's very good, Henry. Very good. I like it. I like it a lot.'

'There's plenty more where that came from. We can use these murders to slay the Government. Of course, we'll condemn the murders as such. We don't want to appear to be condoning the act.'

'Of course not.'

'But once we've done that, we can launch into this stuff about the "unwitting agents of monetarism". It'll knock 'em cold.'

10

'Henry,' Crichton-Potter told him, 'it promises to be one of your best. I've got a lunch at the Garrick. Or possibly it's Boodles. Anyway, I've got a lunch. Have it typed ready for me afterwards – say about five thirty.'

Crichton-Potter left Reform Party HQ well satisfied. He might not have brains, he reflected, but he did at least have judgement. Why else would he have appointed Henry, who was excellent value for money, especially given the pittance he was paid. As Crichton-Potter descended the stairs, a figure shot frantically past him, bright red in the face, and vigorously rubbing the seat of its trousers. Madam Sin gave excellent value for money too.

If, thought George Cragge, there was one form of pond life lower than the press officer it was the personnel officer, and Mr Fortescue was a prize specimen. He had a rule book where his brain should have been and he possessed but one talent, that of frustrating talent in others. Chairing a disciplinary interview – ideally with a victim more gifted than himself and with a job more exciting than his own – was one of the great pleasures of his wretched life and brought out the worst in him. Such an occasion made him feel important and enabled him to lord it over actual broadcasters or producers, forgetful for the moment of his own irrelevance to anything of the slightest moment. With George Cragge, a real live journalist, in the role of prisoner at the bar, Mr Fortescue was in his element. He was flanked by the Editor and the Deputy Editor, whose presence testified to the solemnity of the occasion, but Mr Fortescue was in the chair. He adjusted the pince-nez on his long nose, coughed delicately and began.

'Mr Cragge, I think I should start by reminding you that this is a disciplinary interview as provided for in Staff Instruction Number 167. A written record will be taken of the meeting and you are, if you wish, entitled to be represented by an official of a union recognized by the Corporation in accordance with the terms of the

11

Employment Protection Act, 1975.'

'Bollocks,' said George.

It had been a good lunch. Nothing excessive, just good. At the start of it, George had been frankly nervous at the prospect of the interview. To some extent he still was. He had come to the conclusion, however, that if he were going, he was going in style.

Mr Fortescue continued.

'Such an interview may result in one of a number of decisions. It is possible that there will be a recommendation for instant termination; it is possible that we shall decide to issue an official verbal or written warning, in accordance with the terms of the Employment Protection Act, 1975. Alternatively, we may decide to suspend your increment.'

'Bollocks,' said George.

Mr Fortescue was not a bright man – he would hardly have been in personnel if he were – but even he was beginning to suspect that he was not being treated with the respect to which he was entitled. He decided to move on to the attack.

'You joined the Corporation five years ago as a crime reporter. Since then, you have been informed on a number of occasions that your conduct was unsatisfactory and was giving rise to concern.'

'What's wrong with my work?' demanded George truculently.

'It is not a question of your work.'

'How many complaints,' George persisted, 'have you received about the quality of my work?'

'We are not here to discuss the quality of your work. We expect certain standards of behaviour, certain, shall we say, modes, which under the terms of . . .'

'Bollocks,' said George.

This was no time, Fortescue decided, for half measures. It was a fight to the death.

'The proximate cause . . .'

'The which?'

'The proximate cause of this disciplinary interview

12

was your conduct at the Editor's Summer Party.'

Here the Editor – a small, worried, balding man – shuddered. It would be a long time before he forgot that party. It would be a long time before anyone forgot it, as a matter of fact.

'This culminated,' said Fortescue, 'in an incident in which you upset the buffet.'

Prosaic chaps, these personnel officers. 'Upset' is not actually incorrect but it does not begin to do justice to events. What actually happened was this. The Editor's Summer Party, held usually in June, was a very posh affair. It was graced by all the big noises – the Director General, the Managing Director of BBC Radio and even a few BBC governors. In addition, the guest list boasted several MPs and one cabinet minister. Unfortunately for the Editor, he had, in order to justify the expense, to invite the journalists as well, including George. The views of journalists about what constitutes a good party do not necessarily coincide with those of BBC governors and cabinet ministers. George had expected the event to be crushingly dull. Accordingly, he had fortified himself with several large ones, both to render the occasion bearable and to ensure that he arrived late, thereby cutting short the agony.

It became clear to him the moment he walked in the door that he had not arrived late enough. The atmosphere of tedium was stifling and the conversation insufferable. George had walked into a so-called party that was 'going' – if the overstatement may be pardoned – like this:

'I do think a slice of lemon adds just the right hint of mystery to a fried chicken leg, don't you?'

'Naturally, my son would have walked into Balliol, but I did so agree with the headmaster that for mechanical engineering you simply cannot beat Nottingham.'

'I have always thought that the role of the journalist in public-service broadcasting . . .'

George was not a thinker, he was a doer. And it was clear that what this shindig needed was action. At the end of the room was a long table on which was arranged the buffet. Above and behind it was a stage. In order to liven things up a bit, George mounted the stage, stood immediately behind the buffet table and raised his arms above his head. 'Double somersault and turn,' he announced to his audience, 'difficulty, five point five.'

He then plunged into the buffet causing it to be rearranged over substantially half the room. The BBC governor standing nearest made a fascinating discovery, namely that the world contained more lemon meringue pie than he had ever dreamed of. The cabinet minister's wife to whom he had been talking took a sausage roll full on the nose, and being hit by a BBC sausage roll is an experience one does not lightly forget. The Editor, whose party it was supposed to be, was discovered later, crying softly in his room, reflecting suicidally that his OBE had gone up in a burst of chicken legs and cheese sandwiches.

Framing a defence for a crime of this magnitude would have taxed the greatest of legal brains and George could see that the game was not worth the candle.

'Is there anything,' Mr Fortescue asked him, 'you wish to say to this tribunal, before we decide what course of action to recommend?'

Does the prisoner have anything to say? Even George was a bit stumped by that one. Which was the sensible approach? A vigorous, uncompromising defence? A tearful admission of guilt? A passionate plea in mitigation? An oration of silver-tongued eloquence which would have done the Old Bailey proud?

George said, 'Bollocks.'

'Very well. It is our decision . . .'

Typical, thought George. The decision was already taken. Had been taken, in fact, before the interview had even begun. He braced himself for it and reflected that Fortescue's head seemed to have been designed for the black cap. As it turned out, George was in for a surprise.

'It is our decision,' Mr Fortescue went on, 'that you be

14

given an official and final written warning in accordance with the terms of the Employment Protection Act 1975. You will be instructed that any repetition of your most reprehensible conduct will result in a recommendation for instant dismissal.'

Sigh! Was that all? Well, no, actually it wasn't.

'In addition,' (this was Fortescue's big moment and he savoured it) 'it has been decided that it would be to the mutual benefit of yourself and of the newsroom if you were to spend a few months in a different environment. Accordingly, arrangements have been made for you to be attached' – that being BBC jargon for seconded – 'for a period of twelve months to the Complaints and Correspondence Department.'

Ye gods! thought George, the bastard! So that was it. They were postponing death not out of mercy but out of sadism. The BBC receives thousands and thousands of letters of complaint every year. Chiefly, these are letters about too much sex from people clearly not getting enough and about too much violence from people who would clearly benefit from a large dose. Complaints and Correspondence was the department responsible for being polite and mollifying to these people. It was not a popular department; it was known in the trade as Siberia, although a better analogy would have been with one of those Soviet psychiatric hospitals where they used to send perfectly sane people in order to drive them mad. People had been carried out, white-haired and screaming, from Complaints and Correspondence after three months. And they were proposing to send George there for twelve. He could not even bring himself to say Bollocks.

Mr Fortescue was congratulating himself inwardly on his performance. Something resembling a smile almost forced its way on to his features as he drew to a close.

'Your attachment will begin,' he pronounced, 'immed . . .'

Before he could finish, however, there was a knock at the door.

15

Mr Fortescue looked distastefully at George's saviour. It was one of the young sub-editors from the newsroom.

'I'm very sorry to interrupt,' he gasped breathlessly, 'but there's someone on the phone for Mr Cragge and, well, we think he ought to take it.'

'Dammit, man,' the Editor said, 'can't you see we're busy? Say Cragge will ring back.'

'I'm sorry, sir,' the young sub stammered, having never spoken to anyone as grand as the Editor before, 'but, honestly, I think . . .'

George needed no second telling. Before the dreaded Fortescue could finish the sentence of hard labour, George was racing down the corridor.

'Who is it, son?' he asked the young man who had been his angel of mercy.

'We're not quite sure, sir, but he wouldn't talk to anyone but you.'

The call had come through to the Radio 4 Bulletins Desk. George picked up the phone and, fearing a creditor or a discarded girlfriend, tried to sound authoritative.

'George Cragge speaking.'

'Why haven't you been telling them about my murders, George?' The voice was masculine, youngish, well-modulated: a graduate in his twenties you would have said, if asked to guess.

'What murders are those?'

'The bank managers, George. Why do you keep leaving things out?' George's first thought, naturally, was that this was a loony.

'What do you know about those, then?'

'There was a note on the first one.'

The caller gave a word-for-word account of its contents.

'And another note on the second.'

This, too, was repeated, verbatim.

By now, George was frantic with a mixture of excitement and a sort of spookiness. This was not a hoax.

'I'm just ringing to tell you, George . . .'

'Look, where are you?'

'I'm just ringing to tell you that I want all the details reported. Oh yes, and George, there'll be another one. Before midnight tonight.'

Detective Chief Inspector Frank Jefferson was a plain, no-nonsense policeman. He was rough, tough, bluff and gruff. He was nobody's fool. That, at any rate, was his own estimate of his intelligence and it testified, given the quite different view of his colleagues, to an admirable independence of mind. He saw the world in simple terms. There were good, decent, law-abiding people, epitomized by his own family, to whom he was devoted. And there was a criminal class to be caught and locked up. For the latter, he felt nothing but contempt exceeded only by his contempt for social workers, psychologists, *Guardian* readers and anybody else who sought to blur the stark distinction between good and evil on which his view of life depended.

To his family he extended a genial tolerance which he denied to the lawbreakers he was employed to catch. He smiled benignly. He smiled benignly when his wife threw his dinner at him for being late home after he had worked fifteen hours on a case. He smiled benignly when his daughter married a bassoon player from Ongar. And he smiled benignly when his son, reading Politics at university, wrote home to say that he had shaved his head, become a vegetarian and changed his name to Bakunin by deed poll. He was a big one for smiling benignly, was Frank.

Sometimes, in spite of his being nobody's fool, Frank's hard side and gentler side did get a bit confused. When this happened he would take to getting magistrates out of bed to provide a search warrant for his own house, shoulder charging his own front door at three o'clock in the morning and yelling 'I know you're in there.' Even in this mood, however, Frank was not without his deterrent effect on society's transgressors since they became the beneficiaries of his genial tolerance and, as a result, would be haunted throughout the years of their incarceration by the terrifying memory of one of Frank's benign smiles.

The Bank Manager Murders, with whose solution he had been entrusted, were not Frank's sort of crime. Most murders were straightforward and that was how he liked them. In most cases, the murderer was well known, or even closely related, to the victim and was therefore easily identifiable.

Confronted with a madman, the Detective Chief Inspector lost his bearings. There was so little to go on. Aside from their occupation the victims had nothing in common – no obvious mutual acquaintances, nor indeed any similarity of background. All Frank had to build on was what the victims did and how they had been murdered, which between them suggested merely that the killer combined a pathological hatred of bank managers with a fanatical dislike of one-pound coins.

It had been talking to George Cragge which had given the Commissioner the idea. 'Look, all we've really got,' he told Jefferson, 'are the notes. The notes are a sign of arrogance. They'll be his undoing. You mark my words.'

'But what do they tell us?'

'Well,' admitted the Commissioner, 'I'm not actually sure just at the moment. But I've had a thought. You know the BBC?'

'Of course I know the BBC. It's an organization of lefties and subversives who interview terrorists and criminals.'

'Well yes I know that, but . . .'

'It's an organization hellbent on destroying all that's decent in our national life, every traditional value . . .'

'No doubt. And lots of people think the way you do. So what do they do about it?'

'Turn off their televisions.'

'Oh no, they don't do that. They write to complain.'

'I'm very glad to hear it, sir.'

'The BBC's Complaints and Correspondence Department probably has to answer more letters every day than anyone else in the country. So what does that give them?'

Frank thought hard. 'Writer's cramp?'

'It gives them a unique expertise about letters, doesn't it? There's nobody in Britain who knows more about writing, spelling, makes of typewriter, telling people's characters from the way they write, all that sort of thing. Especially since our own people haven't come up with anything.'

'And you think . . .'

'Exactly. I think they're the very people to analyse these notes for us. See what they come up with. Now, as it happens, I know the chap who runs the BBC's Complaints and Correspondence Department. As a matter of fact I had a bit of a run-in with him a while back over a BBC programme.'

'Oh, you mean the one about corruption at the top of the Metropolitan Pol . . . er . . . oops.'

Frank had left the Commissioner's office with the distinct feeling that if he wished to remain a detective inspector, he had better catch the Bank Manager murderer. He sensed that the interview had not gone well.

The Head of Complaints and Correspondence at Broadcasting House did little to raise his spirits. He proved to be a highly excitable man, clearly given to deriving great pleasure from little things. 'Fascinating!' he expostulated on being handed the murderer's notes. 'Typed on a standard Olivetti.'

'What does that tell us?'

'It tells us absolutely nothing. Millions of these typewriters all over the country. Still, don't despair. Let's study the actual texts. Now both letters begin, "Dear Bank Manager".'

'Well they would, wouldn't they?'

'Yes. Yes I suppose so. I must say, it's damned expensive paper they are written on.'

'Never mind the paper. What about the text?'

'Well, he uses very big words. That suggests an educated chap.'

'Brilliant.'

'Now what do you make of "Malthus lives – which is more than can be said for you"?'

'I was rather hoping that you might . . .'

'Do you know what that reminds me of?'

'No,' said Frank wearily. 'What does it remind you of?'

'Elvis Presley.'

'What?'

'Yes. There's a wonderful bit of graffiti at High Holborn tube station. Somebody's written "Elvis lives" and, underneath, somebody else has written, "and they've buried the poor bugger".'

'Look, this is all very well but . . .'

'Yes, yes, I'm sorry. Well now, Malthus. Malthus was an economist with a theory about population growth. So our chap knows a bit about economics. That should cut down the odds a bit.'

'Well it's been very good of you to see me, Mr . . .'

'I'll tell you one thing about this chap. He doesn't like bank managers much, does he?'

'If there's nothing else?'

'Oh, there is one thing. We ran through our computer to see whether anybody had written to the BBC about bank managers in the last twelve months.'

'And had they?'

'No, not a sausage. There was one thing though. I gather these chaps were tonked on the bonce with a bag of one-pound coins?'

'That is correct.'

'Well, we did have a letter once complaining about the introduction of the one-pound coin. From an MP actually. Said he was getting a lot of mail from his constituents saying the coin wasn't as good as the old note, done for the convenience of the banks not the customers and blah blah blah. He said he entirely agreed with them.'

20

'Who was the MP?'

'Wait a minute, I've got it here somewhere. Ah yes. Geoffrey Crichton-Potter. Mean anything?'

'I've never heard of him.'

CHAPTER
3

Henry was not exactly one of life's sexual successes. He was the kind of man who, when regretfully telling his friends that, no, he did not have a spare packet and he did not know whether the pub had a machine, would be told, 'You know what it's like, old chap'. But Henry did not know what it was like. He had a pretty fair idea of what it was like; indeed, he had mastered the details of the theory at a remarkably early age. His attempts to put them into practice had, however, been a series of unrelieved disasters.

He was the kind of man to whom female friends would say, 'I really like you, Henry. Before I met you, I never thought it was possible to have a purely platonic relationship with a man but I just don't think of you sexually at all.' And Henry would smile, wanly, as the buttons on his boxer shorts fired a twenty-one-gun salute to the purity of youth.

Nor was it any good trying not to think about the subject. Henry lived alone in a basement flat in Bayswater. The flat above was rented by a young couple who were deeply, and loudly, in love. At 6.26 every morning – they were astonishingly punctual – Henry would be awakened by rhythmic moans of pleasure that made him climb up the wall or chew his pillow. Worse than that, the female half of the act had a habit of wandering around the house in her bra and panties in a manner which Henry was convinced was pure sadism and had the sole aim of tormenting him personally.

Such things prey on a speechwriter's mind. The speechwriter, if he is to be worthy of his hire, must forever be inventing new and striking images. Unless he is content to be in the Third Division of his chosen calling, he must not take refuge in clichés such as 'This great movement of ours' or 'The overwhelming majority of the British people'. True, most of the time the politician's art is to say nothing at great length. The role of someone like Henry, however, is to provide an endless store of new ways of saying nothing, each calculated to make the headlines, or to sound good in the mouth of the newsreader.

It is not an easy business at the best of times and every speechwriter finds his turn of phrase reflecting whatever his preoccupations happen to be at any given moment. Henry's preoccupation at almost every given moment was sex and, in particular, his lack of it. As a result, Geoffrey Crichton-Potter's imagery was becoming, to say the least, colourful.

It was unfortunate enough that Henry had a habit of appending notes of self-approval to his work. These Crichton-Potter, being Crichton-Potter, had a habit of reading out as if they were part of the text. No great damage was done, admittedly, when he concluded a speech to the Royal Institute of International Affairs, with the words, 'Furthermore, up yours, Winston Churchill'. It had decidedly raised eyebrows, however, when he had advised Cicero to eat his heart out in the middle of an after-dinner speech to the Anti-Vivisection Society.

The speech about bank managers started well enough. The stuff about them being the unwitting victims of public fury at evil economic policies went down remarkably well, particularly given that it was manifest bilge. Yet as the speech had developed, it had taken a turn for which its audience – the Reform Party Women's Federation – were quite unprepared.

If 'Are we content to be the voyeurs of the world?' was a question to which they had given little thought, it was clear that 'together we can make our national bed-springs creak' was a possibility they had not considered at all. The *Times* political commentator called the speech a 'refreshingly original economic analysis', which in a sense it was. So great indeed was its originality that it had caused several members of the audience to faint – overcome, no doubt, by the intellectual vigour of Crichton-Potter's attack.

'Knocked 'em cold, old boy,' declared the egregious MP, back at Reform HQ. 'Had 'em swooning. And that stuff about bank managers went down pretty well. I think we should do some more.'

'Your wish is my command,' replied Henry. 'I think next time we should use it to have a go at the police. You know – all they ever do is arrest people for drinking and driving, or whatever. But give them a real live murderer and they're sunk. Reform the police!'

'Anything you say, old boy. When am I speaking next?'

'You're addressing the Young Reformers' Movement. I think the police angle should go down well with them.'

'I'm sure it will. Right. I'm off to this blessed cheese and wine party to meet our new candidates. Henry, why would anybody want to meet our new candidates?'

'At least you're being paid for it,' Henry told him. 'Think of the poor voters.'

'There is that, of course.' Crichton-Potter shifted his ample frame towards the door. 'Well, bash out another rant about the police for our beloved youth movement. Oh, and Henry, don't overdo the anti-police thing. I mean, make sure you start off by saying all our policemen are wonderful, won't you?'

'What the hell are you doing here?'

'I just escaped from Complaints and Correspondence Department.'

'So have I,' said George. He and Frank Jefferson were acquainted of old and respected each other. To Frank, George was as near to decency as any journalist could get. Frank liked him for his abhorrence of the modern trend to committed investigative journalism. To George, Jefferson was as near to decency as any policeman could get. 'Neither of us,' as Frank had once

24

told him, 'goes in for the flash-bang-wallop style.'

'You mean you never wallop your suspects?'

'No more than you bang the newsreaders.'

George was delighted to hear that Jefferson was in charge of the Bank Manager Murders. As he related the story of his phone conversation with the maniac, Jefferson's expression became grim.

'George, are you sure he gave you all those details? I mean, if the Commissioner had already told you – without letting me know, I may say – you might have imagined . . .'

'I didn't imagine anything. This guy knew all about it. This is the real thing, Frank. I don't think he's bluffing.'

'All right. Well, look, we've put out a warning to every bank manager in London to be on his guard. I don't see there's much else we can do.'

'There isn't.'

'And, George, I want to ask you a favour. I know this is a big story for you . . .'

'But you'd be eternally grateful for my cooperation. Yeah, yeah, all right. Except that I want your cooperation too. When it's safe, I get this story. Exclusively, with no strings.'

'Done.'

'And I don't see how we can keep it quiet for long. I mean, if there's another one, you can't suppress the fact that we were worried about it.'

'I appreciate that but, just for now.'

'All right. Just for now.'

As George left his friend, a slow smile of triumph spread across his face. He was not a callous man and he did not wish murder on anybody: On the other hand, this was the biggest story he'd been involved in for years. It was not lost on him that the development had certain other advantages too.

Three floors up, on the sixth floor of Broadcasting House, Mr Fortescue of Personnel, together with the Editor and Deputy Editor of Radio News, had been sitting in some confusion for more than an hour and a half. There was no precedent for this and when there was no precedent, Mr Fortescue became perplexed. When it came to reciting the rule book, Mr Fortescue's proficiency was a by-word. If he had a weakness – and his annual report said so, so it must be true – it was in the area of decision taking. Mr Fortescue did not care for decisions, save when they were in line with established practice. The discussion, therefore, was becoming heated.

'This disciplinary interview,' Fortescue told his colleagues, 'has not formally ended and, according to Standing Instruction Number 497, it cannot be formally closed until it has.'

'But George has buggered off,' the Editor told him reasonably.

'We can't just sit here,' put in the Deputy Editor.

'I cannot declare the hearing formally terminated until and unless the correct procedures have been observed.'

'Well, do something, then.' The Editor was beginning to reflect that if this was what it took to get rid of George Cragge, then it was hardly worth the effort.

'I will telephone Mr Cragge and instruct him to re-present himself.'

Well, he did try. He rang George's office, he got through to George personally and he began to remonstrate with him. He did not manage to finish.

'Mr Cragge, I must respectfully request . . .'

'Bollocks.'

'But I must absolutely insist . . .'

'Bollocks.'

'Your attachment to the Correspondence and Complaints Department . . .'

'Bollocks.' And George, having made his position clear to even the simplest mind – that of Mr Fortescue – replaced his receiver.

The Editor and his Deputy had had enough. 'We're going,' they told the Personnel Officer.

'This disciplinary interview,' whined Fortescue, 'will continue to sit.' And alone in an office on the sixth floor, with neither sandwiches nor Thermos flask, the disciplinary interview sat.

Downstairs, on the third floor, George Cragge did the same. Naturally, his provisions were more than adequate. He had sent his secretary out for several bottles of the best, and was now well into the second one. He was, however, perfectly sober. Any feeling of lightheadedness was due to a mixture of excitement and disquiet at that excitement. He ought not to want the phone to ring. Yet he desperately wanted it to ring.

Mr Fortescue, too, was in an agony of indecision. On the one hand, he wanted desperately to ring George Cragge. On the other, it was clearly beneath his dignity to make two attempts to contact a recalcitrant employee whom until the critical moment he had handled, he thought, with such skill. Ultimately, Cragge would have no alternative but to comply with the regulations. Fortescue was not a quitter. He would sit it out. He would sit there all evening if necessary. It was and he did. He would sit there till midnight if he had to. He had to. He was still sitting, wondering whether it was compatible with his dignity to attempt a chorus of 'We shall not be moved', when, three floors down, George Cragge's phone rang.

'George, it's happened.' It was the voice of Detective Inspector Jefferson. 'The victim's name is Inchcape.'

It was not Jeremy Inchcape's fault that he had become a bank manager. He had never really felt that he had much choice in the matter. His parents had worked hard to give him a decent education. They had made genuine sacrifices to send him to a Direct Grant school, the poshest school in Plymouth, where he had been born. It was not, strictly speaking, a public school. But it had a clear idea of what a public school ought to be – an idea which the genuine articles had discarded decades before. Thus, in the 1960s, as real public schools became more liberal and humane, so Mayflower

College became more illiberal and brutal. As the Anglican high church is more catholic than the Catholics, so Mayflower School became more public school than the public schools, to an extent that would have turned nineteenth-century headmasters into campaigners for pupil power. Mayflower College's pupils possessed no power whatsoever. They were beaten, thrown into cold showers and forced through exams like meat through a sausage factory. After seven years of the privilege for which his parents had given up so much, Jeremy Inchcape emerged with eight O levels, two A levels and an irresistible sexual urge for receiving chastisement at the hands of buxom ladies.

What he had been required to deliver in return for the selflessness of his parents was security. Security and respectability. Of course, he was allowed to dream of glamour and fame. He was allowed not merely to dream of wealth but actually to administer it and gloat over it. In progressing through the graduate training scheme of a major clearing bank, to his present position as manager of a small London branch, he had repaid his debt to his parents by insisting with marked acerbity that other people repaid theirs. He had done everything that was required of him and had acquired something in return; the chance to get his own back.

Jeremy Inchcape hated the world. Beneath his respectable, repressed exterior burned an adventurer, a rebel against the profit and loss account, a rebel against the system which made him yawn from nine till five. His thirst for vengeance found its outlet in the cold, curt refusals to those who begged him for loans to set up their own businesses and liberate themselves from their own slavery. The callous scepticism with which he greeted their requests was his only release.

Well, not quite his only. For beneath the seat of his trousers burned the handiwork of Madam Sin, testimony to his unnatural upbringing. His occasional visits to Berwick Street offered his only regular chance of admission into a world of fantasy which his everyday life frustrated.

And undoubtedly she was good at her job. Indeed, on learning that he was a bank manager, she had evinced an enthusiasm that was positively excessive. Jeremy felt on returning from his trips to Soho that he had climbed the walls of ecstasy, only to fall heavily over the other side. Just because her own bank had refused her a loan for her 'equipment', as she put it. 'What I do isn't respectable, dear,' she had told him. 'I'm not respectable. The way you are.'

Following his fortnightly visit to Madam Sin, Jeremy Inchcape was working later than usual. He had already foreclosed on two clients, refused three overdrafts and bounced two cheques. He felt inordinately satisfied with himself as he had reached for the letter marked Private and Confidential which had just arrived on his desk.

As he did so, his phone rang. 'Inchcape,' he barked. ('Inchcape, Inchcape,' they had teased him at school, 'You and your arithmetic, you'll probably go far.')

'Would you please open your window and stick your head out of it?' The voice was young, well-bred and educated.

'I beg your pardon.'

'I said would you please stick your head out of your window? I think you'll find something interesting.'

There was something about the voice, something that suggested adventure. Inchcape's parents had insisted that he got a steady job and worked from Monday till Friday. They had not suggested that he devoted the hours in between to sticking his head out of windows. Jeremy Inchcape rose. He opened his window. He stuck his head out of it. And a one-pound coin, travelling with terrific velocity, struck him in the middle of the forehead and killed him.

'The private and confidential letter,' George asked, 'was it a note from the maniac?'

'Yes. "Dear Bank Manager, I have just paid a deposit into your account. Death to the pinstripes!"'

'So how was the letter delivered?'

'We don't know. It appears to have been dropped at the reception desk when no one was looking.'

'Do we know where the missile was fired from?'

'It appears to have been fired from the ground. Needless to say, nobody saw anything.'

'And was there anything else unusual about the crime?'

'Well, yes. Except that we don't know whether it actually has anything to do with the crime. The victim had . . . well, the blow from a one-pound coin on the forehead appears to have caused severe reddening of the buttocks. The mark of cane, as it were.'

'What?'

'Yes, I know. I don't understand it either.'

'And what about the note?'

'The same typewriter, or kind of typewriter, as before. The usual sarcasm. And what on earth do you make of "death to the pinstripes"?'

'Well, I suppose it suggests somebody with a grudge against City types. Or against people who are obviously successful and respectable. Or against men,' George added thoughtfully. 'When was the body found?'

'About an hour ago,' said Jefferson. 'Apparently he was working late. He'd been out for some time this morning – at a meeting or something, nobody seems to know where – and so he stayed on to catch up. The night porter found him and rang us. He thought Inchcape had been shot.'

'You can't expect me to keep this quiet, can you?'

'I don't want you to keep it quiet. I want it given every publicity. That's our only hope of finding anyone who noticed anything.'

'Right. Shall we do an interview then?' George took out the portable tape recorder that is the radio reporter's trade mark.

'Do you want to go somewhere quiet?'

'No no. Let's do it here. Our reporter at the scene of the crime and all that.'

*

30

Some hours previously, Mr Andrew James of Mysore Road, Battersea, London SW11, eyed the ticket clerk at St James's Park tube station distastefully. 'Do you have to give me those horrible things in my change?' he demanded as he pocketed four shining one-pound coins.

CUE. 'Another London bank manager has been found murdered, the third in six weeks. The body was found around midnight at the St James's Park branch where the victim, Mr Jeremy Inchcape, was manager. Reporting from the scene, our crime correspondent, George Cragge.'
INSERT: CRAGGE + ACT.
'Thirty-seven-year-old Mr Inchcape was found by the night porter at the branch where he had been manager for two years. Although the case contains some unusual features, police are certain that this is the work of the homicidal maniac who has already killed two London bank managers.'
ACT: JEFFERSON
'There are definite links between this and the previous killings. We are now convinced that there is a psychopath at large in the community with a grudge against bank managers. We advise all bank managers – not just those in London – to be constantly alert to any sign of danger. And we are anxious to hear from anyone who was in the St James's Park area between 9 p.m. and midnight last night.'
CRAGGE – PAY OFF.
'The police have already begun interviewing members of the public. But so far they've little to go on except they're sure the three killings are the work of one person.'
END

The Editor of BBC Radio News put down the script of George's piece for that morning's *Today* programme.
'This is bloody good stuff,' he remarked.

'It's a bloody good story,' George told him, 'and I reckon it'll keep us in lead items for some time.'

'Who the hell wants to murder a bank manager?'

'Everybody.'

They were interrupted by the telephone. The Editor had three telephones on his desk as an indication of his importance. He inevitably picked up the wrong one and then the other wrong one before finding someone on the other end.

'Editor!' he snapped, impressively. Well, he thought so, anyway. 'Oh,' he continued lamely, 'it's for you.' He handed over to George, pained that calls for someone else should come through on one of his telephones.

'Hello.' George had a feeling about this call and he was right.

'That's much better, George.' It was the same voice, young, well spoken and spooky.

'What's much better?'

'Your report this morning. I liked it. It had colour.'

'Who is this speaking?'

'Oh come on, George. You know perfectly well who's speaking. No, I liked your stuff this morning. Except I don't think I really care for being called a maniac. I think I would prefer public servant. After all, I am performing a public service, wouldn't you say?'

'Where are you calling from?'

'George, for an experienced reporter your questions are depressingly banal. Oh, and one other thing. You haven't told them about the notes. Why not?'

'Now look . . .'

'I think you ought to tell them about the notes, George. I think they'd enliven your copy. I don't want to have to send one to a newspaper. That would be terribly vulgar.'

Another of the Editor's phones was ringing now. To his intense annoyance, it proved to be another call for George.

'He's on the other line,' he snapped.

'I really must insist on speaking to him.' The voice was

weary, but unmistakable. 'The disciplinary interview has not been formally concluded and . . .'

'Oh, fuck me,' said the Editor. 'George . . .'

'Not now!'

'But George. I think you ought to speak to him.'

'I can't.'

The Editor pushed the phone into George's hand. His other conversation was still continuing.

'You are going to tell them about my notes, aren't you, George? They add such a sense of fun to the occasion.'

'Mr Cragge. I must insist that you begin your attachment to Complaints and Correspondence Department.'

'Bollocks!' George roared at him.

'I beg your pardon?' The maniac did not sound amused.

'I didn't mean you,' George told him.

'I'm very relieved to hear it,' said Fortescue.

'Now about my next murder,' said the maniac.

'Murder!' shrieked Fortescue, 'you can't murder the Head of Personnel and Administration, Radio News and Current Affairs. To do so would be a clear contravention of Staff Instruction Number . . .'

'Oh, bollocks!' George wailed.

'Manners, George, manners,' said the maniac.

'What about your attachment?' demanded Fortescue.

'Oh, I've no intention of using an attachment,' said the maniac, 'although I have come up with something that I think you'll find rather amusing.'

At that moment the Editor's third telephone rang. 'May I speak to Mr George Cragge, please?'

'This is the limit!' the Editor bellowed. 'Who is it this time?'

'This is his bank manager.'

33

CHAPTER
4

'Beware of words,' said Henry, 'for with words we lie.'

Crichton-Potter chortled. 'How very true, Henry. And how very clever of you to say so.'

'It would have been even cleverer if W.H. Auden hadn't said it first,' sighed Henry.

'Who?'

'Oh, never mind. Look, you've got to say something about economics.'

'Oh God. Have I? Why?'

'Because economics is the most important issue in politics. Damn it, every election for years has been decided on economic issues.'

'Oh dear. Well, yes, I suppose you're right.'

'Look, I suggest something like this: "This party – this great party – cannot continue to straddle the Marxist fence."'

'Why not?'

'We must say firmly . . . what?'

'Why can't we straddle the Marxist fence?'

'Because we'll get the barbed wire right where it hurts.'

'Oh I see.'

'This is hopeless. Look.' Henry prepared to explain the elementary facts of Reform Party structure to his leader. 'The trouble with our party is that it's got a right wing.'

'A right wing,' parroted Crichton-Potter.

'Yes. And they want people to be free to get rich and stay rich.'

'Hear hear. Oh absolutely. I completely agree.'

'And then there's a left wing.'

'A . . . left . . . wing.'

'Yes. They want to redistribute wealth to promote social justice and help the poor.'

'I say, what a first-class wheeze!'

'You mean you agree with them as well?'

'Oh yes indeed.'

'Well that is, if I may say so, profoundly symptomatic of the intellectual confusion that is the defining characteristic of this organization.'

'I shouldn't wonder,' assented Crichton-Potter in a cheery fog of corpulent incomprehension, 'and you want me to say that?'

'Of course I don't want you to say that. I want you to find a way of marrying these two . . . well, at any rate, these two differences of emphasis.'

'Oh, aah. Tricky one that. How do you think I should go about it?'

'By committing the Reform Party to steering the economy upon a responsible course.'

'Exactly,' said Crichton-Potter, 'just what I was about to suggest. Steer the economy on a responsible course and everything will be tickety-boo.'

'But where will this course take us?' demanded Henry.

Crichton-Potter thought hard. 'The Garrick?' he suggested brightly.

'What are you talking about?'

'My lunch. Mustn't keep you, old boy. I'm sure you've got masses to do.'

'Oh honestly!'

'No no, really. I'm sure you work better undisturbed.' And Crichton-Potter departed for his club reflecting that nobody should go about marrying differences of emphasis on an empty stomach.

Left alone, Henry muttered to himself. Before Crichton-Potter had arrived, it had been a decent, productive morning. If Crichton-Potter used the draft Henry was preparing, and he invariably did, he would the next morning be asking the Secretary of State for Trade and Industry whether he did not deserve for his callousness towards unemployment to be buried up to his neck in natural wastage. That'll teach the swine, thought Henry as he sat back to savour a job well done.

And then it happened. An apparition, a mirage in the desert of his sexual frustration, came through the door. It had adorably long blonde hair, perfectly proportioned breasts and a trim, shapely bottom. It was wearing a devastating trouser suit. Its voice was deep and masculine, in an utterly feminine way.

The deepness of its voice seemed to compel Henry's vocal cords to rise several octaves as if in compensation.

'Hello,' drawled the apparition.

'Hello,' squeaked Henry in return.

'I'm the new PA,' she continued. 'You did know I was coming?'

At this point the author has to admit to some difficulty. It is not immediately obvious what constitutes the best verbal representation of what began as an expression of polite reassurance but turned unintentionally into a strangulated groan of lust. It would be doing Henry an injustice to report that what he said was 'Cor'. On the other hand, accuracy forbids that his response be recorded as 'Of course, please come in'. Possibly 'Aaargh' would not be a total distortion, although 'O . . . pl . . . aw . . . waugh' would be even nearer. At any rate, Henry was clearly in the grip of a powerful emotion.

The new PA, on the other hand, was ice cool and it was impossible to think of her ever being anything else.

Her name, it transpired, was Laetitia Tone. She was the daughter of the leader of the Reform Party in the House of Lords who was known to the lobby journalists as Mono Tone because he was the most boring person in Parliament. His tediousness had clearly not rubbed off on his daughter, whose every word and deed seemed to Henry to be invested with intense sexual significance.

Laetitia seemed to interpret her duties as PA to be confined solely to saying 'OK, fine' down the telephone at regular intervals. London is full of people who are employed to say 'OK, fine' down telephones. But not the way she said it. Moreover, Laetitia possessed a versatility lacking in the merely competent 'OK, fine' types. She could say 'Soupah' as well and frequently did. She could even say 'OK, fine, soupah – loveleh'. Henry struggled vainly, that first morning, to think about natural wastage. He failed. Drastic action was clearly needed. Excusing himself from her presence, Henry paced up and down the corridor, squirming in an agonized frenzy of sexual desire. He tried to think. Cold showers were supposed to be the answer on these occasions. The Reform Party's modest headquarters did not provide for such luxuries, however. Distraught, he wandered into the kitchen. He wondered whether running up and down the corridor would do any good and decided it would not. Then seeing the kitchen sink, he realized the answer. After all, there was no one about. It was quite inconceivable that Laetitia would ever condescend to enter a kitchen. She looked as if she had never been in one in her life. And, if he could not have a proper cold shower, he could at least have a localized one. If that did not cool his ardour, nothing would.

It was not often that Crichton-Potter went back to the office having just left it. There were indeed entire weeks when he never went near the place. On this occasion, however, it was borne upon his mind that he had been rather hard on his young wordsmith. Perhaps some soothing words would cheer him up. Anyway it wouldn't do any harm to look in. So Crichton-Potter looked in.

There are, no doubt, some excellent books of etiquette. They will tell you how to address an archbishop and what to say to dukes. They will tell in what order to put 'MP', 'MBE' and 'MA (Cantab)' if you are writing to someone who bears all three distinctions. They are, however, united in one striking deficiency. Not one of them contains a chapter entitled 'What to do when Apprehended by your Boss Whilst Pursuing Intimate

Personal Cleanliness in the Kitchen Sink'. On this point, they have no advice to offer and it was clear that Henry needed some. If they were to rectify the omission it is doubtful whether they would recommend saying 'Oh', which is what Henry did. It was the best he could manage but it was not adequate. It lacked wit and verve. It was not calculated to soothe.

The dilemma was no less acute for Crichton-Potter. He was accustomed to being told what to say by Henry. For once, however, following Henry's lead was not conducive to eloquence.

'Oh, oh, oh,' said Henry.

'Ah,' said Crichton-Potter. 'Um . . . ah . . .'

'Oh dear,' said Henry.

'Ah . . . oh dear,' said Crichton-Potter.

'Can I do anything for you?' asked Laetitia.

'No you bloody can't,' shrieked Henry.

'Well, I wouldn't say that,' said Crichton-Potter.

'You would if I wrote it for you,' bawled Henry furiously.

'Yes, that's very true. I knew I came back for something. I wanted to thank you for all your endeavours. He's my speechwriter,' he explained to Laetitia. 'He's working hard on a speech.'

Two days later, George Cragge and Frank Jefferson met to review the case over lunch at the BBC Salad Bar in the Langham Building opposite Broadcasting House.

'So basically you want to know who's been drawing a lot of one-pound coins from his bank in the past few weeks. That shouldn't be too difficult, Frank.'

'We're looking into that angle. Nothing so far, though.'

'And you've got no fingerprints, no bits of hair, or clothing, or anything?'

'No; the murderer seems to have been rather professional.'

'We're looking for a nutter with a grudge against bank managers strong enough to want to murder them and the professional skill to carry it out.'

'That's right. And, the trouble is, we have absolutely no idea where he's going to strike next. There are hundreds of bank managers in London. We can't put a twenty-four-hour watch on all of them.'

'Well, anyway, you know I'll do what I can to help. Do you think there's any point in us broadcasting his voice? I suppose there's always a chance someone might recognize it. In any case, it's a bloody good story.'

'I'm sure it is,' Jefferson told him, 'but I'd rather you didn't. If we do, absolutely everybody will recognize it. We'll get thousands of calls from people who want to get their own back on their husbands, or boyfriends, or neighbours, they'll take us months to investigate and they'll get us nowhere. No, let's hang on to the voice for the time being, if you don't mind. It's all we've got.'

'Well, all right.' George was disappointed but he had promised his cooperation. 'We'll keep it dark for the moment if you insist. You know Parliament's been recalled? I gather the Home Secretary is making a statement about the murders. I suppose that will keep me in copy for a bit.'

'I appreciate your help, George. Meanwhile the murderer's doing another one next week?'

'That's right.'

'But no clue about where or when or how?'

'No,' said George, 'except that he said he thought we'd find it amusing.'

Jefferson did not look amused. He looked shattered. The tedious routine which makes up a murder investigation was well under way and, so far, it was leading nowhere.

'Nobody saw anything,' he complained. 'West London in the middle of a summer evening and nobody saw anything. It makes you sick.'

'What do we know about the victim?' George asked him.

'Well, what you'd expect really. In the week before his

murder he'd refused ten overdrafts, called in eight loans and written fifteen rude letters.'

'You mean he was a sod?'

'Exactly.'

'What about personally?'

'Well, I talked to his staff. They say he nurtured a grudge against the world.'

'Which is why he became a bank manager?'

'No, it's because he became a bank manager. Apparently he was forced into it by his parents. He used to talk about how he'd rather have been a poet or a . . .'

'A bassoon player?' suggested George.

'Very funny.'

'So how did he find his creative outlet? What did he do outside work?'

'That's what I'd like to know. What do you suppose MS stands for?'

'MS? Why?'

'Because he had an appointment with MS at eleven a.m. on the day he was killed. You remember, he'd been away from the office in the morning. That's why he was working late.'

'Yes. MS? Manuscript? Missa Solemnis? Marks & Spencer?'

'I don't know. And what do you make of the mystery of the red buttocks?'

'Well, I certainly don't see what it has to do with the way he was killed. Do you have any idea how the coin was fired?'

'Our ballistics chaps think it must have been from a catapult. Over a distance of about three hundred yards.'

'Good God. So whoever fired it . . .'

'Yes. Was a very good shot.'

'On which subject,' said George.

'Yes?'

'Have a Scotch.'

'Oh all right. Incidentally, one of your people is having a listen to the tapes, to see if the voice suggests anything.'

'I know. Was this another of your Commissioner's bright ideas?

'You guessed it,' said Jefferson morosely. 'All we've got to go on are the tapes. What we need is an in-depth analysis of the voice. That voice will be his undoing. Mark my words. And where do you go for expert voice analysis?'

'The home of BBC Radio.'

'Precisely. Go to Broadcasting House, he says. They know everything there is to know about the human voice. And I just happen to know this chap who's head of announcers.'

'Presentation Editor, Radio 4,' George corrected him. 'Yes, it may do some good and it may not.'

'You don't sound very hopeful.'

'I'm not. You see, the head of announcers isn't actually looking at it himself.'

'Isn't he?'

'No. He's given it to one of his people.'

'Well, that's all right then.'

'Oh no it isn't. He's given it to Jemma.'

'Who?'

'Jemma the Stoned Newsreader.'

'Oh my God. Who is Jemma the Stoned Newsreader?'

'Jemma is the only woman ever known – although not by the management – to have smoked a joint in the Radio 4 Continuity Suite.'

'Oh no. Is this something she does regularly?'

'Well . . . oh, hello Jemma.'

To the millions of Radio 4's devoted listeners, Jemma was the reassuring voice of calm, sober reason. Which just goes to show how much you can tell from voices.

'What could you tell from the voice?' asked Jefferson.

'Wheeeeeeeeeeee,' said Jemma.

There was something about her appearance quite apart from her behaviour that did not inspire confidence. It may have been the enormous baggy white shorts. Or possibly, it was the luminous pink legwarmers.

'You're not seriously telling me that she's a Radio 4 newsreader?' Jefferson whispered furiously.

'And a damn good one,' George told him. 'Put her in front of a microphone and she's sober as a judge.'

'But she's not in front of a bloody microphone.'

'There is that, of course.'

'But newsreaders don't dress like that!'

'Yes they do. They just sound as if they don't.'

'But what's the matter with her?'

'Nothing's the matter with her. She's just been smoking a bit.'

'A bit of what?'

'A bit of . . . um . . .'

'George, I'm a police officer.'

'There is that, of course.'

'I ought to arrest her.'

'You can't arrest her. She's our expert analyst. Buy her a drink.'

'Madam, I am a police officer.'

'I know. Fearless Frank!' wailed the drug-crazed announcer.

'Will you please tell me about the voice?'

'Oh, the voice. Yes, well, I think it's a wheeee!'

'What?'

'A wheeee!'

'You think it's a what?'

'I think it's a woman.'

'A woman?' asked George incredulously.

'Mind you,' she conceded, 'I could be wrong. Nobody else thinks so, Frankie. They all think it's the voice of an educated young man in his late twenties or early thirties, social group AB, from the south of England.'

Frank scribbled furiously.

'But I think they're wrong. That, I told them, is the voice of a woman. And what's more . . . oh hello, it's the Controller of Radio 2. I want to say hello to CR 2. Hello, Controller person!'

The Controller of Radio 2, seated at a nearby table, was in no mood for saying hello. He was looking instead at the Controller of Radio 4 and both wore extremely worried expressions. CR2 was admirably qualified for his job, in that, under normal circumstances, he would rather have been dead than have listened to Radio 2. He was an educated, cultured man who liked nothing more than to retire to the country house where he spent his weekends. He hunted, fished and shot. He was the sharpest and the most cynical political operator in the BBC. His colleague, CR4, gestured to him to come closer.

'That swine,' he said, 'has got to go. My network is the principal speech network in the country. It has the most authoritative news and current affairs, the most exciting drama and the most interesting documentaries. It has . . .'

'Yes,' CR2 interrupted him, 'but we aren't just talking about your network. What we have here is a Director General who doesn't care about radio. He began in television, he middled in television and he finished in television. He doesn't understand radio and he doesn't care about it.'

'Our main problem,' said CR4, 'is that we don't have television's money and we don't have television's clout.'

'Our main problem,' said CR2 more accurately, 'is that we don't have television audiences. The fact is that listening to radio has been declining for years and it shows no sign of stopping. And, on my network at least, I still number my listeners in millions. There'll always be an audience for popular music. But you've got a terrible . . . I mean,' he said diplomatically, 'I have every admiration for your programmes but the fact remains that the audience research department have to use tracker dogs to find anybody who's actually heard any of them.'

'My network,' retorted CR4, becoming agitated, 'represents public service broadcasting in its purest form.'

'You mean nobody listens to it?'

'Look here . . .'

'Oh look; we're not supposed to be having an

argument. We're in this together. We both agree that radio directorate' (in the BBC, radio is always radio directorate, whereas television is the television service) 'is under serious threat.'

'Exactly. The Corporation is in the middle of negotiating the licence fee increase. If that increase isn't as big as we need, there will have to be cuts. And we both know where those cuts will fall.'

'On us,' said CR2 gloomily. 'There'll be an increase in bloody administrators, the television service budget will survive intact and radio will get hammered. There won't be BBC Radio in a few years' time.'

'Quite,' said CR4, 'and our main problem is that the Director General doesn't give a damn. Our dilemma is this: How do we, shall we say, deal with the Director General?'

'Or, to put it another way, how can we welly the swine?'

'Precisely. And the question we have to decide is — what the hell is that smell?'

'Jemma, I don't think you ought to be smoking naughty cigarettes in here,' said George.

'Madam,' said Detective Inspector Frank Jefferson, 'I must warn you that anything you say will be taken down and may be used . . .'

'Wild,' said the blitzed broadcaster. 'Have you heard the new single by Razzmatazz?'

'Have I heard what?'

'Razzmatazz. They're going to be number one. What made you think I'd lay off the drink or even give up the dope, Frankie honey?'

'Smile, Frank,' advised George.

'I have no intention of smiling. All I want to do . . .'

'All I wanna do is rock and roll.'

'What?'

'That's how it goes. It goes:

Sureties. Securities.
Capitalist impurities.

44

Working their corruption in my soul, yeah.
Giving loans, hearing moans,
Mortgages and second homes,
All I wanna do is rock and roll, yeah.

'Stone me,' said George Cragge.

'What we need,' said the Controller of Radio 4 slowly, 'is to secure DG's support for a scheme that will turn out to be a disaster.'

'And make it look as if the whole thing was his idea,' said CR2.

'Something so big – so calamitous – that when it breaks he'll have no option but to resign.'

'And we want something that will make the governors choose a completely different type as his successor. Somebody who cares about radio.'

'Yes. Somebody who cares about radio,' agreed CR4.

Slowly a scheme took shape in his mind.

Perilously clutching the bar, Jemma smiled fatuously as the world slowly lost shape in hers.

'Well,' she declared, 'I must be going.'

'You're not going anywhere. I arrest you in the name of the Law.'

'Oh no you don't,' said George. 'Frank, stop being silly.'

'Now look, I'm not going to tolerate . . .'

'Look, you've got what you came for.'

'I haven't got anything.'

'Yes you have. Now we know that we might be looking for a young man. And we might be looking for a young woman. Now you can't say fairer than that, can you?'

'I am going to detain . . .'

'Right, that does it.' George mounted the bar.

'Oh no. George, I absolutely forbid you.'

'Do you agree to drop all charges?'

'Well no, but . . .'

'Right. That's it then. Ladies and gentlemen,' declared George, 'back flip, triple twist and dive. Difficulty seventeen point six.'

What the Controller of Radio 2 needed was inspiration from above. What he got was George Cragge from the bar.

'Wild,' breathed Jemma.

'Oh God, I give up,' sighed Frank.

So for some weeks did the Controller of Radio 2.

Mr Andrew James of Mysore Road, Battersea, London SW11, whistled the tune of 'Bank Manager Blues' by Razzmatazz happily to himself in his stripped and squalid bedsitter as he arranged his file of newspaper cuttings about the Bank Manager Murders.

'That song,' he mused contentedly, 'is going to be a very big smash.'

Madam Sin brought her hand sharply down upon a pinstriped trouser seat. 'Naughty naughty boy,' she chided, 'and we know what happens to naughty boys, don't we?'

Geoffrey Crichton-Potter, MP, sighed blissfully in the Smoking Room of his club. The trouble with British politics, he reflected, was that you had to pretend to be stupid. You could get away with murder as long as you convinced people you were stupid.

At Reform Party Headquarters Henry put down his pen, stretched and surveyed his work with satisfaction.

I've just invented Reform Party economic policy, he told himself. Completely wasted on somebody as stupid as Crichton-Potter, of course. He's probably never even heard of Malthus.

The Controller of Radio 2 moaned softly in his bed. Why did the BBC employ a man like George Cragge, he wondered. A tabloid journalist. Because he packed them in, that's why. The BBC would be taking advertising next. Commercialism was destroying everything he believed in. It was wrecking his chances of becoming Director General (and that was everything he believed in). 'Vengeance is mine,' said the Controller.

46

CHAPTER
5
***

In 1986, the wind of change blew through the City of London. The Stock Exchange was de-regulated. This came as a considerable shock to those who felt that its activities were quite unregulated enough to start with. It came as an even bigger shock to the gentler, more civilized firms of stockbrokers who found the new dynamism too much for their traditional ways.

It is widely believed that City stockbrokers are invariably restless, rapacious people, ready to cut a rival's throat for a short-term pecuniary gain. This is not so. And nowhere was it less so than in the fine old firm of Clarence Twist, just up the road from Bank tube station in the direction of Moorgate. The men – for they were mostly men – of Clarence Twist ranged from the fat to the gargantuan. Certainly, they had to make money – the firm would not survive if they did not, a fact which in 1986 was greatly occupying the minds of their senior partners. For the less exalted staff, however, money was not the only thing in life. They felt that life revolved around lunch. Lunch at Clarence Twist was an extremely serious matter. It was considered a severe clampdown when a missive from on high requested that those who went for their midday meal at eleven thirty should endeavour to be back by a quarter to four or, at any rate, thereabouts. Why, the Christmas lunch of 1982 had lasted several days. And there was an employee in a hotel in Brighton who was reputedly still consuming a business lunch he had begun in 1978. He had definitely been spotted working on the fish course in the summer of 79. And there were some who swore that he had started in on the sweet trolley some time in the late spring of 1981.

But a man must have time to enjoy his coffee and brandy. At Clarence Twist they didn't mind. They did not sack him or anything vulgar like that. No no. They made him South of England Hotels Partner and said they were quite happy for him to stay where he was as long as he found the occasional new client, something a man as congenial as he had no difficulty whatever in doing.

Certainly the dealers – those who bought and sold shares – showed occasional signs of animation. Even at Clarence Twist these men were indistinguishable from professional gamblers, since that is precisely what they were, backing their hunches about the value of enterprises of which they knew little and cared less. Like members of so many other professions they managed to persuade their clients that they had access to arcane mysteries, wholly inaccessible to the rest of humanity. Yet, bogus as this claim may have been, it went unquestioned by their clients as long as they made money. Few, if any, ever stopped to reflect that the stockbroker's art was both a game of mere chance and a strange way to run an economy.

Insofar as the dealers' hunches were backed up by knowledge – and, at Clarence Twist, very few of the dealers possessed any knowledge of anything whatsoever – this was due to the analysts. Their job was to assess the state of individual enterprises within their particular sector and to provide the back-up assessments and information on which the dealers based their dealings. Getting information meant meeting people. And meeting people meant lunch.

Clarence Twist's banking analyst, Oswald Nicholas, knew very little about banking but he did know about lunch. Oswald's cry of 'another bottle of poo' was legendary in wine bars throughout the square mile. In Sweetings Oyster Bar, Oswald's consumption of oysters was reminiscent of one of those disturbed individuals who occasionally pop up on television trying to break the world record for speed-eating raw eggs. At Mr

Garraway's Wine Bar in Gresham Street they still spoke reverently of the day Oswald had consumed an entire side of smoked salmon and declared that, having dealt with the fish course, he would now proceed to the beef. It therefore occasioned no surprise when one afternoon in August 1986, he gurgled during the soup. Oswald often gurgled. Not for nothing did waiters refer to him secretly as His Imperial Flatulence. Nor did it cause remark when he began to hiccup violently in the middle of conversation with the journalistic contact whom, in theory, he was tapping for information. It was, however, thought unseemly, and indeed even rather bad form, when to conclude his performance, he choked on a one-pound coin and dropped dead.

In the first place, Oswald was lunching at the branch of Balls Brothers in the Great Eastern Hotel at Liverpool Street, and at Liverpool Street Balls Brothers there is simply no room to drop dead. Like most City wine bars at lunchtime it was packed to the gills and possessed all the dignified comfort, and much the same smell, of a rugby changing room. In the second, it was Oswald's round and whatever might be said about Oswald, he was a man who bought his round. In the third, his sudden death meant that he missed the saddle of lamb and, a colleague at Clarence Twist observed, one simply did not expect Oswald Nicholas to depart, even for the great blue yonder, before doing justice to the saddle of lamb.

Not that his colleagues were unfeeling. On the contrary, they were profoundly disturbed. When a bulwark of the City like Oswald Nicholas measures his length, and for that matter his breadth, on the floor of Liverpool Street Balls Brothers the shock waves reverberate from Aldgate to Aldwych. An American banker caught the mood when he remarked, 'Oswald's clogs did not pop; they holocausted.'

But the senior partners had to think of the good of the firm. They knew that the next day's City gossip would be. 'Well, it was always going to happen one day that somebody would hand over his nosebag in the middle of a Clarence Twist lunch. Amazed it hasn't happened before. I mean, everything in moderation, eh, old boy? Two more large tawny ports!'

And that indeed was the gossip. For the gossipers did not know. And the senior partner did not know. But the detective inspector did know. He knew precisely what he was looking for and, in the breast pocket of Oswald's enormous pinstriped suit, he found it.

'Dear banking analyst,' it said, 'I fear your consumption has become somewhat conspicuous. Your futures market is far from bullish.'

'The cause of death,' said Frank Jefferson to George Cragge back at the BBC Salad Bar, 'was asphyxiation.'

'So who put the sixpence in the pudding?'

'They hadn't got to the pudding' – literal chap, our Frank – 'it was the soup.'

'What soup was it exactly?'

'Cream of vegetable. It was very thick.'

'Which is more than can be said for our murderer.'

'How do you mean?'

'Well,' said George, 'the middle of a City wine bar at lunchtime. I mean, it must be the easiest thing in the world. Anybody could have done it.'

'Yes,' said Jefferson, 'and there's another thing.'

'Which is?'

'This one wasn't actually a bank manager. It looks as if our man . . .'

'Or woman. Remember, Jemma says the voice could be a woman.'

'Jemma is going to end up in serious trouble. That young woman . . .'

'Yes, well never mind that. What were you saying about the murderer.'

'That whoever it is is broadening their scope,' said Jefferson.

'Well, the victim did work in banking in a sort of way, didn't he?'

'Yes, but he was a banking analyst. That's not the

same thing as a bank manager. Where on earth will the maniac strike next?'

'Well,' said George, 'perhaps we shall learn something from the Home Secretary's statement.'

'Incidentally,' said Jefferson, 'I think I've discovered the identity of MS.'

'Well, now we could be getting somewhere. Who is it?'

'I've been right through Inchcape's diary. And there's a name in his list of useful phone numbers. It's heavily crossed out, but I think it says "M. Sin". Mean anything?'

'M. Sin, and a phone number,' said George. 'Doesn't that suggest anything to your innocent mind?'

'I was thinking of trying Chinatown.'

'Yes,' said George, 'that sort of area, certainly.'

The Home Secretary had risen to the top by methods that were not for the squeamish. On the face of it, his was a distinguished, if conventional, career for a Conservative cabinet minister. Head boy at Eton, president of the Cambridge Union, leader writer on *The Times*. And then from hopeless Conservative seat to safe Conservative seat. PPS, junior minister, senior minister. Indeed the impression given by that curriculum vitae was not wholly misleading; it suggested cleverness and there was a real sense in which the Home Secretary was clever. He was the cleverest cheat in British politics. Yes, he had become head boy at Eton – but he would not have done so had not cannabis been mysteriously discovered in the study of his closest rival the night before the decision was taken. Yes, he had been president of the Cambridge Union, and some of those who had been induced to vote for him had almost been able to retire on their inducement, so lavish was his generosity when pursuing his own ambitions. He was a patrician Tory; that is to say, he had been born rich, he intended to stay rich and he had a clear view that the Conservative Party's one and only role in the great scheme of things was to help those who had the loot to hold on to it. Ironically, he held a Marxist view of society. That is to say, he fully believed that the capitalist system existed to oppress the masses. The difference between him and the socialists he hated was that he thought oppression the natural and proper condition of the masses and felt that they had been bred to it. 'My job,' he once told George Cragge, 'is to retard the onward march of the braying hordes – the relentless rise of the seething masses.'

Where the Home Secretary took his leave of those who controlled the Conservative Party in the 1980s was his view of how this suppression could best be achieved. It was not that he actually disagreed with the pursuit of ruthless monetarist policies. It was rather that he thought that if one were to retain support for such an approach one had to pretend to be doing something quite different. 'My job as Home Secretary,' he said, 'is to provide diversions from economic reality.' And that is precisely what he did. He talked expansively of patriotism and paid his ever-growing fortune into foreign bank accounts. He talked too about law and order – 'It's always a vote winner for us,' he maintained. And although in private he held extreme views, he was careful in public to strike a moderate, reasonable tone, seldom committing himself to anything. He was a deft, acute and consummate politician.

In George Cragge's opinion he was a fat pillock. It was clearly high time somebody told him so and the Bank Manager Murders seemed to George to provide the ideal pretext. For the murders were, to the Home Secretary, a considerable kick in the teeth. His performances at the annual Conservative Party Conference turned on his skilful deployment of the law and order card – and, since this event was the one time in the year when he could let his true opinions show, he had played that card with consistent vigour, limiting his moderate balanced approach to the assertion that it was perfectly acceptable to hang criminals as long as one had flogged them first.

It was now dawning on his not inconsiderable intellect that, in the law and order issue, he had bred a monster that threatened to devour him. He was in charge of the police, he was deemed to hold ultimate responsibility for the crime statistics. Thanks to the maniac, whoever he or she might be, those statistics had now acquired a momentum of their own. They did not appear on the front pages when the Home Secretary's mastery of news management decided that they should. They appeared because a wave of murders was sweeping London. The Home Secretary did not like it. He did not like it at all. The demands for his resignation were growing. The mere fact that the House of Commons had had to be recalled during a recess suggested crisis. As he sat waiting to deliver his speech to the Commons that afternoon he was aware that the Opposition looked maliciously expectant. The Leader of the Opposition appeared exceedingly cheerful as he mulled over a speech which he had prepared at length and with relish. The Leader of the Reform Party looked exceedingly cheerful as he mulled over a speech which he had not prepared and had not even read.

One of the salient features of the British House of Commons is that the chamber is too small to accommodate the number of Members of Parliament. This is inconvenient to MPs but it does have the advantage of creating a scintillating atmosphere when the House is full and, that afternoon, it was packed. They sat in the gangways, they stood in the aisles, they packed the entrance to the chamber.

In the BBC's commentary box sat George Cragge, ready to give expert analysis as the BBC broadcast the speech live. 'This,' said George, 'is going to be one of *the* parliamentary occasions.'

The points of order had been taken, the objections overruled. 'Statement, the Home Secretary,' cried the Speaker of the House and the Home Secretary, taking the text of his speech from his PPS, a young Tory merchant banker, rose to make his case.

'Mr Speaker,' he declared, 'I appeal to this House.' (Hon member: 'No you bloody don't.' Mr Speaker: 'Order!') 'I appeal to the sympathy and decency of this House.' (Hon members: 'Ho ho.') The Home Secretary continued, 'This is a law and order Government. We shall do everything in our power to assist the police in their quest for the Bank Manager Murderer. Mr Speaker, there are eight compelling reasons why the Government deserves the support of this House and now you're on your own, you old bastard.' (Hon members: 'What?')

The Home Secretary stopped. Partly he was aghast at what he had just read. But he was even more aghast at the fact that in his hand was not the speech that he and his advisers had prepared. It was not the speech that the Prime Minister had grudgingly approved that morning with the words, 'Well at least if we go down, we'll go with all guns blazing.'

But the guns they did not blaze. They were silent. So, for a moment, was the Home Secretary. Then he found his voice. He also found his parliamentary private secretary. 'You bastard,' shrieked Her Majesty's Secretary of State for Home Affairs. 'You fucking swine!' (Hon members: 'Oh!') 'You backstabbing, two-timing shitface!' (Hon members: 'Hear, hear! Go it, sunbeam!') 'I'll kill you for this. I'll bloody murder you!'

It took fifteen Conservative backbenchers to prise the Home Secretary's hands from the throat of his young colleague. When they succeeded, the Home Secretary slumped on the green House of Commons bench. His political life was over, his career lay in ruins. His Parliamentary Private Secretary also lay in ruins but it was a moment before anyone noticed that anything was amiss. It was Crichton-Potter who drew the House's attention to something that, strictly speaking, was not allowed to happen. For it is said to be a tradition that technically no one ever dies within the precincts of the House of Commons. Honourable members who expire on the premises are usually deemed to have died on the way to hospital. As Crichton-Potter bent over the PPS, however, it became clear that this honourable member had not died on his way to hospital. This honourable member was stone dead.

George Cragge was not a regular parliamentary journalist. He did not normally spend his time in the House of Commons commentary box and he neither knew nor cared about Westminster's rules concerning precisely who might go precisely where. All George knew was that when a professional journalist saw a story he went for it. George saw one and went for it. Racing down the steps of the Press Gallery he leapt over the balcony and landed safely on a Labour backbencher. Yet to the majority of MPs his intrusion was less of an affront to their dignity than it would usually have been. Their dignity had after all been somewhat more affronted already. Certainly George was to be hustled away by the Sergeant at Arms and a formal complaint registered with the Editor of BBC Radio News. That Editor, whose collection of complaints about George ran to several volumes, was for once quite unworried. Whilst other journalists fumed in the Press Gallery George had the story. Through the mêlée of MPs, he fought his way to the body. The PPS, Peter Anderson, MP, lay surrounded by the blank sheets of paper which someone had substituted for the Home Secretary's speech. Of course Anderson might have substituted them himself. George Cragge's opinion of the Home Secretary was widely shared and undoubtedly the Minister's PPS led a dog's life, which might have prompted him to want revenge.

There was another possibility, however – a possibility confirmed by George's discovery before being bundled out of the building. Inside the PPS's breast pocket was an envelope. The envelope contained a one-pound coin and a note:

'Dear Banker, The inflation has just been squeezed out of your system, by means of a knock-on effect.'

So who would have had the opportunity to insert the

note in the PPS's pocket? Who could have substituted the speech? As the hands of authority landed on George's shoulders, his eyes came face to face with Geoffrey Crichton-Potter, kneeling over the body.

At 10 Downing Street, the Prime Minister was livid. 'That swine,' he told his colleagues, 'has committed the worst crime any politician can commit.'

'Certainly,' said the Secretary to the Cabinet, 'I don't think there's any precedent for a Home Secretary being charged with murder.'

'Murder?' bellowed the PM. 'I'm not talking about murder, for pity's sake. What that swine has done is infinitely worse than murder – he's precipitated a bloody by-election!'

His cynicism found an echo in George Cragge as he reviewed the case with Frank Jefferson in the St Stephen's Tavern, a pub opposite the House of Commons. 'Well you've got to admit it, it's a bloody good story, Frank,' he told the harassed Detective Chief Inspector. It was not that George was indifferent to murder; it was just that nor was he indifferent to personal commendations from his Editor like the one he received for his on-the-spot coverage of the latest outrage. 'I mean it's not every day the Home Secretary bumps somebody off.'

'The Home Secretary didn't though, did he? I mean, technically, he may have been the instrument. But the real murderer is the maniac.'

'Yes, I suppose so.'

'Mind you, I think he set a precedent that someone else will be following before much longer.'

'How do you mean?'

'I think the Commissioner will throttle me if I don't catch the murderer pretty soon. Where on earth is he going to strike next? I mean, admittedly this one did have some connection with banking but there just doesn't seem to be any pattern.'

'There must be,' said George, 'if only we could discover it. Tell me about Anderson.'

'Well, Daddy was a merchant banker. The son went

to Lancing College and then . . .'

'Became a trained lancer?'

'No, you idiot. He went on to Cambridge. He was chairman of Cambridge University Conservative Club. I think that's how he came to be at the Home Office – the Cambridge connection. The Home Secretary was a Cambridge man, remember. Anderson seems to have found a safe seat very young and very easily. After that he became the Home Secretary's protégé.'

'Poor him,' said George.

'Why do you say that?'

'Because he must have had even more contact with the bugger than I had. I bet he hated him. I must say, if he substituted the speech himself, I wouldn't blame him. It must be bloody tempting to say, "Now you're on your own, you old bastard" when all you get to do is to write speeches for someone else.'

'You mean it was a sort of speechwriter's revenge?'

'Well, I wouldn't rule it out.'

'But there was a note, George. Surely this must tie in with all the other murders?'

'Oh yes. This is one of the sequence all right. But . . . well look, how does this grab you? Anderson hates the Home Secretary. He hates him so much that he wants to destroy him. So how does he do it? By hitting the Home Secretary where it hurts – in the law and order issue. A series of apparently inexplicable murders. And they have the added advantage of having a sort of economic angle.'

'Why's that an advantage?'

'Because it discredits the whole Government. Perhaps he wanted revenge on the lot of them.'

'Umm,' said Frank doubtfully.

'And because he murders bank managers he becomes a popular folk hero. Do you know that that "Bank Manager Blues" thing is number one in the charts? Anyway, tell me more about Anderson – did he keep up the merchant banking connection?'

'Oh yes. He was a partner in Daddy's firm, lucky boy.'

'Well, it would be interesting to know whether he had lunch in the City the day Oswald Nicholas copped his whack.'

'Well all right,' said Jefferson. 'There just could be something in that. But then what about the last note?'

'Just a bit of arrogant gloating.'

'Which is why he planted it on himself?'

'Oh.'

'Yes, oh. Are you suggesting he planned his own murder? And if he didn't, how did he know anyone would find the note?'

'Ah,' said George, 'oh shit.'

'Oh no, don't get me wrong. It's a beautiful theory except that it isn't true. You see, if you look at the note he refers to a knock-on effect. Now I think that means the murderer knew, or at any rate was prepared to gamble, that Anderson would get throttled.'

'It's one hell of a gamble.'

'Not if the Home Secretary was the arrogant, egotistical individual you say he was. He was made to look a prize idiot in front of the whole nation. I gather it's the first time a Home Secretary has been described by a BBC journalist on Radio 4 as a total plonker.'

'Well, I was doing live commentary,' said George, 'I wanted to describe the atmosphere.'

'You did that all right. No, I'm sorry, George,' said Jefferson, 'but I think this political stuff is irrelevant. I think we're going to find that these are sordid little crimes by a sordid little criminal.'

'You may be right. I can't help thinking that this speechwriter's revenge angle must have something in it. Being a speechwriter must be like being a Press Officer.'

'Must it?'

'Yes. And you know what I think about Press Officers. All your life writing stuff and other people getting the glory. I bet a speechwriter feels really frustrated — "wearing out his time, much like his master's ass, for nought but provender"', he concluded in a rare burst of lyricism.

'I beg your pardon?'

'*Othello*,' George told him. 'Perhaps we're looking for a sort of Iago figure, a faithful servant who isn't so faithful after all.'

'We are looking for an honest to goodness criminal. Anyway,' said Jefferson, 'I'd better get back. I'm afraid this faithful servant has to face the music.'

'Well, have another one before you go. You know my motto, Frank – if you've got music to face, get so pissed you can't see straight.'

For once Jefferson's normally iron self-discipline failed him. He grumblingly bought two more large ones.

'Now look,' said George, 'let's suppose you're right and that Anderson, who was a banker, actually was the intended victim. Who might have hated him? What were his responsibilities at the Home Office apart from general factotum to his boss?'

'Well, as far as I can make out, he's only done two things of any note. And one you know about, of course.'

'No, I don't.'

'Of course you do. He had some responsibility for broadcasting. He was the one who made recommendations to the Home Secretary about broadcasting policy. How much of a licence fee increase the BBC should get, that sort of stuff. I thought you'd know that.'

'I'm a crime reporter, mate. Not a bloody BBC politician. So he was the man depriving BBC Radio of its money?'

'The only other thing he did was to draft the reform of the laws on prostitution – you know, the one making it more difficult for them to ply their trade. But I can't see that that's got anything to do with it. Look, I really must go.'

'What's your next port of call after seeing your chief?'

'Well, I've got to find out who Anderson was with during the time leading up to the debate. And I've got to call on MS.'

'M. Sin.'

59

'Yes, M. Sin. Whoever he or she may be.'

This time Jefferson refused George's offer of another large one. He made his way out of the crowded pub and prepared to endure the apoplectic wrath of his superiors. As he left, he bumped into an inconspicuous young man sipping lager and tearing up the remains of a pass to the House of Commons public gallery.

Mr Andrew James of Mysore Road, Battersea, London SW11, had never visited the House before. What a rare treat it had been.

Outside the House of Commons, as he waited for a taxi, Jefferson noticed a man he did recognize – a Conservative backbencher. Had he seen anything?

CHAPTER
6

'Well, frankly, no. Nothing you'd call suspicious. I came into the central lobby about one, or just before. I was supposed to be meeting some constituents but they had not turned up. I saw Peter talking to some people and invited them to join me for a drink.'

'Do you know who these people were?' Frank Jefferson was irritated by the MP's vagueness.

'I think they were friends of Peter's from the City. He used to spend more time there than he did here, you know; he was something big in banking.'

'So I understand,' said Jefferson. 'So you all went on to the terrace.'

'Yes, we nipped out and Peter said, "Why don't we have some champers?" Seemed a good idea, you know, so we had the Perrier Jouer Belle Epoque. Lovely stuff, actually.'

'Really, sir?' Jefferson was a pint of bitter man, and as far as he was concerned, wine was for homosexuals, a view which the young MP did nothing to diminish.

'Then, what?'

'Well nothing. I mean we sat and talked; we thought we'd have another Perrier Jouer, quite delicious, you know – utterly unlike most of the champagne one gets.'

'Yes sir, but I am not researching a book on champagne.'

'No. No, quite. Well, we had that bottle and we thought we'd have a third and I said no because I was hoping to speak in the debate and Peter said no because he had to check over the speech.'

'So you saw him again, when?'

'I saw him in the chamber. He handed over the

speech, just as the PM was saying. "I refer my honourable friend to the answer I gave some moments ago" and he said . . .'

'But you noticed nothing unusual about him?'

'No. Not at all. We were both sitting there . . .'

'Where were you sitting in relation to him?'

'Two rows back.'

'Were you the first person to reach Mr Anderson after he was attacked?'

'No, actually. Crichton-Potter was there first.'

'How many MPs were there in the chamber at the time?'

'About six hundred of us, actually.'

'And you all gathered round him?'

'Yes, but there was nothing we could do.'

'You realized he was dead?'

'Yes, at once. Crichton-Potter felt his heart and his pulse and we opened his eyes and – well – and that was it, really. Oh, yes, and somebody found a letter in Peter's pocket. But you know about that.'

'Yes sir. Now, if I may take you back to your drinks on the terrace. You were drinking this wine . . .'

'We were sipping Perrier Jouer Belle Epoque, Inspector.'

'Chief Inspector, sir.' Jefferson was not normally a pompous man, but he had been mixing with some pompous people of late. 'How many guests did Anderson have?'

'There were three of them, two chaps and a filly.'

'Did you happen to find out who they were?'

'One was a stockbroker, or something, or an analyst. Or he may have been an accountant.'

'Did you catch his name, sir?'

'No. Frightfully sorry. I remember who the other chap was, though. He was the Governor of the Bank of England's brother, Dominic D'eath, and he had his girlfriend with him. Plucky filly. Goes mountain climbing, you know.'

'Her name?' Jefferson was beginning to think that

murdering MPs was not a crime at all. It was a public service. It ought to be rewarded with its own honours system – the Guy Fawkes award for ridding the world of potential legislators. He obtained the name of Dominic D'eath's girlfriend and, with a supreme effort, bade the honourable member farewell.

'I hope you are going to catch this chap, Sergeant.'

'Chief Inspector, sir.'

'Whatever you are. I don't think very much of it if you people are going to let MPs get murdered in the House of Commons. I shall have something to say about it in the House. Heads will roll, Constable.'

'No doubt they will.' But why was it always the wrong heads?

'Is this the headquarters of the Reform Party?'

'Er, yes, that's right. What can I do for you?'

'I'd like to join, please.'

'You'd like to do what?'

'I'd like to join, please.'

'Join? You mean join the Reform Party?'

'Yes please. I'd like to become a member. How much does it cost?'

'How much can you spare?'

'Would ten pounds be sufficient?'

'Ten pounds? Good God!'

'I suppose I could make it fifteen pounds.'

'We'll take it. Look, are you absolutely sure?'

'Quite sure, thank you. Shall I give you the money now?'

'Well, yes. I'll fill in a membership card for you.'

'Thank you. I understand there's to be a by-election in Talbotting. I'd like to help, if you could give me the address of the local headquarters.'

'Yes, yes, of course. May I just have a note of your name and address to put on your card?'

'Certainly. Mr Andrew James of Mysore Road, Battersea, London SW11.'

*

'All we need,' Henry told Crichton-Potter, 'is another couple of hundred thousand people like him. Then we'll be able to afford to fight this by-election. Now, you know we're expecting a visitor.'

'An important, rich visitor,' agreed Crichton-Potter.

'The vital thing,' said Henry, 'is to stress the value to rich people like him of a Reform Party victory in the by-election.'

'How will it benefit people like him?' asked Crichton-Potter, looking puzzled.

'It won't. In the first place, if the Reform Party ever did win power, we'd have to take all his money several times over to do one millionth of the things we are committed to do. And in the second, if we do win this by-election, the Government probably won't take the slightest notice.'

'Well, in that case, how on earth am I going to persuade him to come across?'

'Lie to him,' said Henry patiently. 'I mean, we need his money. We can't fight this by-election without it.'

'That's certainly true. The party's on the verge of bankruptcy. We can hardly afford to pay our staff.'

'I know. I am your staff.'

'Well, yes, quite.' Crichton-Potter changed the subject hastily. 'Anyway, I stress that victory for us will be a good thing for the country.'

'No you do not. You stress that a win for the Reform Party will help him to hold on to his loot. Tell him the Government's becoming complacent, that it takes people like him for granted. A by-election shock will be just what it needs to bring it to its senses, halt the sense of drift at the top of the administration and restore sanity to our national affairs. Then you ask him to make with the lolly.'

'What do we actually know about the chap? I mean, he's some lord or other, isn't he?'

'He's Lord Gate. His friends call him Creaky. He's about eighty or ninety or something. He's half-blind, half-deaf and half-witted. That's why I suggested him.'

'And how does he come to be connected with the Reform Party?'

'He's on one of our advisory panels. He devotes himself to good works and is particularly interested in education. We invited him to join our education panel so we could have the benefit of his money – I mean his advice.'

'I see. Good, fine. Well, he should be here at any moment. Now what was it again – a victory for the Reform Party will bring the Government to its senses, restore sanity . . .'

Outside, the source of the Reform Party's hopes was alighting from a taxi. He paid the driver with a £20 note and did not wait for change. This was no doubt due in part to generosity but it reflected also the waning powers to which Henry had alluded. Lord Gate was an amiable old soul but he had not been an intellectual kind of person in his day. And his day, like the party itself, had been long ago. It *was* Berwick Street? Or should he have gone to Poland Street? Or possibly Frith Street? Lord Gate had always done everything through process of trial and error and, since Berwick Street is where he was, he thought he had better explore that first. The door was open – the Reform Party's door was always open – and he took the lift which creaked almost as much as he did to the third floor.

On the second floor, which was where he should have gone, Crichton-Potter was becoming impatient. 'Where is the old fool?' he demanded.

'Look, keep calm. Remember, we need his cash. We've got to be absolutely charming to him.'

'That's all very well, but I've got lunch at the Oxford and Cambridge in ten minutes.'

'Don't you want us to fight this by-election?'

'Of course I do,' said Crichton-Potter. 'It's just that I want my lunch as well.'

'Be grateful you can afford lunch,' said Henry sharply.

'Ar, um.' Crichton-Potter was anxious to avoid the

subject of his speechwriter's salary. 'Look, shouldn't the old boy meet our candidate if we are expecting him to cough up?'

'We haven't got a candidate,' said Henry. 'The selection process hasn't started yet. We're going to have to make jolly certain we rig it when it does, mind you. The Young Reformers are arguing that what we need is a candidate for youth.'

'Ye gods,' said Crichton-Potter.

'They say the country needs somebody who'll put youth issues at the top of the political agenda.'

'Hell's bells. That's all we need. Do you know, there are times when I'd like to take the leaders of our so called Youth movement and give them a damn good . . .'

Lord Gate's brief association with the Reform Party had taught him that it contained some unconventional people. He was a civilized sort of person and, if the secretary at the Reform Party Headquarters made a habit of opening the door in black bra, panties and suspender belt, well that was nothing to do with him. For her part, Madam Sin was impressed. She was used to clients in advanced middle age but this one was a record breaker.

'Come in, darling,' she bade him. 'Now what can I do for you?'

'My name is Lord Gate. My principal interest is in education.'

Madam Sin liked a client who entered into the spirit of things. 'Oh, so is mine, love. It's fifteen pounds.' Business before pleasure was the rule with Madam Sin.

'Er . . .oh.' Lord Gate had expected to be asked for money but he had not expected the subject to be introduced so early and bluntly. On the other hand he had expected to be touched for a good deal more than fifteen pounds. 'Is that really all it costs for a seat nowadays?'

'Cheap at the price in'it? Now, come to Miss.'

'I beg your pardon?'

'We've been a naughty boy, haven't we?'

'Have we?'

'We've been a very naughty boy. And we know what happens to naughty boys?'

'Er . . . do we?'

'When we've been a naughty boy' – Madam Sin was nothing but professional – 'we get sent to Miss. Miss has to get out her cane. And then she pulls these down. And these . . .'

'Where the hell is the bloody old idiot?' Crichton-Potter's stomach took a great deal of filling at the best of times. He was now painfully empty and victory in the Talbotting by-election was coming to seem trivial in comparison with the need for lunch.

Henry, whose sense of political priorities was somewhat surer, attempted to soothe him. 'I'm sure he'll be here soon. It's very important, this by-election, you know. It's vital to the entire future of the party that we do well.'

'Oh, all right, all right. I just hope he comes across. I mean, suppose he says no? We'll be sunk.'

'I'm sure he won't say no. He's a good-natured old stick, in his way.'

'I just hope you're right. No, I think that the direct approach is the best one. I think that I'll say to him: "Lord Gate, this party is desperately short of funds. Basically, we need your money. All we're asking is a few thousand quid." Now what do you say to that?'

'Aaaaaooh!' said Lord Gate.

'"I mean,"' continued Crichton-Potter, '"we're not asking for much. Just think, your donation could help to change the face of British politics. Now how about it, eh?"'

'Bloody hellfire!' said Lord Gate.

'"And I think I can say – not that I'm in any way offering a bribe or anything, you understand – that when I form my first Cabinet, we shall certainly be looking for some chaps from the Lords. Chaps with your extensive experience of the world, what?"'

'Ow! Ouch! Sodding hell!' Lord Gate's extensive experience of the world had in the past couple of minutes become more extensive. He had always been, in a mild sort of way, opposed to corporal punishment, but he had never thought about it seriously. He was now thinking about it more seriously than he had ever thought about anything and there was nothing mild in his objections. He was expressing his revulsion with a passion which would have done credit to an evangelical preacher. For her part, Madam Sin reflected that she had never known a punter play his part with such conviction. She was actually having a struggle holding him down. She was managing it, though; she had very strong arms, Madam Sin. Lord Gate could testify to this.

'Look, I can't wait about here all day.' Crichton-Potter had had enough. 'If he turns up, tell him I've been called to the House for an urgent division, and fix another date. I'm going to lunch.'

Henry gave up the struggle. 'Oh, all right. I just don't understand it. He definitely said ten thirty. I was told by the people on our education panel that he's usually very prompt.'

'Well, they're wrong, aren't they?' Crichton-Potter's stomach rumbled and when Crichton-Potter's stomach rumbled, it sounded as if it were playing the *1812 Overture*. 'Oh, and we must get together and talk about the candidate selection,' he said as he opened the door. He took one pace outside and then six back in, having collided heavily with what he took to be the world champion in the over-eighties hundred metres. It took a moment for Crichton-Potter to recognize the geriatric sprinter but, to be fair to him, having done so he overcame his longing for food and got straight down to business. 'Lord Gate,' he called down the stairs, 'as leader of the Reform Party . . .'

'The Reform Party,' shrieked the noble Lord, 'my ass!'

'Do you think that means no?' asked Crichton-Potter.

CHAPTER
7

'Personnel officers don't go on hunger strike.'

'This one has. It's something to do with one of the journalists.'

'It would be. All right, I'll look into it. Where is he?'

'He's in room 621, on the sixth floor. He says he won't come out until he obtains satisfaction under Staff Instruction 153.'

'Oh, leave it with me.' The Controller of Radio 4 put the phone down and turned to greet his counterpart from Radio 2. 'Have you ever come across a chap called Fortescue?' he asked.

'I don't think so. What is he? Some sort of trouble-maker?'

'He's a personnel officer.'

'That explains it.'

'Anyway, to business.' CR4 made sure the door was firmly closed and looked suspiciously around the room as if worried that it might be bugged. The overthrow of the Director General was not something he wanted noised abroad – not, at least, until after it had happened. He handed a large cigar to his colleague and took one himself. 'So,' he began, 'any ideas?'

The Controller of Radio 2 was an elegant, silver-haired, vain man. Like so many top executives he had reached the top, first and foremost, because he looked the part. His career in broadcasting as such had been undistinguished but he had learned at an early stage that the key to success was not to be too brilliant but rather to avoid doing anything disastrous. He was a cultured, civilized man who, in the normal course of things, would no more have listened to Radio 2 which he now ran than he would have danced naked down

Oxford Street. He was also an extremely shrewd political animal.

'Harold Wilson,' he told CR4, 'once said politics is ninety per cent presentation and that what isn't presentation is timing. That seems to be the essence of our problem. As far as timing is concerned the main consideration is this: the Corporation is now in the middle of negotiating an increase in its licence fee.'

'Yes.'

'That is the only time when the job of the Director General really matters. All right; the DG is the Chief Executive of the BBC. He is also the Editor-in-Chief.'

'But in fact,' said CR4, 'he does precious little editing. The show basically runs itself.'

'Quite so. The only time the Director General really becomes important is in dealings with the Government about money. Consequently our task is to contrive a situation in which the BBC receives an obviously inadequate licence fee settlement. Only the Director General can be held to blame for that and if things are really bad – if, say, the BBC got no licence fee increase at all – it is perfectly possible that the DG would have to resign.'

'But I thought you and I had agreed,' said CR4, 'that a poor licence fee settlement would hit radio's budget which is exactly what we're trying to avoid. Television is where the power and the money are, nowadays. How do we benefit from this scheme?'

'I'm coming to that. In the normal course of things, everything you say is perfectly correct. However,' CR2 paused to draw on his cigar, 'if the failure of the licence fee negotiations were to be due to a television series . . .'

'Oh, I see.'

'One so bad. So terrible. And so grossly offensive, especially to the Government.'

'Oh, I like it.' CR4 rubbed his hands with glee. 'I like it very much.'

'You see, I think that, under those circumstances, it would be difficult to sustain the case for constantly reducing our budget and increasing theirs. I think we might, at least for the time being, actually reverse the tendency.'

'All right,' said CR4, 'I like what I've heard so far. But what sort of programme had you in mind?'

'The essential thing about this new series is that it must be in absolutely gross bad taste. It must upset everybody – but Government ministers in particular. If you look at the history of the BBC, it's clear that there's only one kind of programme capable of causing that kind of outrage – a late-night satirical programme.'

'And it will have to be one that goes further than any such programme has ever done before.'

'Precisely so. Now as I see it,' said the Controller of Radio 2, bringing his master plan to conclusion, 'there are two problems about the scheme. The first is, how do we cause this series to happen without the slightest possibility of our names being associated with it?'

'Well, that should be easy enough,' said CR4. 'What we do is to sell it to one of the Controllers in the Television Service. Incidentally, are you thinking of BBC1 or BBC2 for this show?'

'Oh, it must be BBC1,' said CR2. 'More people watch it, and we want the maximum possible exposure.'

'In that case, the obvious course would be to plant the idea in the mind of the Controller of BBC1. Only we make sure we do it without any official meeting and leave it to him to raise the matter formally. As long as there's nothing on paper there's no way they can link it with us.'

'Right. Well, your contacts are better than mine. Shall I leave it to you to handle that side of things?'

'Oh, I think we can both do our bit,' said CR4, who had no intention of running the entire risk on his own, which he guessed correctly to be what his colleague had in mind. 'You said there were two problems – what's the other one?'

'The other one is a little more difficult. How the hell do we ensure that the programme when it eventually gets on the air actually satisfies our criterion of awfulness? Are there in fact producers in the Television Service of the standard of incompetence we're seeking?'

'No,' said CR4, 'they're all in management.'

The Controller of Radio 2 smiled. 'Yes. Yes, quite. So where do we find. . .'

'A complete idiot.'

'A moron.'

'A toerag.'

'Who's guaranteed to drop the biggest clanger in broadcasting history.'

'Ideally,' said CR4, 'it should be someone who's never produced a programme before in his life. Someone who's a bureaucratic imbecile. Someone who's . . . who's . . . a personnel officer.'

'My God!'

'Exactly.'

'It's breathtaking.'

'It's brilliant,' said CR4, 'and I know just the chap.'

'You mean . . .'

'I do.' CR4 pressed his intercom. 'Jenny – can you get me a phone number for this Fortescue character. I'm going to talk him out of his hunger strike.'

The cause of Mr Fortescue's hunger strike was not feeling any too special that morning. He sat in his office, clutching his head, moaning softly and praying that nothing would happen in the world to merit his attention. When his telephone rang it took him about thirty seconds to recover from the effect on his tortured head.

'George Cragge speaking,' he groaned.

'Hello, George. It's Frank Jefferson. I thought I'd better put you in the picture about the latest murder. Not that there's much of a picture.' Jefferson recounted his discussion with the MP at the House. 'So I don't think we're much further forward,' he said, 'except that – if he'll strike at the House of Commons, where on earth will he strike next?'

'Yeah,' said George, 'and there's been a hell of a row about security at the House.'

'Don't talk about it. The Prime Minister is going berserk. He says absolutely anybody can wander into the House of Commons at will. And basically he's right.'

'This is supposed to be a democracy.'

'Yes, but democracy isn't supposed to mean that anybody who feels like bumping off his MP just goes ahead.'

'Well, I don't know,' said George, 'I think it is a pretty logical extension.'

'Anyway, the thing is, I want you and me to get together and pool all our resources. I want you to bring the tapes of the phone calls so I can have them analysed again by voice experts and see if that leads anywhere. And I'll draw up a chart with the names and addresses of the murder victims.'

'You mean that, given that this guy's a nutter, he's probably working to some sort of system – crazy, but with some sort of inherent rationale.' George thought for a moment. 'OK. What about this afternoon?'

'This afternoon will be fine. I'm going to catch this bugger, George. I really am.'

'I've set the date of the selection meeting for ten days' time,' the Chairman of the Talbotting Constituency Reform Party told the secretary, Miss Cartright.

'What is the exact procedure for these meetings?'

'There isn't one really.' The Chairman, who had been around the Reform Party a long time, refrained from pointing out that often Reform Party candidate selection did not involve choosing from a range of possibilities but inducing the weakest individual present to make a prize ass of himself in public. The outcome of such meetings was not usually 7–6 in the 5th; it was more 1–nil after extra time.

On this occasion, admittedly, it was different. Three people had applied for the privilege of fighting the Talbotting by-election. The Chairman considered their chances. 'There's Gil Slack,' he said, 'he's the Chair of the Young Reformers.'

'I don't think he'd be suitable for Talbotting, do you?' said the Secretary, a rather prim woman in her mid-dash forties. 'I expect he's frightfully left wing.'

'Well, I think he is on the, er, radical wing of the party, yes. But, on the other hand, a lot of young people have moved into the constituency recently. They might be likelier to vote for us if we have a young candidate.'

'Yes, possibly.' Miss Cartright sounded doubtful. 'Who else is there?'

'There's John Lowther. A stockbroker.'

'Oh, he sounds much more suitable.'

'Mid-thirties. He lives in the area, which is something, I suppose. Smart, clean-cut, affluent, moderate views.'

'Then why are we holding this meeting at all? He's obviously our man.'

'I know he looks a good prospect in a number of ways.'

'So what's wrong with him?'

'Well . . .' The Chairman found it difficult to explain to Miss Cartright but he had a stab. 'He's the leadership's candidate. He's a personal friend of Geoffrey Crichton-Potter.'

'Why didn't you say so? In that case, he is obviously our man.' The suggestion that Miss Cartright's unflagging efforts for the Reform Party were a substitute for her frustrated sexuality would, no doubt, have been unkind. To reveal the details of her dreams about the preposterous leader of her party would not have been unkind but positively indecent. Suffice to say that any friend of Crichton-Potter had her vote before the selection meeting had even started.

The Chairman was made of sterner stuff. 'This party,' he protested, 'has a tradition of local democracy. We've got to make up our own mind. Do we want to be just the lackey of the leadership?'

'Yes we do.'

'Do we want to have a candidate foisted on us by the leader?'

'Yes we do.'

'Well I don't agree. Anyway, there is a third applicant. He's the only one who's actually fought a parliamentary election before. Larry Boot-Heath. He fought one of the London seats at the last general election.'

'How many votes did he get?' demanded Miss Cartright.

'Not very many, actually.'

'How many?'

'Well – er, one, actually.'

'One?'

'But he's been a member of the party for thirty years. He knows our policies backwards.'

'Best way to know them,' said Miss Cartright dismissively.

'Anyway, we must have a look at him. It's our duty.'

'Oh, very well,' she conceded reluctantly. 'So what do you want me to do?'

'Send out calling notices to all the members of the local association.'

'Six calling notices,' wrote Miss Cartright.

'Tell them there's to be a meeting at which each of the candidates will speak for five minutes and then answer questions. After that, we'll vote and the winner becomes our candidate.'

'John Lowther becomes our candidate,' wrote Miss Cartright.

'Whoever wins,' the Chairman repeated. 'This is a democratic party.'

'The trouble is,' said Henry ruefully, 'that this is a democratic party. In any sensible organization the leader would simply inform the local party of who the candidate was to be. Then we'd all get on with it. I mean, it's obvious that Lowther's got to fight this seat. At least he looks like a human being.'

'What are his views on policy?' asked Crichton-Potter.

'He hasn't got any views on policy. That's another of his advantages. He's a respectable member of the community, he wears pinstripe suits, he works in the City and he wants to be an MP because he thinks it will help his business. Politically, he will do just as he's told. He's ideal.'

'And what about the others?'

'Well, I ask you. There's Gil Slack – all very well in his way, of course.'

'Oh, quite,' said Crichton-Potter.

'I mean the party needs the voice of youth. But in a by-election at Talbotting? Can you see those people voting for a red-haired left-wing loony?'

'No, frankly, I can't.'

'And, as for the other possibility, it's just too ghastly to contemplate. Larry Boot-Heath.'

Crichton-Potter shuddered. Larry Boot-Heath had once talked to him for three and a half hours about land taxation. Admittedly the party was in favour of land taxation, but Crichton-Potter had never had the faintest idea what it was or where he stood on the issue. He knew exactly where he stood, however, on the question of people who talked to him for three and a half hours abut any aspect of policy.

'The only trouble with this selection meeting from my point of view is that it all looks so straightforward.' Henry liked to think of himself as a one-man dirty tricks department. He had the feeling that on this occasion his talents in that direction would not be needed. 'All I need to do,' he said, 'is to write Lowther's speech for him. Oh, and I suppose I'd better plant a few questioners amongst the audience. And make sure he's got his answers ready. Piece of cake as far as I can see.'

'I'm relieved to hear it,' said Crichton-Potter. 'We don't want any cock-ups.'

'I don't see how that could happen.'

Henry telephoned John Lowther. 'It is scarcely possible,' he told the candidate, 'to underestimate the intelligence of any given electorate. They don't want to be bothered with politics. And I don't want you to bother with politics either. I want you to look smart, and shake as many hands as you can and to smile a lot. If you do that, it's in the bag.'

John Lowther agreed deferentially. He was an ideal candidate. His suit and his quiet and obviously silk tie were immaculate. His hairline was receding but not too much. His eyes were bright, his teeth were white and his head was empty. 'Of course,' he said, 'I can't claim to know much about this political business.'

'Don't worry about a thing,' Henry told him. 'I'll write your speech – you just read it out – and I'll have so many questions planted in the audience that no one will have time to ask any proper ones. The whole thing will go like a dream.'

'Ar, *mon pauvre* Hastings, you must learn to use the little grey cells.'

'But, my dear Poirot, usin' the bally grey cells is so common – makes one feel such a frightful ass, what?'

'Lord Peter, you are – as you say – *imbécile.'*

Frank Jefferson poured George and himself another large whisky. They had had a great deal of whisky that afternoon to console themselves for their singular lack of progress in deciding who or what sort of who they were looking for.

'I', said Lord Peter Cragge, 'shall gather my thoughts, whilst nonchalantly tossing off a couple of Beethoven sonatas on my Hungarian nose flute.'

'Listen to those tapes again,' Jefferson told him. 'They're about all we've got to go on at the minute. I'm off to visit the Governor of the Bank of England's brother.'

Dominic D'eath lived in some splendour in Eaton Square. Jefferson was admitted with distaste by the butler and shown into a large and sumptuously furnished room on the ground floor. He felt decidedly uncomfortable. He thought the carpet too good to stand on and the chairs to smart to sit on. He moved around the room, admiring what he recognized – for he was not as ignorant as he would sometimes have liked to pretend – as a Tintoretto.

His host, Dominic D'eath, entered in a crisp and businesslike fashion. He was a large imposing man, with broad shoulders. He had grey hair and intelligent, piercing blue eyes. He would indeed have been handsome were it not for his nose. This nose was monstrous. It was truly a nose amongst noses. It would have stood out in a crowd. Unfortunately for Dominic D'eath, it stood out on his face instead and mocked the ordered elegance of the rest of his appearance.

'Chief Inspector, I'm so sorry to have kept you waiting.' There was an affected Cockney tinge to the accent, denoting D'eath's aristocratic origins.

'That's all right, sir. I'd just like to ask you a few questions concerning the murder of Peter Anderson.'

'Yes, of course. Ghastly business.'

'I believe Mr Anderson was with you shortly before he died.'

'It sounds terribly sinister put like that. Yes, I had lunch with Peter. Well, not so much lunch, really, just a few drinks on the terrace. My girlfriend, Kelly Sharpe, was there and some stockbroker chap. Peter wanted my professional judgement on some aspects of Government policy.'

'Yes, sir. What is your profession?'

D'eath coloured slightly. 'I am an economist,' he said with some hauteur. 'Obviously you have not come across my book, *Inflation, Money and War*. It is the definitive work on the subject.' He relented. 'Oh, I suppose there's no reason why you should have heard of me. It is my misfortune to be known only as the Governor of the Bank of England's brother. Carstairs has achieved a much greater degree of prominence than I have – demonstrating in the process that intellectual limitation need be no bar to advancement in a democratic society.'

'Er, quite so, sir.' Jefferson was rather stunned by the venom of the remarks. 'If I might take you back to the day of Mr Anderson's murder.'

'Yes, yes, of course. How can I help?'

'You were drinking with him on the terrace. What did you drink?'

'At first I drank Campari. So did Kelly. The stockbroker had a Pimms and Peter a gin and tonic. Then we drank some champagne. I don't know why. Most of our legislators could not distinguish a Perrier Jouet Belle Epoque from a bottle of Lucozade.'

'How many drinks did you have?' Jefferson was anxious to steer D'eath away from the merits of democracy, since plainly he thought there were none.

'Oh, a few glasses. I think we had about three each.'

'Did you notice anything unusual at all? Did you speak to anyone who struck you as odd?'

'Have you ever met a stockbroker, Chief Inspector?'

'Well, yes sir, but anyone else?'

'No, I don't think so, except – well, there was this one chap. But that wasn't on the terrace, it was in the central lobby whilst we were waiting for Peter. Or rather, just after Peter had joined us.'

'What exactly happened, sir?'

'A young chap came up to us and asked where he could get a copy of some white paper or other that had just been published. His manner was decidedly odd. He obviously didn't know his way around the House and I distinctly remember that he was wearing odd socks – one red, one grey sock. He seemed – I don't know, agitated or excited, or something. And he looked at Peter in a strange sort of way. But I am sure none of this is any use to you, Chief Inspector. I expect it's all totally irrelevant.'

'Oh no, sir; it doesn't sound irrelevant at all. Can you describe this man for me?' Jefferson felt his heartbeat increase. The first solid sighting of what he was sure would turn out to be the murderer.

'Certainly. He was young – about twenty-five, I should imagine. He was well spoken, he had rather curly hair, brownish in colour, and spectacles, and, as I say, he was wearing odd socks.'

'Can you remember what else he was wearing?'

'I'm afraid I can't,' said D'eath, 'I was so struck by his socks, you see.'

'Yes, yes of course. Tell me, Mr D'eath, do you think you'd recognize his voice if you heard it again?'

'I'm not sure that I would, to tell you the truth.'

'Pity,' said Jefferson. 'Still, that's a great help. Just one or two more questions. Your drinks were brought to you on the terrace by a waiter?'

'That's correct. Incidentally, I am sure I have seen him around the place for years.'

'Quite so, sir. We interviewed him at length and eliminated him from our inquiries. Now, once you had your drinks did Mr Anderson's mood seem at all unusual? He didn't seem on edge or anything?'

'No. No, nothing like that.'

'Then how the dickens did he do it?' Jefferson wondered aloud.

'Is one permitted to know what are your main lines of inquiry?' asked D'eath.

'Oh yes, sir. We don't believe Mr Anderson tampered with the speech himself. We think someone else did because . . . well, for reasons I cannot really go into.'

'I see. Well, none of us tampered with the speech, if that is what you are suggesting.'

'No no, sir. I am sure you didn't. I won't take up any more of your time. You've been a great help.'

'Not at all, Chief Inspector.'

'I wonder if I might ask you to drop in at the Yard sometime and listen to some tapes for me. Just to see if they ring any bells.'

'Of course. I have a good deal of free time. *The World at One* does not invite me to pronounce on the great topics of the day as it does my illustrious brother. Shall we say tomorrow afternoon?'

'Thank you, sir. That will be fine.' Jefferson took his leave, feeling more cheerful than he had felt since the case began. Someone, at least, had seen the murderer.

CHAPTER
8

'This is the first lead the police have had in their hunt for the so-called Bank Manager murderer and they say they hope to issue a description shortly of a man they want to interview.'

'That was our crime reporter, George Cragge,' said the drug-crazed newsreader, 'and now one piece of late news. The Reform Party has chosen Larry Boot-Heath to be its candidate in the forthcoming by-election at Talbotting in Surrey. The by-election – for which the writ is expected to be moved within the next few weeks – is due to the murder of the sitting MP, Mr Peter Anderson, thought to be one of the victims of the Bank Manager murderer. BBC Radio News.'

Henry wondered as he turned off the midnight news whether the word 'sorry' would begin to do justice to the magnitude of his offence. He was travelling back by car from the selection meeting and wondering how to explain to Crichton-Potter that the leader's favoured candidate had, in a word, been wellied. Anyone can make a mistake, Henry told himself. The trouble was that this was not a mistake; it was a megalulu.

The trouble with being involved with politics twenty-four hours a day, thought Henry, is that one loses one's sense of perspective. One tends to be over elaborate. A more sensible course would have been to keep things simple.

Henry had been over-anxious not to leave anything to chance. He knew that the Talbotting Reform Association had only six members, including its Chairman and Secretary, and that that was not enough. He had therefore decided to bus in as many Reform supporters as he could find, with clear instructions of their duties.

His reasoning was, first, that if the local newspaper were short of a story, it might send along a reporter to the selection meeting. It would not be impressive if he found only a handful of people, and Henry thought it essential for publicity purposes that the meeting should be a large one. Admittedly, only the paid-up members of the local association would actually be allowed to vote but the reporter would not know that. Second, even without voting rights, a good crowd, properly primed to cheer the favoured candidate and disparage the others, would create an atmosphere conducive to the right outcome.

The crowd Henry brought to Talbotting certainly created an atmosphere. Then they created a disturbance. Finally they created a riot.

Possibly they had misunderstood or, at any rate overzealously interpreted Henry's instructions. The truth was that Henry had been extravagant. He had booked a coach to take the John Lowther supporters to Talbotting. The Reform Party could not afford to go about booking coaches and, in order to justify the expense, Henry had moved heaven and earth to ensure that the coach was full. It was not easy to raise a coachload of Reform Party supporters at short notice and, in desperation, Henry had combed the pubs of Soho around Reform HQ to bribe the patrons with offers of a night out and free alcohol. They were not all committed Reform supporters – some of them, indeed, had never even heard of the Reform Party – but they had availed themselves freely of Henry's generosity and most had managed to get hold at least of the basic idea to cheer Lowther and boo the rest.

That is precisely, and abundantly, what they did from the first. The Chairman and the three applicants mounted the platform to a chorus of 'One John Lowther, there's only one John Lowther', complete with scarves held above heads. The Chairman of Talbotting Reform Association blinked over his spectacles with amazement. He had never seen the Church Hall of St

82

Mary and All Saints, Talbotting, so full. He gave a little cough and began. 'Ladies and gentlemen, may I begin by extending a warm welcome to all our visitors.'

'Ere,' said one of the warmly welcomed visitors to Henry, 'who's this cunt?' in a stage whisper audible for several miles.

Henry fixed the platform with what was supposed to be a reassuring smile but was in fact a demented grin. His questioner was not to be deterred. 'Is that John Lowther?' he demanded.

'No,' Henry hissed furiously.

'Right, mate.'

'After each candidate has spoken,' said the Chairman, 'there will of course be a chance to . . .'

'Turn it off, ya wassock!'

By now the whisper had gone round: 'Not Lowther – this one is not John Lowther.' The warmly welcomed visitors had their instructions for such a contingency and acted upon them. They followed cries of 'Get off', 'We want Lowther' and a selection from their extensive repertoire of animal noises with a chorus, to the tune of 'Amazing Grace', of 'Sod off, sod off, sod off, sod off'.

Sensing that he had outstayed his welcome – he was a perceptive man – the Chairman called upon Gil Slack, Chairman of the Young Reformers, to give his address.

The sight and sound of this red-haired mental case would have been enough to raise even a more placid audience than the one Gil now faced. By the time he had finished telling them that 'This election is about Nicaragua – and Guatemala – and Chile' – everywhere in fact except Talbotting – the warmly welcomed visitors had concluded that here was a special case requiring actions rather than words. It was no doubt appropriate that, just as Gil said 'I now turn to Ireland' a Guinness bottle should have flown past his left ear. The symbolism was lost on Gil, however, whose idea of a good fight was one conducted by urban guerrillas thousands of miles away from him. Admittedly his hair was red anyway, so that the tomato cannot be said to have done much damage, but the watermelon put the matter beyond doubt. There is something imposing and not-to-be-denied about a watermelon. A watermelon looks you in the face and says what it thinks. What Gil thought was that solidarity with the working class was one thing; catching their watermelons with your nose was quite another. In any case, if catching watermelons with his nose were to become a permanent feature of Gil's act, it would clearly need extensive rehearsal. Gil fled, reflecting as he scrambled through the lavatory window that the education of the proletariat into a left-wing perspective was going to be a longer process than he had realized.

Back in the hall the Chairman decided on a change of plan. He had intended that Larry Boot-Heath should be the next speaker but the continuing shouts of 'We want Lowther' made it clear that this was not the sense of the meeting. 'Ladies and gentlemen,' he declared, 'John Lowther.'

The hall erupted. After experimenting with a variety of chants and slogans the meeting finally settled on 'Lowther is the chap – the others all are crap' and proceeded to bellow it for fully five minutes before allowing their hero to begin. The sun was shining, the night was young, the audience were on John Lowther's side, and John Lowther's speech was on the train.

It was a pity because Henry had worked hard on it. It had been brief and to the point. It said Talbotting was in the heart of the Home Counties stockbroker belt, and that John Lowther was a stockbroker. It stressed that he understood stockbrokers' problems (the only one of which, as far as Henry could see, was where to store their money, but he did not put that in the speech). It ended with the assurance that, if elected, John Lowther would be a quietly conscientious MP. He would not in other words bother his constituents with politics. With his prepared speech, thought Henry, John Lowther would be smooth, elegant and vacuous.

Without it, however, he managed only one of the

three. After what the audience took to be a pregnant pause, he attempted an 'Er well' and, possibly encouraged by the fact that it had not earned a watermelon, he gave them another 'Er well'. Next he essayed an 'Rhhhh' and rounded off the exhibition of his oratorical versatility with an 'Um'.

Henry was aghast. So, for that matter, were the warmly welcomed visitors. 'Are you trying to tell us,' demanded their self-appointed leader, 'that you brought us all this way to support that?'

Henry, like his protégé, was lost for speech. The audience were not. 'Lowther,' they declared with the fickleness of the voting public, 'is a toerag. Lowther is a toerag.' When one of their number gave his considered opinion that here was a joint in need of wrecking they needed no second opinion. They wrecked the joint.

As a political pro, Henry had a strong sense of self-preservation. Both he and the Chairman were safely locked in the loo for the duration. Outside in the hall John Lowther was being mobbed by his fans. Over it all sat the benign and smiling figure of Larry Boot-Heath. He liked people with fire in their guts, he thought, as a pomegranate bounced off his own. Pity he had not been able to deliver his speech about land taxation. That would really have raised their passions.

At Talbotting police station, a call from an irate neighbour of the church hall was received with weary exasperation. 'Not the Parochial Church Council again?' expostulated the constable who took the call.

On arriving he realized that not even the PCC could stage a shindig like this one. Wisely waiting until reinforcements had arrived, the officer led the first of several baton charges before breaking up the rumpus. He could not understand what it was about except that the combatants repeatedly shouted the word 'Lowther'. When order was established he demanded to know who or what Lowther was and, being answered with an 'Er well' he fulfilled one of his life's ambitions. 'Right,' he said, 'you're nicked, mate.'

When it was finally safe to emerge, Henry and the local Chairman discovered Larry Boot-Heath still smiling serenely upon an empty hall. The Chairman recalled that there was business to finish. 'It will have to be him then,' he said, pointing at Boot-Heath.

'Him?' shrieked Henry.

'My dear chap. One of the candidates made a run for it and the other one's in the clink. That leaves us with no alternative. Can I leave it to you to draft the press statement?'

Jim Wilkes was not an intellectual. He had built his entire BBC career on not being an intellectual and he had been highly successful. He had begun, in the late 1950s, as a light entertainment producer and, at heart, that was what he would always remain, a creator of what he liked to call 'gentle shows for gentle people'. By the early 1960s, however, it had become clear to him that light entertainment on its own was not enough. He watched people younger than himself, usually with dazzling Firsts from Oxbridge, joining the Corporation's Current Affairs Department and racing up the promotion ladder. Seeing the writing on the wall, Jim had applied for a job on the BBC's early evening magazine programme. His superiors in light entertainment were incredulous and discouraging.

'But you don't know anything about politics,' they protested.

Of course, they were perfectly right. His political ignorance was woeful and, having inexplicably secured the job, he began by performing disastrously. He was responsible for producing the first-ever post-Budget interview with the Chancellor, an achievement marred somewhat by Jim's interruption during the rehearsal: 'Never mind that, Chancellor – what my viewers want to know is, what's the latest joke going round the Treasury?' Jim was probably right about the preferences of his viewers but his tone sat ill with the air of high seriousness and intellectual superiority which his

Lime Grove colleagues affected. He felt he was out of his depth and few were disposed to disagree. His attempts to bring the values and techniques of light entertainment to current affairs television reached their nadir when, after a well-known by-election in 1962, he attempted a documentary entitled, *Orpington Man – can he sing and dance?* His vulgar populist approach led to his being dubbed 'The man who put the po in politics' and he found himself increasingly producing marginal items for marginal programmes, expecting no more than to be sent back to light entertainment with his tail between his legs.

Then came the 1964 General Election and the rescue of Jim's career. The Labour Party had been out of office for thirteen years and, aside from the Prime Minister, none of the new ministers had ever held high government office. For once, not only was Jim ignorant of who the leading political personalities were; so was everyone else. Moreover, the accession of Harold Wilson marked the beginning of a period in which show-biz and politics became difficult and often impossible to distinguish. Britain now had a Prime Minister who apparently believed that winning the World Cup and the Eurovision Song Contest were governmental achievements and substantial ones at that. A Prime Minister who invited footballers, rock stars and stand-up comics to Downing Street and told them, 'Jack Kennedy's parties at the White House had nothing on this.'

Jim saw his chance and seized it. Clinging precariously to his post in current affairs, he began a series entitled *They Rule our Lives* which set out to present politicians not as administrators, or philosophers come down from the mountain, but rather as entertainers. George Brown came on the show and sang a song. Reginald Maudling came on and fell asleep. Jeremy Thorpe appeared and impersonated Edward Heath. Edward Heath appeared and impersonated Edward Heath, but then no show can be a winner all the time. The important thing was that the programme was a huge success. The politicians liked it because it made them look human. BBC management liked it because it was a genuine broadcasting innovation. Most importantly, the public loved it.

They Rule our Lives rapidly transformed Jim Wilkes from black sheep to blue-eyed boy. From current affairs he went back to light entertainment as Departmental Head. From light entertainment he became Head of Series and Serials, where he guessed that the most popular serials would be those suggesting that the rich and famous were as miserable as sin, thus establishing a principle to which soap opera adheres to this day. And, from Series and Serials he rose to what is almost the most coveted job in British Broadcasting: the Controllership of BBC1. He was still regarded by many as a 'bums on seats' broadcaster but now he could afford to revel in the description. When nowadays he declared 'I'm just a plain man' there were still those who would whisper 'How true' but it was noticeable that they whispered more furtively with each succeeding year.

Even the Controller of BBC1 has his troubles, however, and that lunchtime Jim Wilkes was feeling thoroughly cheesed. This was not solely because he was being given lunch by the Controllers of Radio 2 and Radio 4. They were certainly boring company but, on the other hand, they had at least taken the trouble to find out that his favourite London restaurant was Inigo Jones in Garrick Street, Covent Garden, and had booked his favourite table there. In public of course Jim was a 'give me egg and chips every time' man. In private, if occasionally they gave him quail's eggs on a bed of smoked salmon instead, he was not disposed to complain.

About his network, however, he found himself moved to complain a good deal. 'What the bloody hell is wrong?' he demanded of his hosts.

'With the brandy? It's an Armagnac.'

'I don't mean the brandy. The brandy's lovely. In fact why not get me another one? No, I mean with the BBC?'

Jim lit a cigar and continued. 'Look, I'm a ratings man, right? What people say about me is: old Jim may not have too much up top but he knows how to pack the viewers in. That is what they say, isn't it?' he demanded truculently of CR2. 'I bet you say it as well, you supercilious bastard.'

CR2 attempted an indulgent smile. Humour the ghastly prole, he told himself, and stick to the task in hand.

'So when the ratings are in trouble, I'm in trouble. And the fact is that BBC1's figures are bloody awful. And it's not even as if they're all going to the other side. People just don't seem to be watching television any more. What is it? Is it because they've all got those whatever you call 'ems?'

'Video machines,' said CR4.

CR2 was anxious not to let the conversation drift away from its main purpose. 'I suppose it's the weekend figures that give most cause for concern,' he suggested.

'You said it,' Jim Wilkes agreed. 'Look at my Saturday night programmes. I mean, nobody else does.'

'Yes, I know,' said CR2, 'it's very worrying.'

'Yes it bloody is. Hang on a minute,' said Wilkes, 'what's your angle? Why is radio so worried about my figures all of a sudden?'

CR4 heard alarm bells ringing and leaned over to his friend. 'He's not pissed enough,' he whispered.

'What?'

'I said, he's not pissed enough.'

'You're bloody right, I'm not pissed enough. Where's that brandy?'

The Armagnac having been replenished, CR2 made his play. 'Look,' he said, 'radio and television don't always see eye to eye.'

'That's certainly true,' said Wilkes.

'But, with a new licence fee settlement in the offing some of us have decided it is time to take a broader view. The fact is that getting a decent licence fee increase depends on the BBC commanding roughly fifty per cent of the television audience. And, if you're talking about television audience, you're talking, first and foremost, about BBC1.'

'I still don't see why this concerns you.'

'It concerns us,' put in CR4, 'because if we don't get a big enough licence fee increase it'll be radio that suffers most in the long run. Our interest now lies in seeing that your ratings go up.'

'Well, I've been saying all of that for years,' said the Controller of BBC1, 'but I must confess it still strikes me as odd to hear you saying it.'

'We're saying it because we're worried,' said CR4.

'We don't want to find ourselves fighting over shares of a cake so small that it won't save either of us from starvation,' said CR2.

Jim Wilkes thought for a moment. 'All right,' he said, 'I'll buy it. After all, if we don't get a proper increase, you two are in dire trouble. One of your networks may have to go.'

'Exactly,' said CR2, casting a look of relief at his fellow conspirator. The first part of the battle had been won.

'So tell me,' continued Wilkes, 'how I go about boosting my audiences.' He listened as CR2 outlined the plan.

'But it's been done,' he objected. 'A late-night satire show on a Saturday? I mean, it's not exactly original.'

'No, but this one is going to be different,' said CR2, 'because you're going to bring in somebody new and different to produce it. Someone who's not hidebound by the conventions of television satire. Someone who'll make satirical shows like they've never been made before.'

Hercules Fortescue was a proud and stubborn man but he knew in his heart, and indeed every other part of his body, that he could not continue the unequal struggle. Rules were rules and his devotion to upholding them had been total, throughout his fifteen long years with the Corporation. Even he could not believe, however, that his duty to the rule book obliged him to starve to death. It had been three weeks since George Cragge had made his premature exit from the disciplinary interview. Since then Hercules – he had been given his father's idea of a name which was perhaps why he had not turned out to be his father's idea of a son – had consumed nothing but bread and water. It was not that which truly galled him. It was the fact that, in all that time, he had received not an iota of support from senior management. He had taken it for granted that they would back him to the hilt, bring this errant journalist to book, and pat Hercules on the head for a job well done. Instead, he had been given to understand that he was a thoroughgoing nuisance, that there were higher political considerations to be taken into account and that his conduct might very well conclude with himself on the receiving end of a disciplinary interview.

Hercules was scandalized but he was also worried. Even he had enough sense to know that after fifteen years as a BBC Personel Officer he was totally unemployable anywhere else. He had the distinct feeling that his refusal of an invitation to discuss the matter with the Controller of Radio 4 had not been a wise move.

'I haven't had a happy life,' he blubbed to his water glass. 'It's not much fun being a personnel officer. You sit here, watching other people producing programmes, being on television, interviewing the famous, travelling the world. And what do I get out of it?' he sobbed. 'Sick notes, annual leave applications. Pension arrangements. Disciplinary interviews. Oh God,' he bawled, 'disciplinary interviews. I can't stand it. I can't stand it, I tell you!'

He flung open the window and stood on the ledge. 'This is it! I've had enough. You wouldn't support me when I needed you. You wouldn't back me up, would you? Well, see how you like this. It is a far, far better thing I do – even if it is in contravention of Staff Instruction No. 456, section A, sub-section 3. Goodbye world. I go ...'

At that moment the telephone rang.

*

91

CR2 suppressed a shudder when Jim Wilkes passed the port the wrong way for the third time. At last the words came which made it all worthwhile. 'I think your idea brilliant,' said Wilkes.

'Our idea? Oh, it wasn't our idea. It was yours.'

'Mine?'

'Oh, yes,' said CR4. 'I mean we just had a germ of something . . . something very nebulous. We needed your expertise in the light entertainment field to put flesh on the bones.'

'Precisely,' said CR2. 'We don't deserve any of the credit. We'll be happy enough if this show takes off and the BBC's licence fee increase is big enough for all of us. That's what we're in it for.'

'What I really like about it,' said Wilkes, 'is having it produced by this Fortescue. Think how good it'll look when I tell the DG we are actually moving the bureaucrats out of the offices and into the studios to make programmes. It's a stroke of public relations genius.'

He was interrupted by the manager of Inigo Jones. 'Excuse me sir, but it's almost four thirty. I feel we must close for lunch.'

'Then, damn it man, we'll stay for dinner,' said Wilkes. 'Bring us some more port and bring me a telephone. Oh, and there'll be someone else joining us for dinner.'

'Very good, sir.'

Inigo Jones' prices were formidable. The manager shuddered as he thought of the combined bill for lunch and dinner. Still, they looked as if they could afford it. His not to reason why. He fetched the telephone for Jim Wilkes who dialled Broadcasting House and asked to be put through to 621.

It would make an awful mess if he jumped, thought Fortescue. It would require forms to be filled in in triplicate and, anyway, the phone call might be to tell him that George Cragge had backed down and that he had won after all. If it were not he could always take the call and jump afterwards. He climbed off the ledge and picked up the phone.

'Is that Hercules Fortescue? This is Jim Wilkes, Controller BBC1. I wondered if it would be convenient for you to join me and two of my colleagues for dinner at Inigo Jones. I've got a proposition to put to you.'

Dinner at Inigo Jones? They'd hardly be buying him dinner at Inigo Jones if they were going to sack him. He had won – that surely could be the only interpretation. 'I'll be there right away sir,' said Hercules.

'Is that all, Superintendent? I really must get away. I'm going to the country for the weekend.'

What it is to have money, thought Frank Jefferson. An elegant flat in Hay's Mews, Mayfair and a place in the country too. Still, at least she had called him Superintendent. In any case, he had always wanted to meet Kelly Sharpe, the deb who climbed mountains.

She was not exactly beautiful; she was rather too big and masculine for that, with thighs like a second row forward. Moreover, she suffered as did her boyfriend Dominic D'eath from a nose that did not fit her face. Jefferson found himself wondering how they ever managed to kiss given the size of their respective conks. On the other hand, she undoubtedly had a presence. She was forceful and self-assured and gave you the impression that, whilst convention obliged her to quaff Pimms, she would have been happier sinking pints of real ale.

'I think that's about it, miss,' Jefferson told her. 'You say he had curly, gingery hair, and spectacles, wore a white shirt and green corduroy trousers.'

'And odd socks,' said Kelly.

'And you didn't notice anything odd in the way he looked at Mr Anderson.'

'No, but I wasn't really looking.'

'And you had never met Mr Anderson before?'

'No. He was a friend of Dominic's.'

'How long have you known Mr D'eath, miss?'

'About five or six years. I was going through my radical days. I read a book of his about war and economics and wrote to him, saying it was a load of balls. He invited me to dinner.'

'Mr D'eath doesn't strike me as the kind of man who would take kindly to that description of his work, miss,' said Jefferson.

'No. He was livid at first. But he forgave me. I think I fascinated him.'

Jefferson could well believe it. 'Well, I won't detain you any longer, miss. I know you are anxious to get off for the weekend.'

Leaving Hay's Mews, Jefferson hired a cab and told the driver to take him to the BBC Club, Langham Place.

George Cragge was already there, in a thoroughly bad mood. It had been one of those days when absolutely nothing had happened and he had not been required to broadcast a single item. Such days were the bane of George's life. Nothing to do, but he had to be around, just in case. It was no wonder he drank, he told himself. That evening, he had not even forced himself to listen to the six o'clock news.

'You didn't miss anything, dear boy,' said Max Parker, joining him. Max was the BBC's Economics Correspondent and was described by George as 'the oldest journalist in the world'. He was actually only fifty-nine but a lifetime of dissipation had left him looking much older. He had grey hair and he took perverse satisfaction in his perpetually ruddy countenance which, although the result of his fondness for whisky in huge quantities made him look the picture of health. 'Why the hell,' he demanded, 'does the BBC employ sub-editors who can't tell less from fewer or enormity from magnitude or . . .'

'Or their own arses from a hole in the ground,' George put in helpfully.

'Why don't these bloody people go and learn their trade before they come here? Why can't they go to the *Middle Wallop Gazette?* Or the *Western Morning News?* Or the *Coventry Telegraph?*'

'Why don't they just piss off?' said George.

'Something wrong, dear boy?' asked Max, for he was quick on the uptake.

'I'm bored. Bored, bored, bored.'

'Yes, it has been a quiet week, hasn't it? Nothing but foreign stories. I remember when I was Night Editor of the *Daily Mirror . . .*'

'Oh God,' said George wearily.

'I was the best night editor that paper ever had,' Max continued, 'and I knew what to do with foreign stories. One thousand dead foreigners – no bloody use to me. Two thousand dead foreigners? It might rate a small par. Come back when you've got ten thousand dead foreigners, I used to tell 'em. That's the way to treat foreign stories.'

'Why do any of us come and work in this dump?' asked George. 'Fleet Street was so much more fun.'

'It was. I remember when I was Chief Sub on the *Express* – it was under C.J. McKinley. Remember C.J?'

'I remember him all right,' said George. 'He had a drinking problem.'

'We all had drinking problems, dear boy.'

'But C.J. had the worst one. He drank so much that, every so often, in the middle of his editorial conferences, he used to throw up into his wastepaper basket. Then carried on as if nothing had happened.'

'He was a damn good journalist, though.'

'He was an old pro.'

'Exactly. An old pro,' said Max. 'And look at 'em nowadays. Prats, the lot of them. Can't write, don't wash.'

'Why did we come here, Max? Why didn't we stay in Fleet Street?'

'You're getting morose, dear boy. Buy me a drink – that will cheer you up.' Being the Economics Correspondent, Max never had any money.

George duly ordered a couple of whiskies. 'I wanna retire.'

'You can't retire at your age. I'm the one who ought to be retiring. I've been in this business, man and boy, for forty years. I remember when I was Chief Reporter on the *Bournemouth Echo*.'

'Aw, put a sock in it, you daft old twit,' said George affably.

'I'm just telling you . . .'

'I know what you're telling me. You've told me that one a hundred times. Tell me what I'm doing in the BBC; that's what I want to know.'

'Well, I don't know. What am I doing here? All I ever really wanted to be was a sports reporter.'

'Typical of the BBC, isn't it?'

'It is, dear boy, it is. I remember when I was Sports Editor of the *Daily Mail*. I got a phone call, it was from the Director General in person.'

'Was it hell?'

'It was too. "Max," he said to me, "you're the finest journalist in Fleet Street, we need you at the BBC. Name your price."'

'Name your price, indeed! What they actually said was: "Come over here to the BBC, you clapped-out old fool, get out of real journalism before you do any more damage."'

'It was not − "the finest journalist in Fleet Street". Only then he said, "Do you know anything about economics?" And I said, "No." And he said, "Good. I want you to be our Economics Correspondent."'

'Typical,' said George, 'typical of this bloody institution.'

'Can I get you one, George?' It was Jefferson. 'I've just come from D'eath's girlfriend. I think we've got enough to put out a description.'

'What?' George's manner changed dramatically. He waved away the offer of a drink and at once he seemed to come alive.

'I thought you should be the first. I was going to tell the papers . . .'

'Don't you go telling the papers before you tell us,

96

mate. The BBC is the principal news medium in the country.'

'I thought I just heard you describe it as "this bloody institution".'

'Frank,' said George Cragge, 'I love you very dearly. But if I hear you say one more word against the BBC, I'll bop you one. Where is this description, let's get on the air.'

George disappeared, clutching the police statement.

Max introduced himself to Mr Jefferson and accepted his offer of a drink. 'Strange lad, George,' said Max, 'I remember when I was Psychology Correspondent of the *New Delhi Times* . . .'

Laetitia Tone was like Kelly Sharpe with the brains left out. She had had a similarly debby upbringing but, in Laetitia's case, it had worked. She felt no urge to climb mountains. Nor indeed had her schooldays been marked by any academic distinction. After twelve months at a finishing school in France she had been wholly unable to speak a single word of French. Laetitia had majored in sex. She had taken a congratulatory first in the subject and her tutors had remarked upon her outstanding grasp of detail.

Back in England, however, Laetitia was frustrated. She had no doubt that most of the men she met were turned on by her and lusted after her. In almost every case, however, they were stark terrified of actually doing anything about it. Laetitia, the sex kitten, went home alone more often than many plainer but less intimidating females and came painfully to the realization that, for English men at least, smouldering, assertive female sexuality was something to be safely contained in their fantasies; its reality scared them limp. For the modern male activist feminism was both an intellectual commitment and a genital deterrent.

This time she did not intend to be thwarted. Henry clearly needed a woman. Whatever the brilliance of his political mind Henry was a shambles, badly in need of someone to take him in hand. Laetitia intended to be that someone. As she sat typing plaintive appeals for money at Reform Party headquarters, she felt bound to admit that she had no idea how to go about it. She had realized at their first meeting that Henry ran from women like a frightened rabbit and he clearly had no sexual experience whatever. She had only to smile at him to set his knees knocking. Her reflections were interrupted by a knock at the door.

'Can I borrow some sugar, dear?' inquired an apparition in black underwear.

'Yes, yes, of course,' stuttered Laetitia, 'I . . . I don't believe we've met. I'm Laetitia Tone.'

'Madam Sin, dear, from upstairs.'

'Oh yes, of course.' Laetitia, like everyone else in the building, had heard Madam Sin at work. 'Would you like some coffee? I was just going to take a break anyway.'

'That would be lovely, dear. Business seems a bit slack today.' Madam Sin seated her ample frame on the rickety chair the Reform Party kept for its visitors. 'You're new here, aren't you?' she inquired.

'Fairly new, yes. I'm Geoffrey Crichton-Potter's PA.'

'The fat geezer?'

'Er . . . yes, yes that's right.'

'Oh yes, I know him. Seems a nice feller.'

'Yes he is.' It had been suggested many times to Laetitia by embittered men that she saw herself as an up-market prostitute. Never before, however, had she met a down-market one. 'Have you been here long?' she asked.

'Oh years. Years and years.'

'Are you – I mean, excuse me asking this question, but are you happy in your work?'

'Happy?' said Madam Sin with a throaty chuckle. 'Course I'm happy. Money for old birch twigs.'

'What do you actually do?'

'I smack their backsides, dear.'

'Lucky you,' sighed Laetitia, 'I wish I could sometimes.'

'Having man trouble, are we?'

'Yes, I suppose we are,' said Laetitia. 'Look, you must be an expert on the subject. I mean you've met an awful lot of men.'

'Thousands. Mind you, they all look much the same from where I see them.'

'Well, anyway. Look, give me your advice.'

The object of Laetitia's designs was not having the happiest of times. Having to explain to Crichton-Potter that John Lowther had not been selected for Talbotting was bad enough. That in addition to not being selected he had been arrested was even worse. That, on top of everything, the local party had chosen Larry Boot-Heath as their candidate was the clincher. Crichton-Potter was an extremely placid man, content as a rule to let his young acolyte do most of what he should really have been doing himself. Given his own abilities, this was normally a sensible course. On this occasion it had been disastrous.

'It's really not like you to make a mistake like this,' he told Henry. 'This by-election is expected for early October – just before our Party Conference. How am I going to face the conference after a humiliating defeat? And just think of that . . . that man, under the sort of media scrutiny you get in a by-election. The idea's appalling.'

'I know,' said Henry glumly.

'And what am I going to say about the fact that half our selection meeting wound up in clink? It's not exactly an auspicious start, is it?'

'I know,' said Henry glumly.

'I tell you, Henry,' said Crichton-Potter, warming to his theme, 'we've got a crisis on our hands. If we get massacred in this by-election it will raise big questions about my leadership.'

That contingency had already occurred to Henry. He knew that in politics he who lives by patronage shall die by patronage. If Crichton-Potter fell, Henry would fall with him.

'So what do I do, then?' demanded Crichton-Potter.

'Well,' said Henry, 'what I think we need is an exercise in damage limitation.'

'You mean we assassinate Boot-Heath?'

'No, I don't mean that. I mean that the first thing you have to do is to issue a statement about the disturbance at this selection meeting.'

'Go on.'

'Of course, you totally dissociate yourself from the violence. But you go on to say that it shows how vibrant and alive the party is.'

'You mean alive and well and living in Wormwood Scrubs.'

'No. You say that it was part – admittedly a reprehensible part – of a vigorous internal debate about the direction of the nation's affairs and the way our party should rise to the challenge.'

'Ar, um. Well, it's better than nothing, I suppose.'

'You then announce that this by-election is of such vital importance to our national future that you've decided to take personal charge of the campaign.'

'Oh God, do I? But damn it, I shall be out of the country during September.'

'You'll have to take a holiday after Party Conference instead. If you take charge, with any luck the media will concentrate on you and not on Boot-Heath. It's the only way.'

'I suppose you're right. It's a blessed nuisance, though. If you'd only got Lowther chosen in the first place none of this would have been necessary.'

'I know,' said Henry. 'I said I was sorry.'

'You're not seriously suggesting I put Henry across my knee?' said Laetitia.

'No, dear. But what I do for a living is just an extreme example. All men want to be ruled by women really. It's just a question of taking the initiative.'

'Taking the initiative. Do you know, I think you're right. I can't sit around waiting for him to make the first move. I'll invite him out. I'll treat him to a really expensive meal. That will make my intentions clear.'

Inigo Jones was deserted, save for three BBC executives who greeted Hercules with a courtesy that baffled him and insisted that he consume the most expensive meal of his life.

'You know, Fortescue, I've had my eye on you for quite some time,' said Jim Wilkes.

'Have you, sir?' Fortescue was mystified. He was also extremely full and somewhat drunk. After weeks on bread and water he was rather overcome by the succession of snail sausage, fillet of sole, pink duck and Inigo Jones' superlative puddings, each looking like a Salvador Dali. He was even more overcome by the succession of gin and tonic, sancerre, Aloxe Corton, Sauternes and port. Even in this state, however, he was baffled to learn that the Controller of BBC1 had been watching him for quite some time. Head of Personnel and Administration, Radio News and Current Affairs, was not exactly a conspicuous post in spite of Fortescue's attempts to make it so.

'I'm going to put my cards on the table,' said Jim. 'I've asked you here because the BBC, as you know, is within sight of its next licence fee increase.'

'You do understand that we are discussing high policy here,' said CR2 conspiratorially. He had judged his man correctly. Fortescue's ears pricked up and his little pink nose wriggled with pleasure. High policy!

'We've got to demonstrate to the Government that we are increasing our efficiency and giving people value for money.'

'Yes,' said Fortescue slowly, 'I see.'

'And part of that means moving our best chaps into positions of . . . Shall we say, conspicuous responsibility?'

'Precisely,' said CR2, 'preparing the best and brightest for positions of senior management.'

'And that means you,' said Jim Wilkes.

'Does it?' gasped Fortescue.

'Certainly it does. I've always admired your personnel skills, your tact, your diplomacy, your acumen, your foresight, your – success.'

'But I'm not having a success,' Fortescue complained. 'I have specifically ordered that a BBC journalist should be required to undertake an attachment . . .'

'Oh yes, yes, we know all that,' CR4 put in hastily – a true picture of Fortescue's ability was the last thing he wanted – 'but, if you see yourself occupying a top position in, say, a couple of years, you really must learn to take a relaxed view.'

'I take a relaxed view,' intoned Fortescue reverently. 'Commenting on the industrial dispute in BBC Television,' he hallucinated, 'the Corporation's Director of Personnel, Mr Hercules Fortescue, said management would take a relaxed view.'

'Now, let's get down to brass tacks,' said Jim. 'I've got a very big job and I need a rising star to take it on for me. Now what do you say?'

'I take a relaxed view,' the demented personnel officer orgasmed obliviously.

'What?'

'I mean, I'd be delighted, Controller,' said Fortescue, coming to what, stretching a point, might be termed his senses.

'Basically, I'm launching a new satire programme on Saturday nights and I want you to produce.'

'Me? But, Controller, I've never . . .'

'Damn it, man. I know you've never. That's exactly why I want you. I want new ideas, new attitudes, a new approach and new bloody viewers. Well, will you take the job or won't you?'

'I . . . I shall be honoured,' stuttered Fortescue incredulously.

'Now, to get down to the details.'

Jim was interrupted by the waiter. 'Excuse me, sir, but it is well after midnight.'

'Well then we'll bloody well stay for breakfast,' Jim

told him. 'Bring me some more port.'

For once George Cragge's head was not the most painful in the Corporation the next morning. That honour was equally divided between three controllers and a personnel officer. George arrived at his office, keen to discover what developments there had been in the Bank Manager Case.

'Oh, we had a public response all right,' Frank Jefferson told him. 'Hundreds and hundreds of calls, including several from Plymouth and one from Crianlarich.'

'I suppose it's not definite he's a Londoner,' said George, 'I mean maybe he comes up here to do the jobs and then goes home.'

'Well, possibly. But I don't believe that, do you?'

'No, not really. Anyway, what can I tell them on the one o'clock?'

'Oh, you can say the police are extremely gratified by the public response and are following up every suggestion.'

'All right. That'll have to do, I suppose.'

In the office next door to George's, Max Parker, Economics Correspondent of the BBC, was wondering whom he had not recently touched for a fiver. He was as usual a bit short and his taste buds reminded him that it would shortly be opening time. He would try George, he decided. Admittedly, he owed George twenty already but that was a perfectly good reason for making it twenty-five. The intervention of a sub-editor saved George at least temporarily the annoyance of shelling out yet more cash to his impoverished friend.

'Excuse me, sir,' the sub told Max, 'the Assistant Editor asked me to remind you that the new money supply figures are out today.'

'What of it?'

'Well, we were wondering whether you could possibly do us a piece for the one, analysing their significance.'

'Don't you think I've got better things to do with my

time than analysis of sodding money supply figures? Get somebody else to do it.'

'But you're the Economics Correspondent.'

'Exactly. Now piss off.'

'Well, can I tell him that you'll do it then?'

'You can tell him that if it happens to fit in with my plans for luncheon, which I doubt, I may, or may not, prepare the odd sentence on the subject, if there is anything of value worth saying, which I also doubt. Can you lend me a fiver?'

'I'm afraid not.'

'Well piss off then.'

Next door, George's phone rang. 'Hello, George, we haven't spoken for some time.' It was the maniac. 'I loved your description of me, George. Very vivid. It's not like me at all but it was still vivid.'

'Look,' said George, 'don't you think you've made your point by now? Why not stop these murders and give yourself up?'

'Oh, I couldn't think of doing that, George. I'm having so much fun. And I'm keeping you in work, aren't I?'

George passed over that; it was, after all, true. 'Look,' he said, 'if you gave yourself up we could help you.'

'Oh, I don't think I can accept that offer, George. Even if it is well meant. Especially with the little surprise I've got planned.'

'What little surprise?'

'It's just for you, George. I'm not quite ready for the big one yet. But I thought I'd work up to it with something . . . something close to home. From your point of view, that is.'

'What, exactly?' But the maniac was gone.

As George put the phone down, a familiar face appeared around the door. 'Can you lend me a fiver, dear boy?'

'Oh all right, I suppose so.' George handed it over.

'Incidentally, do you know anything about the money supply?'

'Yes I do. I've got the money and I supply it to you.'

'Very droll, dear boy, very droll. The thing is, I've got to write a piece about the new money supply figures for one o'clock.'

'Yes? Well? You are the Economics Correspondent.'

'Yes I know, but to tell you the truth, I've always found figures a bit confusing. It's all these M0s and M1s and M3s. I can never make out which one is supposed to be which.'

'Well, can't you do something about lies, damned lies and statistics? That'll floor 'em. Anyway, you've got an advantage in your subject. Nobody ever knows what you're talking about.'

'No. But neither do I.' Max retired dolefully to his office and sat staring into space awaiting inspiration. Twice he told the inquiring sub-editor that he was not yet ready to record.

George likewise stared vacantly ahead. Someone close to home? His own bank manager? He might get to like this murderer if that were his intention. But then his own bank manager lived in Talbotting which was not, strictly speaking, London. On the other hand, Peter Anderson had not, strictly speaking, been a bank manager, so clearly the maniac was less predictable than they had first thought. And did one give any credence to his assertion that the description George had broadcast was nothing like him? After all, the evidence for his appearance was very slim. After a morning of such fruitless speculation George turned on the radio to make sure that the brief report he had recorded earlier sounded OK. Police following up every lead, he thought, big deal.

His report was followed on the one o'clock news by a penetrating analysis of the money supply figures, 'by our Economics Correspondent, Max Parker'. After explaining, or rather not explaining, the confusion caused by the various and conflicting definitions of money, Max reached the nub of his report, 'as the *Financial Times* put it this morning,' he declared. There followed eleven lines lifted wholesale from that morning's *Financial Times*. 'In short,' Max concluded, 'these new figures tell us nothing about the true direction of the economy. The Chancellor will be making a statement in the House this afternoon, after which we may have a clearer picture.' Max did not sound hopeful.

'And that house in Ummerton Drive is on the edge of the constituency,' said Henry, 'so we can use that as the divs committee room.'

Crichton-Potter was not familiar with the sophistications of fighting by-elections. He had, of course, been a candidate, but that only involved doing what one was told; it did not have to mean immersion in the nitty-gritty. 'What's a divs committee room?'

'It's the headquarters for all the head cases who volunteer to go canvassing but who you know you can't possibly let loose on the voters. You send them out so they think they're canvassing the actual constituency. But in fact they're just outside it in a completely different constituency. So they're happy because they think they are contributing to the party's effort and we're happy because they aren't.'

'I see,' said Crichton-Potter bewilderedly. 'Well, I'll leave all that kind of thing to you. How do you rate our chances?'

'The first opinion poll gives the Tories thirty-six per cent, Labour thirty-four per cent and us fifteen per cent,' said Henry, 'which actually is nothing like as bad as it might be.'

'But surely that means we haven't a hope in hell?'

'Certainly not,' said Henry. 'For a start it means there are fifteen per cent don't knows. If you add them to our score, we are nearly equal to the other parties. In the second place, what we must do is squeeze the Labour vote.'

'How do we do that.'

'By persuading them that Labour can't possibly win a seat full of stockbrokers, so their sensible course is to vote for us. Actually I think we've got quite a good chance. At any rate we would have, if only.'

'Yes, exactly. If only it weren't for our candidate. Henry, what are we going to do about our candidate?'

'Well, there must be something he's good at. Perhaps he'll be good at charming housewives on the doorstep.'

'If you were a housewife would you be charmed by Boot-Heath?'

'Well no,' Henry admitted, 'but at least if we send him out to knock on doors we'll stand a chance of keeping him away from the media. That's the important thing.'

George Cragge had been puzzled when the invitation arrived. 'I wonder if you would care to join me for a drink at Lime Grove one evening,' it said. 'I would be most grateful for your advice. Bamber Sampson.'

In the first place, thought George, it was most unlike anyone at Lime Grove, the home of BBC Television Current Affairs, to admit to needing advice from anyone. George had once said of Lime Grove that its inmates redefine the boundaries of human arrogance. In the second, he had made that remark to the Editor of *Panorama* whilst on attachment to the programme and had thereby ensured that his name would be mud at the Grove for all time.

What made it especially surprising however was the fact that the request had come from Bamber Sampson, the BBC's ace reporter – or so he said. It was not merely that George thought Sampson a shit and had told him so to his face. It was rather that George thought him a smarmy, ingratiating shit. It should perhaps be said in the interests of balance that part of George's distaste undoubtedly stemmed from the fact that, although ten years younger than himself, Sampson already earned twice George's salary. After Oxford where he had taken an indifferent degree in Politics, Philosophy and Economics, he had secured a BBC production traineeship – the Corporation's equivalent of the Civil Service fast stream – and had risen fast. Today he was paid a massive sum,

chiefly for reporting elections. General Elections, Pres-
idential Elections, Euro Elections – any elections. None
would have been complete without Sampson, snidely
intoning his assessments of the rival candidates in a
manner designed to convey his utter superiority to all
of them. His admirers, and undoubtedly there were
some, said he performed a service to democracy by
debunking the pretensions of politicians. His detractors,
of whom there were more, said he performed a service
to democracy in that, set beside him, even the politicians
looked human.

Nonetheless, as George drove through Shepherd's
Bush on the way to the Grove – and George never
ceased to wonder why the self-styled nerve centre of
British broadcasting was set in such a squalid part of
London – he could not help admitting that Sampson
had made it in ways that he would not have minded
making it himself. Sampson's sexual success, for example, was legendary. He bore out everything that has ever
been said about fame as an aphrodisiac. And you had
to hand it to the little swine, thought George, he had
seized every opportunity that had come his way. 'More
than I did,' muttered George.

It was therefore with no sense of pride and a definite
feeling of discomfort that George entered the Lime
Grove bar. He felt little better for being greeted as
'George darling' by Bamber Sampson, all suavity and
self-assurance.

'What will you have, George? You're a Guinness man,
aren't you, if I remember rightly? I'm afraid I'm just a
tiny port and lemon man myself.'

That's not what I've heard, thought George. The
sexual ambiguity, he thought, was quite deliberate and
he could not help admiring it. Always keep your
interviewee off balance.

Another of Sampson's techniques was suddenly to
come straight to the point when you least expected it.
'You live in Talbotting, don't you?' he asked when they
had found a table.

'Yes.'

'Well, that's why I've asked you here. I'm covering the by-election. I thought you might be able to give me a few hints.'

It all became clear. 'But I don't think there is much I can tell you,' said George. 'I mean, I'm not a political reporter.'

'Oh, I just wanted some background. I'm going to enjoy this by-election,' said Bamber Sampson. 'Do you know, I've heard a whisper that the Reform Party has selected the wrong candidate by mistake. I'm going to have some fun with him.'

CHAPTER
9

It occurred to Frank Jefferson's shimmering intellect that M. Sin was definitely not Chinese. She was blonde, buxom, semi-naked and quintessentially English. She also had an undisguised loathing of policemen.

She had not been easy to find, being neither in the phone book nor on the electoral register. In a sense, Frank had not been far out, at least geographically, in his assumption that the Chinese quarter was the place to look. He had taken the logical course and asked after M. Sin in every Chinese restaurant in Soho. At several, particularly those in the region of Berwick Street, he had had the feeling that, behind the solid wall of sweet and sour inscrutability, there was just a flicker of recognition. On learning that he was a policeman, however, Chinatown had become silent. Such was the mystery surrounding Madam Sin's existence that Frank had begun to think that perhaps the description of the young man which George Cragge had put out might be wholly irrelevant. Perhaps, after all, Madam Sin was the person he was looking for. Clearly, she had something to hide.

Frank was baffled. He was even more baffled to learn that, apparently unlike the rest of London, the Commissioner seemed to know exactly who M. Sin was.

'I . . . er . . . I'm not personally acquainted with her, you understand,' he told Jefferson during one of their regular meetings to discuss the case.

'I didn't suppose you were, sir.'

'No no, absolutely not. I mean, I've never actually met her. But, umm, well, I think if you were to try Berwick Street you might find . . . that is, it is possible that, mind you, this is only a suggestion. I have – I repeat – I have

110

no personal connection with the lady whatsoever, you understand?'

He did now. Jefferson was amazed. He was also appalled, a feeling shared by his interviewee, whose manner had changed pointedly when she had discovered that he was not a client but a police officer.

'Madam,' Jefferson sought to reassure her for the umpteenth time, 'I am not here to discuss your . . . your profession.'

'I should hope not. Don't I know your boss?'

'I believe you may have come across him.'

'Oh no, dear, it was the other way around. Do you know what he likes?'

'I have no wish to know what he likes.'

'He likes me to . . . '

'Madam, I did not come here to discuss my Commissioner's likes and dislikes, interesting as they may be.'

'Oh they are.'

'Look,' said Jefferson, 'I am investigating the case of the Bank Manager Murders.'

'I wouldn't know anything about that; I'm not even respectable enough to have a bank account.'

'One of the victims was a Mr Jeremy Inchcape. On the morning of his death, he had an appointment with someone called MS. It has been suggested to me that MS stands for Madam Sin.'

'I am not at liberty to discuss my clients.'

'But, damn it all, you seem perfectly happy to discuss my Commissioner.'

'Oh, I'll talk about him all right. What do you want to know? The rolled-up copy of the *Police Gazette*?'

'I have no wish to hear about the *Police Gazette*.'

'The tutu?'

'I certainly don't want to know about a tutu. Was Inchcape one of your clients or not?'

'He may have been.'

'Did you see him on the morning of July the sixteenth?'

'I may have done. I can't be sure. They all look the

111

same from where I see them.'

'Can you give me an account of your movements on . . . ?' Jefferson listed the dates of the murders.

'Yes, I was here.'

'What, on all of these dates?'

'I'm always here.'

'Can you prove that?'

'Of course I can't prove it, dearie. My clients expect me to be discreet. I'm the one who gets persecuted, I'm the one who's a second-class citizen. I don't suppose you fancy a bit, do you?' said Madam Sin, changing tack somewhat.

'I beg your pardon?'

'Well, you're a policeman. I'm sure you're interested in crime and punishment.'

'Madam, my interest is purely professional.'

'Yes, but so is mine.'

'Now look,' said Jefferson, attempting a different line of inquiry. 'Have you got any MPs amongst your clients?'

Madam Sin smirked. 'Oh yes, dearie. I get 'em all in here.'

'Was Mr Peter Anderson a client of yours?'

'Never heard of him.'

'You must have heard of him. He's just been murdered.'

'Well, he can't be one of my clients then, can he? Are you quite sure I can't do anything for you? After all, I do have the rent to pay.'

At last Jefferson twigged. 'Are you telling me that you have information to impart but that I have to pay for it?'

'I wouldn't put it as crudely as that. But, since you mention it, yes . . . Well now,' said Madam Sin, pocketing a tenner – well, not exactly pocketing it to be honest; it had never occurred to Jefferson before that this was why money was referred to as knicker – 'you mentioned MPs. Well, if I were you, I should have a look at that lot downstairs. The, what is it, Reform Party. They're very weird people.'

'Are they?' Jefferson wondered what on earth could satisfy Madam Sin's definition of weirdness.

'Especially that fat one. Crichton-Potter I think he's called.'

'Wait a minute.' Jefferson had heard that name before. 'Did you say they were downstairs? In this building?'

'Yes, it's their headquarters. The fat one's always here with his, oh I don't know, his assistant, his speechwriter, I think.'

'His speechwriter?' Jefferson's face became grim. What was it George Cragge had said?

'That's right. Young chap with curly hair. Goes about in horrible green corduroys.'

'Madam,' said Jefferson, 'you've been extremely helpful.'

'Oh, I always try to oblige, dearie. And you're sure there's nothing I can do for you a bit more practical like?'

'No, nothing thank you.'

'Pity. I bet you've got a lovely little botty.'

Frank had only one answer for this kind of situation. He gave Madam Sin one of his benign smiles.

'Do you know,' she observed when she had recovered from the shock, 'I've got clients who would pay you to do that to them?'

Frank left. He was thankful to get away but, for all that, he felt that the interview had been of enormous value. Why was it that the name Crichton-Potter kept cropping up wherever he went? And what about the young chap with curly hair who was a speechwriter?

Mind you, he told himself, on the other hand, he could scarcely eliminate Madam Sin herself. She clearly hated respectable men and not entirely without reason, he had to admit. Of one thing he was certain. Something – something Madam Sin had said – contained a vital clue.

Crichton-Potter's feet were not made for walking. In

fact his entire body was not made for exercise and he took as little of it as he could. Lifting a glass of port at his club, walking to the taxi to take him to Westminster and waving his order paper were, as a rule, his only gestures towards healthy living. When he had agreed, at Henry's insistence, to take personal charge of the Talbotting campaign he had envisaged an essentially supervisory role. It had not occurred to him that the democratic process involved work of an arduous physical nature.

The experience was sorely testing his love of humanity. In the first place, leading an election effort involved meeting the local party activists. In Talbotting there were mercifully few of these but there were enough to persuade Crichton-Potter that the answer to the grass roots was, as he put it, to concrete the entire bloody garden.

Precisely because he had so few helpers, Crichton-Potter found himself consigned to an even worse fate; going out and meeting the voters. Crichton-Potter had no desire to meet the voters. His traditional response to complaints about the remoteness of Westminster from ordinary people was a heartfelt 'thank God'. It was not that he was indifferent to the 'condition of the people', which he genuinely wanted to improve. It was simply that he preferred to luxuriate in his love of humanity as far away from the mass of it as possible. He said as much to Henry as the latter handed him his canvassing cards on the second day of the campaign.

'All this bothering people in their own homes. Surely it's not really necessary.'

'It's essential,' Henry told him. 'I know people complain about being disturbed, but they notice if you don't do it. I gather you don't enjoy the experience.'

'I do not.'

'There are people,' Henry quoted sonorously, 'who enjoy elections. I am not one of them.'

'Who said that?'

'Alfred Duff Cooper.'

'Sod Alfred Duff Cooper.'

'Just as you say,' said Henry. He was decidedly worried by this attitude on what was only the second day of a potentially long, hard campaign. He was also keenly aware that after his mishandling of the candidate selection a good result was essential to restore his status as the party's political guru. 'Look, polling day is only three weeks away,' he protested, 'surely you can't be tired already. Anyway, cheer up, we've got some Young Reformers coming to help us tomorrow.'

'Hell's bells,' said Crichton-Potter. He set off resentfully to one of the more Tory-inclined parts of the constituency. He had insisted on canvassing these first because he thought it less likely that he would be beaten up in a Tory area and second, because Henry had turned down flat his suggestion that he might canvass working-class council estates in a taxi.

'Costa Plenty' declared the garish sign outside the first house he came to. Crichton-Potter rang the bell which was answered by a middle-aged woman in a bad mood and curlers.

'Mrs . . . Biggs?' he inquired, reading the name from the canvass card.

'No.'

'Oh,' said Crichton-Potter, 'is Mrs Biggs in at all?'

'Shouldn't think so. She died two years ago.'

'Ar, um, Mrs . . . er . . . Mrs . . . er.' Crichton-Potter looked appealingly at the stony-faced woman before him. 'Well anyway,' he declared gamely, 'I'm calling on behalf of your Reform Party candidate in the by-election, Alfred Duff Cooper. I mean Larry Boot-Heath.'

'Who's Alfred Duff Cooper?'

'No, madam. Not Alfred Duff Cooper.'

'Who's this Duff Cooper?'

'He's dead, madam,'

'How can I vote for him then?'

'You can't, madam. If I might explain. Our candidate . . .'

'But you just told me that your candidate was dead.'

'Yes, madam. I mean no, madam. Perhaps I should ask my candidate to call on you.'

'What in? A hearse?'

'Madam, the Reform Party is fighting this election . . .'

'I'm not voting for any Duff Coopers. I'm not interested in politics. I'm a Conservative.' She slammed the door.

'The important thing,' Henry had told Crichton-Potter, 'is to register the candidate's name. Never mind policies. Just get the name firmly implanted in the voter's mind.' The candidate's name, that is, not the name of a long-deceased Conservative MP. Oh, never mind, thought Crichton-Potter. Try again. He rang the bell at No. 2.

This time, he thought, he'd give the voter's name a miss and concentrate on the candidate's. The occupant of No. 2 was swarthy and male but at least managed a smile. 'Good morning,' said Crichton-Potter. 'I'm calling on behalf of Larry Boot-Heath. Larry Boot-Heath is your Reform candidate in the coming by-election. I wonder if we can rely on your support?'

It may have been a 'yes' and it may have been a 'no'. The form the response actually took was an extended and expansive burst of something continental followed by a kiss on both cheeks.

'Ah,' said Crichton-Potter. Henry had not prepared him for this contingency. Another quick reference to the candidate's name, he thought, and then hop it. 'Larry Boot-Heath,' he began.

'Boot-Heath,' said the mysterious voter, and kissed Crichton-Potter again.

'No, I'm not Larry Boot-Heath.'

'Boot-Heath,' said the voter from foreign parts.

'Yes, yes, quite.'

'Boot-Heath,' he bawled enthusiastically.

'Splendid, splendid,' said Crichton-Potter and waddled as fast as his burdened little legs would carry him to No. 3.

Meanwhile, at the campaign headquarters Henry was busy writing election leaflets. The Reform Party's approach to the by-election was to encourage tactical voting. This was a highly sophisticated political concept which essentially involved persuading Conservatives to vote for you to stop Labour winning whilst simultaneously inducing socialists to support you in order to stop the Tories. It therefore required the Reform Party not exactly to be all things to all men but at least to be different things to different voters and to hope fervently that the different voters did not compare notes. Thus, for potential Labour supporters, he composed a leaflet which declared, 'It's a two-horse race – vote Reform to stop the Tories'. For those who seemed likely to vote Conservative an alternative leaflet was prepared, urging them to 'vote Reform – stop socialism'. A third leaflet would be delivered to those who either said they would vote for the Reform Party or were don't knows. The technique might have been ethically dubious but it had been effective in the past. Its problem was that it relied on rigorously accurate canvassing and this was not easy to achieve. It was Henry's experience that canvass returns invariably and substantially overestimated Reform support. Reform Party canvassers were on the whole naive souls and it often did not occur to them that voters would promise anything – including a vote for whichever party the canvasser represented – just to get rid of the canvasser.

Reform canvassers, although innocent, were usually conscientious. After all, to go to the lengths not only of joining a tiny political group with no hope of power but of going out on the streets and working for it implied a sincere and substantial commitment. There were, however, exceptions and Crichton-Potter had the air of a man desperate to join their ranks. He had now canvassed twenty houses. It was extremely hot. Crichton-Potter was extremely fat. And it had become rapidly clear to him that Talbotting was not natural

Reform territory – if such a thing existed. Admittedly, he had made a deliberate decision that morning to canvass what he knew would be a predominantly Conservative area. He had, however, been shocked, not so much by the degree of material wellbeing the inhabitants enjoyed as by the indifference this seemed to breed to the welfare of the country as a whole. The only genuinely political questions he had been asked concerned the level of taxation. The considerable reductions effected by the incumbent Conservative administration were apparently not enough for the people of Talbotting who seemed prepared to consider voting Reform only if that party committed itself to the total abolition of income tax.

As a rule, Crichton-Potter did not frequent pubs. A decent claret or a good white burgundy were more his mark. Close contact with the voters of Talbotting, however, had persuaded him that what he needed above all else was a long, cool and alcoholic drink. The last straw came when he knocked at the door of No. 21 and declared, 'I'm calling on behalf . . . half . . . half of lager and lime.' The time had clearly come for a break and Crichton-Potter settled himself in the Old Blue Chip to reflect, he said in self-justification, on his morning's work. At first he intended to have just the one, or possibly two, before resuming his labours. Having persuaded himself that he needed a third he began to see the world in a different light. This canvassing lark, he considered, was no way for the leader of a political party to carry on. Party leaders should be above such things, quite apart from which it had been a considerable blow to his ego to discover that nobody he had canvassed appeared to have heard of him. He studied his canvass cards. By rights, he should be finishing his drink and knocking on the door of No. 22. On the other hand, No. 22 was occupied by Mr and Mrs D'arcy. How on earth could you be called D'arcy and not vote Conservative? The thing looked so certain that there scarcely seemed any point in actually going to the house and ringing the doorbell. Such a formality was hardly necessary. Now he came to think of it Crichton-Potter decided that much the same was true of No. 23, whose inmates were named Blenkinsop. A good solid Labour name.

Looking down the list, Crichton-Potter came increasingly to suspect that his method had a universal application. If your name was, for example Middleman, then you could surely be put down as an undecided voter. If you were called deVere Smith there would be no point in any but the Conservative canvassers troubling you. Crichton-Potter bought his fourth half and settled to develop the now famous Crichton-Potter Sedentary Canvassing Thesis.

At campaign headquarters Henry had just put the finishing touches to his leaflets when he was interrupted. 'I wonder if I might have a word with you, sir?'

'Yes?'

'I am Chief Inspector Frank Jefferson from Scotland Yard. I am investigating the Bank Manager Murders and I have reason to believe that Mr Geoffrey Crichton-Potter may be able to assist us with our inquiries. I would like to speak to him.'

'I'm afraid you can't at the moment. He's out canvassing, he's gone to meet the voters.'

'Good God, has he?' said Jefferson, 'I didn't know politicians had to do that.'

'Neither did he, to tell you the truth.'

'And you are?'

'I'm the agent. I'm running this by-election.'

'Oh, I see. Well, have you any idea where I can find Mr Crichton-Potter?'

Jefferson left armed with Henry's directions and set out to retrace Crichton-Potter's steps. He had no idea that he had just been talking to Crichton-Potter's speechwriter. At campaign headquarters he had left behind a young man anxiously mopping his brow.

Jefferson had travelled to Talbotting certain that Crichton-Potter could provide a vital link in his hunt for the killer. He had also been fascinated to learn from one of his subordinates that Talbotting, as well as being the constituency of the murdered MP, had also been the home of the late Oswald Nicholas banking analyst of Clarence Twist. That struck him as a highly important fact.

At the Old Blue Chip, Crichton-Potter was wiping his forehead and mopping up a good deal of lager and lime besides. Jefferson, meanwhile, became the second man that morning to disturb Mrs Biggs.

'Good morning, madam. I wonder if, by any chance, you have seen a Mr Geoffrey Crichton-Potter?'

'You mean Alfred Duff Cooper.'

'No, I don't.'

'Yes you do. You can't see him, he's dead.'

'No really, madam. I'm looking for Mr Geoffrey Crichton-Potter.'

'Would he be the one who knocked on my door earlier?'

'He would. And . . . '

'He's a maniac.'

'That, madam,' said Jefferson grimly, 'is precisely what I am trying to establish. What gives you reason to suppose that he is . . . a maniac?'

'Because he knocked on my door to tell me that Alfred Duff Cooper was dead. And then asked me to vote for him. Anyway, which lot are you from?'

'I'm calling on behalf of the Metropolitan Police Force.'

'I didn't know they were fielding a candidate.'

By the time he left the first house Jefferson felt baffled. By the time he left the second he felt dazed. He had been favoured with kisses on both cheeks and had received the 'Boot-Heath' response to his every question. Reflecting that the politician's life must be a harder one than he had appreciated, Jefferson left. Eighteen houses later the trail mysteriously dried up. Crichton-Potter had vanished.

The first appearance of a candidate is often a depressing experience for an agent. This is his raw material for the next three weeks. They did not come much more raw than Larry Boot-Heath.

Larry Boot-Heath was politically green in both senses. He was a man who Cared. A man who was Angry, a man to put the 'Grr' in Green. He cared about animals and despised people. He was ozone-friendly and human-hostile. For Larry Boot-Heath, wasps did not sting; they creatively self-expressed.

'I intend,' he told Henry, dismounting from his ecologically sound bicycle on to his ecologically sound Hush Puppies, 'to fight a campaign of high political principle.'

'Oh no you don't,' Henry told him. 'You intend to fight a low-down campaign of ruthless expediency. You are going to attack the other parties from morning to night.'

'But this is a unique chance,' Boot-Heath protested, 'to put over Reform policies. We shall attract huge media attention.'

'That's what worries me,' muttered Henry.

'And, that being so, we shall be admirably placed to promote the causes which made us join the Reform Party. Take site value rating for example . . .'

Ten minutes later, with Henry still wondering whether murdering one's candidate could be held to be justifiable homicide, Boot-Heath drew to a close. 'That's what the people of this country are yearning to hear.'

'Larry, old son.' Henry thought he had better begin with the friendly approach. 'I think you may be under a slight misapprehension about your role in this campaign.'

'I'm the candidate,' said Boot-Heath haughtily.

'Exactly. You're the candidate – the most important person in the whole show. That's why I'm here to help you. To allow you to concentrate on higher matters without having to worry about mundane considerations like – well, like what to say and when to say it.'

'I insist on fighting this election my own way,'

declared Boot-Heath.

'Of course you do. But you're a great servant of the party. You've been around a long time; no one knows this party better than you do. And you'd be the first to admit that a by-election candidate isn't there just in his own right. He's there to serve the whole party.'

'Exactly,' said Boot-Heath, 'which is why I shall be putting over our policies in a totally uncompromising way. Do you happen to know whether Talbotting has a badger rehabilitation centre?'

'Holy shit,' said Henry.

'Well, there you are then. This is the kind of issue that only the Reform Party is prepared to take up. And I firmly believe that the voters are desperate for our message.'

'Now you just get this message,' Henry told him, the gentle approach having manifestly failed. 'You are the candidate in this election. That means you will bloody well do as you are told. It means you keep your mouth shut except when I tell it to open. When I do tell it to open, it will speak words that I put there. If you have ideas in your head they will bloody well stay in your head for the duration. Do I make myself clear?'

'Yes,' said the candidate.

'Good,' said Henry.

'But I fear,' declared the badger's fearless champion, 'that I cannot possibly accede to your request. I am persuaded that what we need is a drastic change of direction.'

'So am I,' hissed Henry, 'off a bloody cliff at high speed.'

'I wish to make it absolutely clear that I will not be muzzled.'

'Hello, hello, hello, hello,' breezed Crichton-Potter, returning from his strenuous round of canvassing. 'Hello, hello, hello,' he added for good measure.

'Are you drunk?' asked Henry.

'Certainly not,' Crichton-Potter lied affably. 'Merely intoxicated by the joys of meeting the good people of

122

Talbotting. Ah, Boot-Heath,' he beamed, 'splendid. Splendid.'

Henry was baffled. Crichton-Potter could not normally bring himself to speak to Boot-Heath. It must have been a good morning's canvassing. 'Well, are we going to win then?' Henry asked.

'Dear boy,' said Crichton-Potter, 'dear boy, dear boy, dear boy. I would say – dispassionately, objectively and without prejudice – that we haven't got a cat in hell's chance. Not a hope, old son. I shall be sacked. You will be sacked. We shall all be sacked. We're doomed. Doomed!' With which guarded assessment of his party's chances, Crichton-Potter fell heavily into a chair and began to snore loudly.

'Oh hell,' said Henry. He could not bring himself to be angry. He appreciated Crichton-Potter's feelings. In fact, after his briefing session with Boot-Heath he had some claim to feel even more strongly than his boss did. 'Oh well, he's been under a lot of strain,' Henry explained to Boot-Heath. 'We'd better let him sleep it off whilst we handle this press conference.'

'Where is it taking place?'

'Upstairs. Come on – into the valley of the shadow of BBC television.'

The Chairman of the Talbotting Reform Party was already seated at a table in front of twenty or thirty journalists and an army of television cameras. There was clearly going to be considerable press interest in this campaign. Normally Henry would have been pleased. The local Chairman rose to shake hands with Henry and Boot-Heath, who took their places either side of him.

'Gentlemen,' said the Chairman to the assembled hacks, 'I'd like to welcome you to the Talbotting Reform Party campaign headquarters. This is our candidate Larry Boot-Heath.'

'I would like,' began the egregious candidate.

'And this,' said the Chairman, moving hastily onwards, 'is his adviser. Now, gentlemen, as you will appreciate, Mr Boot-Heath has only limited time because he's anxious to get out and start meeting the voters. This campaign is going to be fought on the doorsteps. But he will be delighted to answer your questions if you keep them brief.'

'I would like . . .' said the candidate.

'Who would like to ask the first question?'

'Mr Boot-Heath, what do you see as the main issues in this election?' asked the London *Standard*.

'I would . . .'

'Mr Boot-Heath believes that the central issue,' said Henry, 'is the appalling performance of the Government, especially in the economic sphere. He believes the voters will take this chance to tell the Government we need a change of direction – or a change of government.'

'Mr Boot-Heath,' asked the *Daily Telegraph*, 'do you believe the Government should be spending more money and, if they do, won't it cause inflation to rise?'

'I will not be muzz . . .'

'Mr Boot-Heath will not be misled by questions from hostile Tony journalists like you,' said Henry.

'Mr Boot-Heath what do you say to the latest opinion poll showing you fifteen per cent behind the other parties?'

'I would like . . .'

'Mr Boot-Heath would like to say that an opinion poll, taken before the campaign has even started, is no guide whatever to the result after three weeks of putting our policies across.'

Boot-Heath was green with passion. This was his moment. How dare this whippersnapper try to take it away from him? He was determined to have his say.

So was someone else. From the middle of the hall Bamber Sampson of the BBC rose imperiously. There was a bristle of expectation in the room; Sampson's ability to put the knife into by-election candidates was legendary.

'Mr . . . er . . . Boot-Heath,' he began in his nasty

waspish little voice that suggested a mixture of sulphuric acid and expensive aftershave, 'isn't it a fact that you were only selected for this campaign because, of the three applicants, one was lynched and the other got arrested?'

Even Henry was momentarily nonplussed by that. He recovered, but not quite quickly enough.

'I would like,' declared Boot-Heath, 'to say a word about badgers.'

'Badgers?' asked Sampson.

'The threat to this nation's wildlife is what this by-election will be about. Unless immediate action is taken, Britain's countryside is . . .'

'Doomed!' bellowed a voice from down below. 'Doomed! Doomed! We are all doomed!'

'Exactly,' said Boot-Heath, 'we are all doomed.'

'But what about my question?' demanded Sampson. He was not accustomed to being treated in this fashion by by-election candidates. He was used to respect. From Boot-Heath, however, he was not going to get it.

'Your question is simply uninteresting. Think of something better and I'll answer it.'

From Sampson's demeanour it was clear that Boot-Heath had not won a friend for life. He had however won the total admiration of the other journalists present. They had never seen Sampson treated like this and they loved it.

'Now to return to what I was saying,' continued Boot-Heath. 'Take the ferret. Think of the stoat. Raise your minds above vulgar economics and look at the world around you. What are we doing to it? And if we don't stop, what is going to become of it?'

'Massacred!' came the answer from downstairs. Crichton-Potter had originally intended to be wide awake and sober for the press conference. He was now managing one out of the two with a vengeance. 'Massacred!' he bawled. 'We're going to be massacred!'

'We are indeed going to be massacred,' said the apparently imperturbable Boot-Heath. 'And those are the issues on which I shall fight this campaign. I shall not lower myself to talk of taxes, of mortgages, of second houses and second cars. I shall say to the people of Talbotting: Why do you need the first car? Think of what you are doing to our atmosphere. Think of what you are doing to this planet. And I have no doubt that when they have been given the chance to discuss these issues, the people of Talbotting will say . . .'

The doors crashed open. Crichton-Potter blundered belligerently into the room. It was Bamber Sampson's misfortune that he happened to be the one standing up. It could have been anybody. It happened to be Sampson. Crichton-Potter grabbed him by the throat and shook him violently. 'We cannot go on, I tell you,' he shrieked, 'we cannot go on. I've had it. You've had it. We've all had it.'

Henry sat with a towel around his head, moaning softly. Beside him sat Crichton-Potter, looking sick with shame and alcoholic excess. 'I said I was sorry, dear boy,' he appealed.

'It's not your fault. It's not as if we've got a bad press. *The Times* actually said we raised the tone of the campaign. We invited the people of Talbotting to lift their eyes above the mundane issues of standard electioneering. The trouble is that we just can't risk it happening again.'

'I have forsworn the bottle for the duration of this campaign,' said Crichton-Potter.

'It's not you I'm worried about. It's him. That man is a maniac. We've got to do something. Something drastic. Damn it, I'm supposed to be a political fixer. Look at the way this campaign's going.'

'I know. But he is the bloody candidate. How do we stop him? You can't fight a by-election without a candidate.'

'What did you say?' Henry removed his head from the towel and sat bolt upright. 'Say that again.'

'I said we can't fight a by-election without a candidate.'

126

'Why not?' said Henry.

'What?'

'Of course we can fight a by-election without a candidate. That's exactly what we'll do.'

'My dear boy, I'm beginning to think Boot-Heath's insanity is contagious.'

'No, listen. Look, you know when I asked you to take personal charge of this campaign – with my assistance of course – and you said you were going on holiday?'

'Don't remind me.'

'Yes, but that's it. Where were you going?'

'I was going to Capri,' said Crichton-Potter with a sigh. 'Four beautiful weeks in Capri.'

'Have you still got the ticket?'

'Yes, I think so. Why?'

Henry gave him a wink. 'Oh no,' said Crichton-Potter. 'Henry! We can't!'

'Oh, yes we can,' said Henry. 'Where is our beloved candidate?'

The beloved candidate was out meeting the people of Talbotting, who had never met anyone like him before. He felt obliged to admit that, on the doorstep, his message did not seem to be making the impact that it had at the press conference. The voters appeared decidedly unimpressed by Boot-Heath's concern for the constituency's flora and fauna. Their own ecological zeal was more of the 'what are you going to do about my drains?' variety. To questions such as these, Boot-Heath had no answer.

Worse than that he had incurred the wrath of Bamber Sampson. Sampson was not accustomed to being humiliated, least of all in front of fellow journalists who, he knew, hated his guts. He was determined to get his revenge.

He could, as it happened, have done so perfectly well just by following Boot-Heath on the doorstep. His canvassing technique was so spectacularly incompetent that it would have made thoroughly good entertainment for the late-night current affairs programme to

127

which Sampson was under contract. It would also have destroyed the Reform Party's claim, such as it was, to credibility. Boot-Heath's trouble was that he simply did not know when to take no for an answer. Like all true bores he could not stop boring people because he did not realize he was doing so. A typical Boot-Heath canvass went like this:

Boot-Heath: 'Good morning, madam, I am Larry Boot-Heath, your Reform Party candidate in the parliamentary by-election.'

Voter: (Wearing kitchen apron and with baby screaming in background) 'Oh yes.'

Boot-Heath: 'I am here to tell you of the issues on which I am fighting this election.'

Voter: 'Well, I'm rather busy at the moment. I'm in the middle of cooking dinner.'

Boot-Heath: 'Madam, lift your eyes above dinner. Think of the starving millions. Think of what we are doing to our planet.'

Voter: 'You see, I've got my husband to think of . . .'

Boot-Heath: 'Ask yourself why we are here.'

Voter: 'Well, thank you, I'll certainly think about what you've said (starts to close door).

Boot-Heath: (Placing foot firmly in door) 'But I'm not just asking for your vote, madam. I am asking for you to change your attitude and your life style.' (At this point the chip pan catches fire, guaranteeing a change in the voter's life style because her house is burning down.)

Boot-Heath was in short an aggressive bore. He counted himself on the radical wing of the Reform Party and, like many who did likewise, he subscribed to a philosophy informed by a basic contempt for ordinary people. Having been affluent, and having remained single, he was oblivious, perhaps wilfully oblivious, of the worries of bringing up children, of running a family and of making ends meet.

In a way then, Boot-Heath was a shit. He was nothing like as much of a shit however, as Bamber Sampson.

Instead of following Boot-Heath, Sampson had been doing a little canvassing of his own until he found what he was seeking. She came in the form of a small, elderly, and ostensibly frail lady which, from Sampson's point of view, was all to the good. What attracted him to her was her attitude towards politicians, which verged on the homicidal. Under the mistaken impression that Sampson was one of the candidates she grabbed him by the throat and began to shake him violently, threatening to set the dog on him if he did not leave her alone. The hound in question was a monstrous mixture of Afghan and Alsatian and appeared to be eating the front door as a prelude to getting out and eating Sampson. Muttering something about being from the Reform Party, just to plant the idea in the psychopathic pensioner's mind, Sampson retreated. He turned to his research assistant. 'Get me Boot-Heath,' he said, 'bring him here.'

Boot-Heath professed to be irritated by the interruption. In reality of course he was delighted at the chance to perform in front of the camera. He found Bamber Sampson outside a flat on the fifth floor of a tower block in that small part of the constituency which voted Labour.

'Ah, Mr Boot-Heath,' said the media megastar. 'Just to show there are no hard feelings about the press conference I wondered if you'd let us film you canvassing an ordinary voter. I've heard such a lot about your canvassing technique.'

'Oh, certainly,' said Boot-Heath, 'I think you'll find my approach unconventional.'

'I'm sure I shall.'

Adjusting his rosette, Boot-Heath confidently rang the doorbell. He thought this time he would vary his approach slightly. Instead of dwelling on the virtues of ecology, he would attack the vices of capitalism, denounce the trinkets of materialism and condemn the evils of the consumer society.

Unfortunately the consumer society got in first.

'What's wrong with capitalism?' demanded the kettle as it connected with his nose. 'I am a trinket of materialism and proud of it,' said the frying pan, aggressively slugging him on the chin. It had been Bamber Sampson's intention that television should have the last word and, in a sense, he was not disappointed. The psychopathic pensioner's portable television caught Boot-Heath amidships and he disappeared over the balcony, declaring to the inhabitants of each of the five floors below as he passed, 'I'm calling on behaaaaaalf . . .'

But it was just not Bamber Sampson's by-election. For the BBC's ace reporter, even in the midst of triumph there was disaster. The trouble was that the psychopathic pensioner's dog was under the impression that he had been given a starring role in the slaughter of the candidate. Finding himself written out of the script at the last moment he was understandably peeved. He determined to enter stage left and to have his big scene whatever revisions had been made to the script. There was no Boot-Heath. On the other hand there was Sampson, and Sampson presumably had a trouser seat like everyone else. The psychopathic pensioner's hound went in search. Sampson made the understandable tactical error of turning his back. He had intended the move as a prelude to running away at extremely high speed. Sadly he did not make it. It was just not Bamber Sampson's by-election.

'My Boot-Heath's going over the ocean,' sang Henry, 'my Boot-Heath's going over the sea. My Boot-Heath's going over the ocean. He's going to old Italy.' Henry parked the van festooned in 'Vote Boot-Heath' stickers and got out to look around. 'Here, Larry, Larry, Larry,' he called, as if to a kitten. 'Oh where is the old fool?' he demanded after ten minutes' fruitless searching. 'Oh bring back,' he began to sing disconsolately, 'bring back, Oh bring back my Boot-Heath, to me.'

Somebody up there heard him. Henry had been all set to leave the council estate and try one of the Tory areas when, suddenly, it was raining Boot-Heaths. The parliamentary Reform candidate landed in the back of the campaign van. His fall was broken by two thousand leaflets urging the good people of Talbotting to give him their support. Henry, who was not of a religious disposition, was momentarily stunned by his candidate's arrival on the scene. On the other hand, this was no time for philosophical speculation. He ascertained quickly that Boot-Heath was alive but unconscious. That was exactly how Henry wanted him.

As he climbed into the van to go back to headquarters, he heard a voice bellowing from some fifty yards away. 'Hello, 'ello, 'ello,' it boomed. 'What's all this then?' Fearless Frank Jefferson had seen a crime committed and, in the best traditions of his profession, he gave chase. Bravely, he made a dive for the back of the van. Stupidly, he missed. Just as he had also missed the critical significance of what someone had said to him that morning.

CHAPTER
10

Max Parker and George Cragge walked out into the sunshine from the headquarters of the BBC's Parliamentary Unit in Bridge Street opposite the House of Commons.

'Those bloody crime figures are a farce,' said George.

'So are all statistics, dear boy,' said Max, 'at least, that's the assumption I've always worked on.'

'Take mugging,' said George. 'Legally, there's no such thing. No exact legal definition exists, right? So what do the police do? If they want to prove how well they're doing, they say the figures show muggings are reduced. If they want more money or more powers they say there's been a dramatic increase in muggings. But they could be exactly the same, it just depends how you define the term.'

'In the case of economics,' said Max, 'in so far as I understand it . . .'

'Which you don't.'

'Oh, all right, all right. Anyway, I've just come from talking to the Financial Secretary to the Treasury, whoever the hell he is. Now he says that the public sector borrowing requirement is under control.'

'Oh good,' said George, 'I'll sleep a lot easier for knowing that.'

'But the thing is,' said Max, 'a short time ago they were talking about the money supply, which is a different thing — I think. Now why have a different statistic? Because the Government chooses whichever indicator suggests they're doing a good job. I remember when I was Chess Correspondent of *TV Accountant* . . .'

'Have we got time for a quick one?' asked George hastily.

'Well, just one perhaps. I've got to get back.'

'Haven't you recorded your piece, then? I thought that was the idea of coming down to Bridge Street.'

'Well no, not exactly recorded it. You see, I think the figures need a certain amount of, um, interpretation.'

'You mean you can't understand them.'

'Well, in a manner of speaking.'

'Oh, let's go and have a drink.'

In the St Stephen's Tavern where, had he but known it, Frank Jefferson had come face to face with Andrew James, George and Max sank their whiskies and ordered refills.

'Government statistics,' declared George by way of a toast, 'are crap.'

'Government statistics are crap,' agreed Max. 'In any case, who cares what the difference is between capital and current expenditure?'

'Exactly.'

'George,' said Max after a pause, 'what actually is the difference?'

'Oh, for pity's sake, current expenditure is the money you're going to use buying the next round, right?'

'Right.'

'And capital expenditure is the money you're saving up to buy me a crate for Christmas, OK?'

'Exactly.'

'Oh, just tell 'em it's all nonsense.'

'I do wish I'd been the Tennis Correspondent,' complained Max. 'I understand tennis.'

'Well, use a tennis analogy when you're talking about public spending,' George suggested. 'That way you'll totally fox them.'

'What a good idea. On the subject of good ideas, you couldn't lend me a fiver, could you?'

'No, I bloody couldn't.'

'Well, it wouldn't be a loan. It would be more of an investment.'

'In what sense?'

'Because if you don't lend me a fiver, I can't buy the

next round.'

George gave in to superior argument. 'I suppose we'd better go after this one if you're going to get your piece for the six o'clock done.'

Max appeared to be beyond caring about the six o'clock news. He'd think of something. He always had in the past. 'Anyway,' he said, 'tell me about your murderer. Any more cosy little chats on the phone?'

'Well yes, there has been, as a matter of fact. The oddest one of the lot, as it happens. He said he was planning the next one as something special for me. Something about it being close to home. What on earth do you make of that?'

'Can't imagine,' said Max. 'You haven't got any bank managers in your family, have you?'

'Certainly not,' said George. 'I'd disown them if I had, anyway.'

'You haven't got a bank manager living next door?'

'No.'

'Well, that settles it. It was probably a hoax. Designed to throw the police off the scent.'

'But the police aren't on the scent.'

'There is that, of course. Well, I wonder who he's got in mind then?'

Larry Boot-Heath woke up in a hotel bedroom with a headache and a hazy memory. He vaguely remembered that television chap and then knocking on someone's door. The rest was a blank. And how had he got in this hotel room? If he had known what a hangover felt like, Boot-Heath would have felt like he had one. He disapproved strongly of drinking, however; it was flatly incompatible with his ecological view of the world which prescribed a steady diet of nut cutlets and fruit juice. Perhaps he had been overcome with political passion. Whatever the reason he was not deterred from his mission by a little thing like a headache. He walked unsteadily down the stairs and resumed the search for voters. The first he encountered was a dark, foreign-

134

looking chap.

'Good morning,' Boot-Heath began. 'I'm Larry Boot-Heath, your Reform candidate in the by-election. I wonder if I might tell you about the issues I'm fighting on.'

'*I Gabinetti?*' inquired the foreign-looking voter, under the impression that Boot-Heath was looking for the nearest lavatory.

'I am anxious,' Boot-Heath continued, 'to make the conservation of our planet the dominant issue.'

'*Inglese! Inglese!*' The foreign-looking voter had perceived that he was talking to an English lunatic. '*Come se dice in inglese, non capisco.*'

'Ah,' said Boot-Heath. 'Are you by any chance on the electoral register or have you just arrived in the constituency?'

'*Non capisco.*'

'Ah. In that case, perhaps I might just give you one of these.' Boot-Heath pulled from his pocket a crumpled leaflet exhorting its recipient to 'vote Boot-Heath'. The Italian studied it for a moment and burst into hysterical laughter. '*Inglese,*' he repeated as if this made everything clear. '*Inglese!*'

For once even Boot-Heath was at a loss for words. He left his cheery companion and tried another passer-by. 'Can you tell me whether I'm anywhere near the Reform Party's Headquarters?' he asked.

'*Prego?*' The second foreign-looking voter was an enormous woman with a look of good-natured concern. Boot-Heath produced another of his leaflets. It seemed to have much the same effect as the first one. The woman roared until the tears rolled down her cheeks. '*Inglese,*' she bellowed, slapping him so heavily on the back that he shot forward several paces. Clearly the woman thought the joke much too good to be kept to herself and was busy summoning her friends. '*Inglese,*' she informed them, pointing at the hapless Boot-Heath who beat as dignified a retreat as he could manage. Why had no one told him that there was such a high immigrant population in Talbotting?

'The Chancellor, this afternoon, brought off a craftily disguised lob,' said Max, taking out the keys of his car.

'No, Max,' said George.

'The Chancellor, this afternoon made a superb running forehand pass,' suggested Max.

'No, Max.'

'The public spending figures are best understood as a delicately chipped backhand volley down the line.'

'No, Max!'

'Oh well, never mind. I'll think of something.' Max and George clambered into the battered old Ford that passed for a company car in the BBC. Max looked at his watch. It was twenty-five to six. 'My God, I'm on the air in half an hour,' he said, 'we'll have to step on it.'

And Max stepped on it. Building steadily up Whitehall he took Trafalgar Square at a steady seventy. He took Lower Regent Street at eighty and collected a fruit stall en route. At Piccadilly Circus he acquired an underground sign and a busker. At first, George enjoyed the experience. There was, after all, a fair bit of traffic about and driving on the pavement was the obvious way to avoid it. 'Fifty bonus points for an Arab,' he shouted, 'a hundred bonus points for an American.' As they hurtled up Regent Street, however, even George was beginning to get worried. Nobody should attempt Oxford Circus at a hundred and ten. 'Max, aren't we going a bit fast?' he asked as Max added a hot dog stall, two rucksacks and a Japanese tourist to his tally.

'Of course we're going a bit sodding fast,' Max said reasonably. 'The sodding brakes have failed.'

'What?'

'I said – oh bugger!'

The traffic lights at Oxford Circus were not working. Nor for some considerable time afterwards, did the traffic warden who had been doing their job. Appropriately perhaps, Max contrived to collect seventy-four parking tickets as he passed, dispatching their owner to an honoured place in the underwear department in a major store several hundred yards away.

The doors of Broadcasting House are extremely robust. BBC employees have been known to have half an hour's complete rest first thing in the morning after the sheer exertion of opening them. They were not, however, equipped to resist an economics correspondent doing a hundred and thirty-five. Probably George summed it up most succinctly when he and Max smashed their way into the home of British Broadcasting with an enthusiasm seldom displayed by other staff; he remarked, 'Holeee Sheeeeit!'

The totally battered car came finally to a halt at, or rather half in and half out of, one of the lifts. It is not easy to rouse a BBC commissionaire but Max had managed it.

'Wot the 'ell!' demanded the smart uniform when it had picked itself up from under the reception desk. George and Max had by this time however convinced themselves that they were still alive and Max was not in the habit of being bossed around by commissionaires.

'Don't just stand there, man,' he roared, 'I'm on the air in five minutes.'

In the glove compartment, George found what he'd known would be there. 'Dear Economics Correspondent,' it said, 'in the best traditions of Keynesianism, I have found it necessary to effect some fine tuning.'

There were those who held that 'I'm an old pro' was Max Parker's mantra and that he intoned it several hundred times a day in the quest for inner peace. If so, his reception in the newsroom proved the wisdom of his philosophy. He arrived, cut and bruised, and his tie around his ear. The Assistant Editor, in charge of the Radio 4 Bulletins desk, drew the obvious conclusion.

'Have you and Cragge been out on the piss?' he demanded furiously.

'I'm an old pro,' Max snapped, 'get me on the air.'

'You were supposed to be here an hour ago.'

'I got held up, didn't I?'

That day's Assistant Editor was a little man bitter with frustrated ambitions. Twice he had been passed over for the Editorship of Radio News, a post which he had no doubt he could have filled with unprecedented skill. If he ever got the job, which everyone else knew he never would, his first act, he reflected savagely, would be to sack Cragge and Parker.

'You're supposed to be doing a piece for the 1800 about the PSBR,' he told Parker.

'About what?'

'Public spending, you imbecile.'

'Oh, that's all right,' said Max superciliously, 'I'll do it live.'

'And look at the state of you.'

'I will have you know,' said Max haughtily, 'that someone has just made an attempt on my life.'

'And the bastard failed,' sighed the Assistant Editor. 'Oh, very well. I suppose you'll have to do it live. You're the third lead.'

'The third lead?' snarled Max. 'What the bloody hell do you mean I'm the third lead?'

'Lots of foreign stories about today. We're leading with two bits of foreign news.'

'Foreign stories! Bugger foreign stories! I'll tell you what we used to do with foreign stories when I was News Editor of . . .'

'I already know your attitude to foreign stories. Fortunately I'm in charge of this bulletin and you aren't. Perhaps you would be good enough to get yourself to the studio.' The Assistant Editor was painfully aware that Max Parker's journalistic experience was much greater than his own. He knew also that, on almost every subject save economics, Max's journalistic judgement was extremely sound. It was one reason why there were not a few members of the newsroom keen to see Max kept in his job as Economics Correspondent, where his manifest incompetence rendered him less of a threat.

Unlike most BBC Radio News broadcasts which are

transmitted from the news studio – studio 3C at the end of the newsroom – the 1800, as it is known, comes from the larger studio, No. 3E, down the corridor, which is in fact the current affairs studio and the home of the *Today* programme and the *World at One*. As Max staggered into it, he found Jemma in situ, luminous pink legwarmers and all, reading over the stories already written.

'Hello dear,' said Max wearily as he crashed on to a chair. She gawped at his dishevelled appearance. 'Wheee,' she observed perceptively.

'I know. I've had a bit of a day. Some bastard tried to murder me.'

'Wild,' she breathed.

'Yes. Quite so. Still, I'm an old pro,' said Max. 'The main thing is to get the bloody paper on the street.'

The half hour before the Radio 4 six o'clock is the newsroom's most exciting and busy time. Naturally, all news broadcasts are live. Not for the journalists the luxury, enjoyed by so many radio producers, of pre-recording at leisure. It is a strange but immutable law of radio journalism that, if the bulletin begins at six o'clock, nothing will happen until a quarter to six at which point everything will happen. At that stage sub-editors crash into each other racing between the newsroom and studio 3E. The Senior Duty Editor is to be found frantically counting words and lines to make sure the programme will run for exactly half an hour, no more or less. The foreign dispatches will usually have been put on tape and another law is that one of the tapes will go missing, the studio insisting that it must be in the newsroom and vice versa. In the midst of the apparent chaos the majestic figure of the Assistant Editor – the boss – paces the newsroom as he dictates the day's headlines to his typist.

Much as he approved of all this strenuous activity Max felt that it displayed a mistaken sense of priorities. He stuck his head outside the studio and accosted a young female sub-editor who was vehemently protesting to one of her superiors that, whoever had lost New York, it was not she. 'Get me a large whisky,' he demanded.

'I beg your pardon?'

'An immensely large whisky, woman. At once.' Having given his instruction Max scribbled a few lines on a scrap of paper and handed it to the announcer. 'Just lead me in with that,' he told her. 'I'm the third story.' It was five minutes to six.

Max Parker's whisky arrived. In the newsroom, a voice came over the Tannoy, 'General News Service. We're getting reports of a coach crash in Devon. A party of children from Liverpool on their way to Torquay. There are no reports of casualties.'

The Assistant Editor broke off from dictating headlines. 'Here you,' he snapped at one of the sub-editors, 'do five lines on that for the top of the programme and update it as it comes in.' It was four minutes to six.

'Where the hell's New York?' demanded the Senior Duty Editor. 'It's all right – Radio 2 has pinched it.' 'Well get it back!' 'I have done.' 'Have you edited it? There's a mistake in it.' 'Oh hell, is there?' Three minutes to six.

The Editor of Radio News sauntered self-importantly into the newsroom to jolly up the troops. 'Anything I can do to help?' he inquired casually. The Assistant Editor gave him a cold and expressive look. Two minutes to six.

The Assistant Editor marched down to the studio and handed copies of the headlines to the newsreader and the studio managers who were busy checking voice levels and making sure the taped inserts were assembled in the correct order. One minute to six.

'Max, where's your cue material?' Max hastily scribbled another copy and handed it to the Assistant Editor. The studio became quiet and calm as they waited for the pips. 'BBC News at six o'clock.' The two foreign leads passed off uneventfully. New York turned out to be a dispatch about the United States' Central American policy and was followed by a report on the situation in the Middle East. Then the reader introduced Max who by this time looked keen, sober and alert. 'At home, the latest public spending figures have been published by the Government. This report by our Economics Correspondent, Max Parker.'

Max took a quick sniff at his whisky and began: 'The Chancellor of the Exchequer,' he declared, 'has never been known for getting a high percentage of first serves over the net.'

'Bloody hell,' said the Assistant Editor.

'The Government's difficulties,' Max continued briskly, 'were best summed up in this week's *Economist*, which said . . .'

Outside in the cubicle a sub-editor handed the Assistant Editor the latest on the coach crash. 'What do you mean, there's been a new development?'

'Well, there has.'

'All developments are new, you idiot. That's why they're in the news.'

In his office down the corridor George Cragge broke into a wide grin as his friend merrily plagiarized or more precisely just read, the *Economist*. It would clearly take more than the odd hundred and thirty-five mile an hour crash to destroy Max Parker's distinctive style of economic analysis. George's own report on the crime figures was the second half lead; in other words, it followed the resumé of the headlines at six fifteen. Since George had pre-recorded it at Bridge Street, he was able to listen in comfort in his office and, satisfied that it sounded reasonably coherent, he switched off. Max came in, obviously exhausted from the combined effects of that attempt on his life and a live broadcast about public spending figures. George poured him a Scotch. 'That was brilliant,' he told his friend.

'Naturally, dear boy. I'm an old pro.'

'And very nearly a dead old pro. Look at this.'

Max studied the maniac's letter. 'You mean that it was this bank manager lunatic?'

'No question.'

'But I'm not a bank manager.'

'Well no. But then neither was Anderson, strictly speaking. Your family does have banking connections, doesn't it?'

'My wife's father was in banking, yes. That's not a very good reason for murdering somebody.'

'Well, perhaps he picked on you because you're a symbol of the economic system or something.'

'He bloody well failed, didn't he,' said Max triumphantly.

'Yes, he did for once,' George agreed. 'I wonder what his response will be.'

At the campaign headquarters, in Talbotting, Henry and Crichton-Potter were in conference.

'But how did you manage it?' Crichton-Potter asked.

'I just had him shipped off to the airport with instructions that he was recovering from an operation and he needs a long period of convalescence. I wonder how he's enjoying Capri.'

'I wonder how Capri's enjoying him, come to that. Anyway,' said Crichton-Potter, 'at least it means this should be a more peaceful campaign from now on.'

'Well, yes. And no.'

'How do you mean?'

'Well, whilst you were out canvassing, we had a caller.'

'A supporter? A well-wisher?'

'No, a police officer. Apparently something to do with the Bank Manager Murders.'

'What could they have to do with us?' asked Crichton-Potter.

'Oh, nothing. Nothing at all. Anyway, I think I managed to shake him off.'

When Frank Jefferson came to, he looked and felt like a man who had been shaken off. He had been unconscious for some time in the middle of the road and all he could remember was that he had seen a man bundled into a battered old van by a young man he had met earlier at the Reform Party campaign headquarters. Talbotting had been the scene of a serious crime.

When he found a telephone box and rang one of his subordinates, he learnt that the quiet Surrey constituency had been the scene of several more.

Andrew James of Mysore Road, Battersea, London SW11, alighted from the six ten from Waterloo to Talbotting. He had devoted the journey to intense study of a map of the area and his first act upon reaching it was to find a telephone directory from which he copied some names. He then made his way to the headquarters of the Talbotting Reform Association on whose behalf he intended to do some canvassing. It fitted neatly with his plans for the next few weeks. At the campaign headquarters he found Henry and Crichton-Potter in conference. Henry handed him some canvassing cards and introduced him to the leader of the party.

'It's a pleasure to have you aboard,' Crichton-Potter told him, 'young people joining the party, supporting the cause, fighting for . . . er, why did you join the party actually?'

'Well, I've always admired you enormously,' said Andrew James.

'It's the only way you can admire him,' muttered Henry as Crichton-Potter swelled with pride, no mean achievement in one whose girth left little scope for further swelling of any description.

'And I want to change the face of British society,' continued Andrew James.

'Oh,' said Crichton-Potter. 'Ah. Yes. Absolutely.'

'And wipe the smile off its bloated features.'

'Er, oh. Well, up to a point.' Crichton-Potter couldn't help feeling that if there had been a Society for the Preservation of Bloated Features, he might well have been its honorary life president, but he wisely forbore to say so.

'What I really like about you is your radical subversiveness.'

'My umm, radical subversiveness. Yes, well, my radical subversiveness is absolutely oojah-cum-spiff, no doubt about that. Would you like some claret?'

'Of course he wouldn't like some claret,' protested Henry.

'No, no, of course he wouldn't. Actually I've got a rather decent white burgundy if . . .'

'He doesn't want anything to drink. He wants to go out and campaign. He's bursting with radical zeal, aren't you?'

'Oh yes,' said Andrew James grimly, 'I certainly am.'

The revenge of the Bank Manager murderer was swift and dramatic. It showed also a reversion to type in its choice of victims after the murder of an MP and the abortive attempt to kill Max Parker. Just two days after that indestructible hack had redesigned the front of Broadcasting House, three bank managers were killed, all of them in Talbotting. Beside each body was a note making it clear who was responsible.

One side effect was that George Cragge achieved one of his life's ambitions which was to write his copy from an armchair at home. Since he lived in Talbotting, there was no need for him to go to Broadcasting House; he simply ambled around the town between the scenes of the crimes and telephoned his reports through to the newsroom.

'It's all right for some,' grumbled Frank Jefferson as he sank wearily into a chair at George's home after a hard and fruitless day.

'So what do you make of this latest lot?' George asked.

'Oh, it's obvious. He's clearly furious with himself for buggering the attempt on your friend. This is his way of showing he's still in business.'

'I guess you're right. It's a bit extreme though, isn't it? Three in one day?'

'Well yes,' said Jefferson, 'and it's also the first time he's struck outside London. I suppose from now on we've got to be ready for him to attack anywhere in the country.'

'Any fresh clues from the latest lot?'

'No, not really. He's always varied his methods. These are no exceptions – a different style of murder in each case.'

'Versatile chap, isn't he?'

'Yes. And the same goes for his choice of victims. Three very different people. Who were they – Abberton, Elliott and Lough.'

'But all bank managers.'

'Yes, but what different kinds of bank managers. One, a director of a City bank leading the life of a gentleman farmer in Talbotting.'

'Until the maniac pushed him into a combine harvester.'

'That's right.'

'What was it the note said?'

'It said, "Dear Bank Manager, I have decided the time has come for you to explore the mechanics of my operation." The second one was just an ordinary manager of a small branch here in Talbotting. Blown to bits as he sat on the loo, poor bastard.'

'"Dear Bank Manager, I have decided to confiscate your assets,"' said George recalling the murderer's note. 'And the third one worked in Talbotting as well.'

'He did. On the insurance side of the bank's operations. He was knocked down. The note said something about him losing his "no claims bonus".'

'And you still don't think you're any nearer catching him? You'll never get to be Commissioner like this, you know.'

'There's no need to rub it in,' said Jefferson bitterly. 'How the hell do you think I feel? Here I am looking for a needle in a haystack and all I get from my governors is: "Get this villain bloody quick." I'm doing my best, aren't I? Anyway, there is just one small possibility.'

'Which is?'

'Well, why are so many people in Talbotting at the moment?'

'Because there's a by-election,' said George.

'Exactly. And I'm just wondering whether that might lead somewhere. After all, there are people in Talbotting now who would normally be in London and who would have been there for all the previous murders.'

'I suppose you're right.'

'One way or another I must talk to Geoffrey Crichton-Potter.'

The effect on public opinion of the new outbreak of murders was considerable. Up to that point, the bank manager murderer had been something of a hero. That someone should wish to murder bank managers struck most people as eminently sane and reasonable and they had difficulty thinking of the maniac as a maniac at all. When he broadened his scope and bumped off an MP it seemed to a sizeable part of the population that here was a murderer with sound ideas. He seemed to deserve reward rather than punishment. Moreover, the murderer provided a field day for sociologists and social observers who wrote of the killings not as criminal acts but as 'manifestations of the national psyche'.

The new round of crimes changed all that, however. Partly this was because the murderer had now moved out of London and people all over the country began to feel threatened, especially since in order to be a victim one appeared to need only the most tenuous link with banking. Partly also it was because the horror of three murders in one day struck home to people who had hitherto taken the whole affair lightly. It also had something to do with the attempt on Max Parker's life. Max's spectacularly uninformed economic reporting was a national institution and to attempt to extinguish a voice known to millions struck most people as lese-majesty.

Consequently there had been a marked shift in the prevailing consensus. The demand now was that the murderer be caught with all due speed. In Talbotting itself the murders were not just a by-election issue, they

146

were *the* by-election issue and Henry, ever alert to changes of political mood, had changed tack in the leaflets and press releases he was putting out in the name of the absent Boot-Heath. No longer did he call bank managers the 'hapless agents of evil Tory policies', suggesting that whilst the crimes were not exactly to be condoned they could at least be understood in the economic climate which the Government had created. Different circumstances required a different tone and it was one which gave Henry immense pleasure. 'What about Law and Order, then?' screamed the headline on the latest Reform Party handout which continued:

> The Tory Party came to power committed to reduc-ing the rate of crime. Especially violent crime. Yet after years of their misrule, no one is safe.
>
> THE TORIES ARE MURDER! And the people of Talbotting know that better than anyone else in the country!
>
> Your Reform candidate, Larry Boot-Heath, will make the physical safety of his constituents his top priority. A defeat for the Government *now* will bring them to their senses and make it clear that the wave of lawlessness now sweeping the country will not be tolerated!

The voters of Talbotting entirely agreed. In fact they agreed so much that, whilst opinion polls showed the Labour vote as static, they revealed a dramatic swing from the Government to the Reform Party which the absence of the candidate did nothing to diminish. Boot-Heath's apparently lofty contempt for such conventions as daily press conferences struck several commentators as masterly.

'He is refusing to allow this campaign to be domin-ated by the media,' they wrote. 'Instead he is going out and meeting the people.'

This would admittedly have been news to the people but then they were mostly indifferent to what the candidate looked like. To judge from Henry's leaflets this Boot-Heath, whoever he was, had the right ideas. Suddenly, what had initially looked like an open and shut by-election for the Government promised to be close and exciting and to raise a possibility which neither Henry nor Geoffrey Crichton-Potter had contemplated. It was a possibility that filled them with horror.

'But damn it,' Crichton-Potter protested to Henry, 'I said I wanted to do well in this by-election. I didn't say I wanted to win it. How on earth could we explain to the voters that their new MP is somewhere on the island of Capri, only we don't know where?'

'I suppose we could always get him back,' said Henry.

'But I don't want him back. Can you imagine what it would do to this party if that idiot became a national political figure? If he gets elected, he'll be on every television programme in the country going on and on about the evils of materialism.'

'But we're supposed to be in politics to win,' Henry protested.

'Yes, but dear boy, look, you're supposed to be the brains of the family. If we win this by-election, either we shan't be able to find our candidate or, worse still, we shall be able to find him. Either way, the effect on our performance at the next general election will be catastrophic. Talk about winning the battle and losing the war.'

'I guess you're right.'

'Of course I'm right. And what about the effect on me personally? I've got quite enough appalling people to put up with at the House of Commons without having Boot-Heath inflicted on me.'

'I can certainly understand your feelings.'

'There's only one thing for it,' Crichton-Potter concluded. 'Henry: I command you to lose this by-election.'

The Reform Party had had lots of practice at losing by-elections; it was something that came naturally. Like many things that come naturally, however, it became fiendishly difficult the moment it was consciously striven for. The canvass returns continued to show a steady advance and, by the Monday before polling day, they put Boot-Heath ahead for the first time. Henry was distraught. The traditional ploy, if you found yourself slightly ahead going into the last week, was to issue a leaflet headed something like 'Nearly There', which implied that you were actually still in second place and needed every vote you could get. The thinking was that if people believed it was in the bag they might not take the trouble to vote and you might therefore lose by default. In accordance with the Leader's instructions, Henry broke all the rules and put out a leaflet entitled 'Miles Ahead'. This suggested that the election was all over bar the shouting and that Boot-Heath was certain to win it. Henry's hope was that some voters who would have supported Boot-Heath might stay at home and thus tip the balance in favour of his opponent.

For once, however, the conventional wisdom was confounded. The news that Boot-Heath was 'miles ahead' seemed only to strengthen the voters' resolve to support him, and a lead in the polls of three points became one of eight. The trouble was that the two major parties had chosen such totally unsuitable candidates that losing to either of them was no easy matter. The Labour representative, a woman with flaming red hair, a flaming temper and a flamingly dislikeable personality, had dropped out of the running at an early stage. Partly this was because, in a Conservative seat during an unpopular Conservative administration, it was traditional that support went to the third party rather than to Labour whose chances of doing well in a cosy and affluent constituency such as Talbotting were never great. The candidate could not exactly be said to have helped matters, however. She aimed her campaign at the women of Talbotting, who were interested to be informed that they were the victims of male oppression and were sexual slaves. Living as they did, in stock-broker affluence and acting as almost full-time cocktail party hostesses, they concluded, quite reasonably, that they had nothing to lose but their jewellery and dismissed the Labour candidate from their minds.

Throughout the lifetime of the Government, political commentators had grown to suspect that there was only one Conservative by-election candidate and that he was simply wheeled on whenever necessary. He was young, chinless and white. He had a respectable job. He had the by-election children and the by-election wife and he totally supported everything the Government was doing. He was perfectly competent as long as his party was ahead and supporting the Government was the correct line. He became a serious liability the moment the Government was in trouble since he entirely lacked a mind of his own and was therefore quite unable to distance himself from Downing Street and Smith Square as the situation demanded.

Losing a by-election to either of these two looked a near impossibility. In such circumstances, Henry's refusal to allow his candidate to appear with his rivals in a public eve-of-poll debate looked entirely sensible. Boot-Heath was in the lead and even if he had actually been in Talbotting as well, it would have made no sense for him to stoop to a vulgar wrangle with his opponents.

Henry put his head in his hands. On Thursday night, against all the odds, he would, barring a miracle, have achieved a brilliant by-election victory. As a result he would probably get fired, quite apart from having to explain to the Returning Officer, and, indeed, the television cameras, why he was unable to produce the candidate. Of course, things might be different if Crichton-Potter would allow him to bring Boot-Heath back. This had, however, been totally ruled out and, in any case, Henry no longer had any idea where Boot-Heath was.

On Wednesday morning the constituency was flooded with party members; the scent of victory had reawakened loyalty in so-called party workers who had not done a stroke for the Reformers in years. Henry's protests that he did not want anyone to do any canvassing were taken as a joke and caused much hilarity. There was a mood of euphoria in the Reform Party camp. It was some years since they had scored a by-election victory of any kind. It was decades since a majority on this scale had been overturned and the Reform Party activists were determined to savour the moment. Henry even had what would normally have been the huge satisfaction of telling Bamber Sampson to get stuffed when the BBC's ace political reporter demanded for the hundredth time that he be allowed to interview Boot-Heath. At Conservative Central Office in Smith Square the preparation had already begun of the 'plea in mitigation' which the Government would make on losing one of its safest seats. At 10 Downing Street, the Prime Minister was giving the party chairman hell.

'First,' he stormed, 'you tell me to get this by-election over quickly because that's our best chance of winning. Then you engineer three murders in the constituency when we're supposed to be the law and order Government.'

'I didn't engineer three murders, for pity's sake. There's a maniac on the loose. It's hardly my fault.'

'Of course it's your bloody fault. You're the party chairman, aren't you?'

'Well, you appointed me, didn't you?'

'A fact of which you will be made painfully aware once all of this is over. Have you got a farm in Sussex?'

'No, I do not have a farm in Sussex.'

'Get one. You're going to need it.'

At New Scotland Yard, the Commissioner was giving Frank Jefferson hell.

'You're supposed to be the best man I've got. And you're being made a bloody fool of. I'm being made a bloody fool of. Do you know the essence of good policing, Jefferson?'

'Yes, sir. I mean, no, sir.'

'The essence of good policing is unobtrusiveness. When the force do a good job people are almost unaware of our existence. When they start noticing we're probably doing a bad job.'

'Yes, sir,' mumbled Jefferson miserably.

'I have known bad times in this job,' said the Commissioner. 'I've known questions in Parliament, searching documentaries on the BBC, opinion polls showing us less popular than tax collectors. But it is your sublime achievement, Jefferson, to have swung an entire bloody by-election with your incompetence. Do you own a farm in Sussex?'

'No, sir.'

'Get one.'

At Reform Party campaign headquarters in Talbotting, Geoffrey Crichton-Potter was giving Henry hell.

'So you're the political genius, are you? You're the one with the brains. The – what's the expression? – political acumen. This, young man, is the biggest cock-up since Watergate.'

'Yes but . . .'

'Don't worry about a thing, you said. Leave it all to me. I'll fix the selection meeting.'

'There's no need to go on about the selection . . .'

'Well, you bloody fixed it all right, didn't you? Bloody Larry, bloody Boot-Heath. The biggest dum-dum in the Reform Party.'

'Hardly the biggest,' Henry muttered under his breath.

'What?'

'Nothing, C-P.'

'And then came your masterstroke. Don't worry about Boot-Heath. Leave Boot-Heath to me. I'll get rid of Boot-Heath.'

'But I did get rid of him.'

'Exactly. And now what are we going to do? "I declare the said Larry Boot-Heath duly elected to serve" – and the swine's in Capri.'

'Well, you wanted me to get rid of him. What you're telling me is that I've done wrong to bring about the biggest victory the Reform Party has had in generations. Is that being fair?'

'I'll tell you what's fair, my lad. When, as a result of tomorrow's débâcle, I have to go back to my farm in Sussex, I'm going to give you a job on it. Mucking out the pigs at five o'clock every morning. And I'm going to get up at that unheard of hour every day just for the pleasure of coming and watching.'

At 51 Lacon Gardens, Talbotting, George Cragge's head was giving him hell. So was his stomach. If there was one thing worse than a lazy summer with no big stories to cover, it was a summer with a massive story to cover. Since the triple murder in Talbotting, George had been having the worst of both worlds. He had traipsed from murder scene to murder scene and broadcast endless reports for the news, the *Today* programme, *The World at One* and, it seemed, virtually every programme on the air. At the same time he had been able to do his reports 'on site' and had not had to go near the dream factory, as the BBC Radio newsroom was affectionately known to its inmates. Free from the beady eyes of Editors and Assistant Editors and constantly within walking distance of his local, George had combined a prodigious amount of work with a prodigious amount of drinking, and the effects were now catching up. He had also been on the receiving end of succinct expletives from almost all of those whom he had sought to interview and, whilst George was no stranger to being told to 'Sod off' by Home Secretaries and Assistant Commissioners, the phrase stung when it came from friends like Frank Jefferson.

What George needed, above all, he decided, was a quiet, sober – well, relatively sober – evening in front of the television. George's viewing was infrequent but it followed a regular pattern. He always watched the BBC out of corporate loyalty. On the other hand, he did so purely in order to snarl. In particular he snarled at the crime reporting of BBC Television News which he considered both totally derivative of, and grossly inferior to, his own. The feeling was intensified because BBC Television's Crime Reporter was a woman, or, as George put it, a tart.

George had enjoyed a restful and refreshing half hour of muttering 'Derivative tart' in the direction of his television when suddenly there was a loud crash outside. He cursed. Of course it might be Charlotte Rampling just happening to be in the neighbourhood and deciding to call. On the other hand, it might be work. It seemed likely, given George's experience of the past few weeks, that it would be work.

It turned out to be Mr Andrew James of Mysore Road, Battersea, London SW11.

CHAPTER
11

The 'Good Morning' leaflet had for some years been a regular part of the Reform Party's by-election campaigns. It was delivered in the middle of the night before polling day so that the voters would find it on their doormats when they rose. As its title suggested, it bade them a cheery good morning and went on to remind them of the Reform candidate's name and of the fact that the election was that day. In theory it sent them off to vote for the Reform Party before going to work. In practice the noise of it coming through their letter boxes, waking their babies and their dogs, and scattering their milk bottles, woke them up in the middle of the night and made them determined to go out and vote – for almost anybody who was not the Reform candidate.

At about 6.30 p.m. on Wednesday, the night before the Talbotting by-election, Henry sat composing such a leaflet as he had done many times before. He had even included an extract from one of Boot-Heath's speeches about the 'real issues'. But he was not hopeful. The by-election looked unshakeable. When he had finished the leaflet he telephoned Crichton-Potter who had become so despondent he had announced his intention of going to his club in London and staying there until the by-election was over.

But Henry was not beaten yet. In whatever way his political career was going to end, he was determined that it would not be finished by Boot-Heath. Not, at least, before Henry had finished Boot-Heath.

'Yes, Henry?' Crichton-Potter had been roused from slumber in the Smoking Room and sounded like it.

'First the bad news,' said Henry. 'The latest poll puts

155

us ten points ahead of the Tories.'

'Oh God. Well, there's nothing to be done, is there? There's no way we can lose now.'

'I'm afraid not. But I think I can see a way out of our troubles. I know what we can do about Boot-Heath.'

'Like what?' Crichton-Potter was wearily sceptical.

'We kill him.'

Crichton-Potter was wide awake and totally sceptical. 'Dear boy, don't you think we've got troubles enough without a murder charge? I mean, I know you'd like to kill him. I'd like to kill him. But . . .'

'I don't mean really kill him, for Pete's sake. I mean we announce he's dead. After the polls close. There's no point in doing it before.'

'Yes but . . .'

'No, listen. For all we know, Boot-Heath actually is dead. None of my contacts in Italy has been able to find him. And if we announce he's dead after the by-election there'll have to be another by-election, right? Which, given the sympathy vote his death will create, we shall win with a huge majority.'

'Ah.' Crichton-Potter was beginning to grasp the idea.

'And the real advantage is that we win that by-election with a different candidate.'

'It could just work. How are we going to kill him?'

'I haven't finalized the details. But I think he probably commits suicide, after leaving a note saying he has found the spectacle of the state the country's in so unbearable that he can no longer face it. I think that's the approach.'

'And when do we make the announcement?'

'Just after ten o'clock when voting's finished. I'll draft something this evening and read it over to you later on.'

'Henry, my boy, this is one of your best. Why, it will . . .'

'Snatch defeat from the jaws of victory,' said Henry. 'Okay, talk to you later.'

The trouble with Reform Party workers is their indecent enthusiasm. No one had told Andrew James that his party leader wanted to lose the by-election. He would not have understood if they had. All he knew was that for his own purposes, it was vital that he threw himself fully into the campaign. Henry could think of no good reason, much as he wished he could, for not letting Andrew James drive the van around the constituency. It was the van with the speakers on top, a traditional sight in British elections, from which usually unintelligible words are bawled at voters in the street.

What interested Frank Jefferson, who drove up to Reform Party HQ as the van drove off, was that it was clearly the vehicle into which Larry Boot-Heath had been so unceremoniously bundled. Why Boot-Heath's photograph was all over the back of the van he neither understood nor cared. He had been flung off the van at high speed, and whoever was inside it was in trouble.

At first the van's progress was sedate.

'This,' declared Andrew James, 'is the Reform Party speaking. Tomorrow – that's polling day – go out and vote for your Reform Party candidate, Larry Boot-Heath.' As he became gradually aware of a flashing blue light in his rear-view mirror, Andrew James' progress became dramatically faster.

'This is the Reform Party,' said the campaign van.

'This is the police,' said Frank Jefferson, through a police megaphone. 'Stop in the name of the law.'

'This is the Reform Party. Go out and vote for Larry Boot-Heath. This is your chance to say to the Government: IT'S THE FILTH! IT'S THE BLOODY POLICE.'

This unconventional election message was clear to the voters of Talbotting, who were already displaying an extraordinary degree of interest in the campaign's latest turn. They were quite accustomed to a candidate going walk-about. Never before had they witnessed a party worker going drive-about, hotly pursued by a Chief Inspector, convinced that, at last, he was closing on his quarry.

'Fine tuning, eh? I'll fine tune you,' shrieked Jefferson. 'Malthus lives, does he?'

'Vote Boot-Heath!' bellowed Andrew James.

Talbotting's principal supermarket had been canvassed before, but never on wheels. Andrew James butchered the meat section and spattered the van in blood. He slashed the special offers. At the check-out section, Andrew James checked out in a hail of one-pound coins. His advice to the voters of Talbotting changed from 'Vote for us' to 'Get out the Sodding Way, you Imbeciles'. In the High Street, he met Bamber Sampson of the BBC.

'Aha,' said Sampson, seeing at last his chance of an interview with the candidate. 'Oh shit,' said Sampson, as, for the only time in his life, a campaign pursued him instead of the other way around. With the BBC in front of him and the Metropolitan police behind him, Andrew James did what the Reform Party had been doing for generations. He went sideways. He careered through George Cragge's front gate, and George Cragge's front gate was a formidable obstacle. Andrew James leapt out of the van, and, as George opened his door, he saw a young man in green corduroy trousers sprinting towards him pursued by the officers of the law. Between them Cragge and Jefferson pinned the young man to the ground.

'We've got him,' yelled Jefferson. 'We've caught the swine.'

'"And I can no longer endure the shoddy, squalid wreck that my once great country has become,"' read Henry. 'And that's it.'

'It's very good, Henry. It should do the trick splendidly. All right; I'll be there some time in the morning.' Crichton-Potter returned to his brandy. Henry bade the last of the party workers goodnight, telling them to be back at three a.m. promptly to deliver the 'Good Morning' leaflet. He stretched wearily and poured himself a drink. For the first time since the by-election campaign had begun, he thought he was entitled to a small celebration. Tomorrow the party would win an election. Its candidate would conveniently pop off. Then the party would win another election. It was all eminently satisfactory. Henry switched on the radio, just in case there was a late opinion poll, or a political story he had missed. There was.

'A man is helping police with their inquiries into the so-called Bank Manager Murders. The man, who's not been named, is in his late twenties or early thirties. He was arrested tonight at the home of our Crime Reporter, George Cragge.'

It was, of course, a moment of great triumph for George. 'Ever since the murders began,' he reported, 'a man claiming to be the murderer has been telephoning me at the BBC. Tonight a man with a voice I strongly believe to be that of my mysterious caller visited me at my home in Talbotting. He was arrested shortly afterwards by Chief Inspector Frank Jefferson of New Scotland Yard.'

But Henry hardly heard George's exultant account of the arrest. He was frantically trying to calculate what this would do to his party's by-election chances. Would the voters forgive the Government now that the maniac had been caught? Surely the news would have come too late? Surely the Reform Party's lead was big enough? On the other hand, suppose it had not? There would be precious little mileage in bumping off Boot-Heath if he lost.

Henry was still pondering when the telephone rang. The slime seemed to ooze out of the receiver. 'This is Bamber Sampson of the BBC. As you no doubt know, the man arrested tonight in connection with the Bank Manager Murders was a Reform Party worker. What is your response?'

'I . . . I . . . I . . .' said Henry, 'that is . . . um . . .'

'Can I quote you on that?' smirked Sampson delightedly.

*

159

They even had a song for such occasions in the Reform Party:

> Our voters have gone down the plug-hole.
> Our support's disappeared down the drain.
> Our candidate's score is so puny and poor
> We've lost our deposit again

it went and it was sung lustily in Talbotting on polling night. You had to have a sense of humour in the Reform Party; there had been so many nights like this.

The joke was, however, completely lost on Crichton-Potter and Henry. The last opinion poll before the election had shown the Reform Party at thirty-seven per cent. In the event they achieved four per cent – one per cent short of the figure needed to save a deposit the party could ill afford. They were, it is true, spared the embarrassment of explaining their candidate's absence because everyone understood that he could not bring himself to appear in public following the morning's ghastly revelations. The papers were full of them. Breakfast television was full of them. Most of all, BBC Radio was full of them. George Cragge had virtually the whole *Today* programme to himself. He told the full story of the telephone calls, he interviewed a jubilant Frank Jefferson at length. He told of the police visit to Andrew James' bare bedsitter in Battersea and the discovery of an extensive collection of cuttings about the murders. He interviewed Andrew James' mother, who declared that her son was innocent and could not possibly have done such things and Andrew James' father who said he had always known his son would come to a sticky end. And the listeners lapped it up. Especially in Talbotting, where the possibility that they might have been canvassed by the maniac filled the voters with a mixture of terror and high excitement and sent them to vote Conservative in droves.

At Berwick Street on Friday morning, Henry was

besieged by telephone calls from journalists furious at George Cragge's coup and determined to upstage it. Had Henry suspected anything about Andrew James? Were the Bank Manager Murders a Reform Party plot? What were Crichton-Potter's plans for the future?

The Reform Party activists, whose telephone calls were as numerous and persistent as those of the journalists, had a settled view of that question. At about eleven o'clock, Henry was rung by the Reform Party Annual Conference organizer. The Conference was just three weeks away. 'We're going to have to make drastic alterations to the conference agenda,' he told Henry.

'But the agenda's already been printed,' Henry objected, 'we can't mess about with it now.'

'We're going to have to. Over the last twelve hours I've received forty-two motions of no confidence in Crichton-Potter's leadership of the party.'

At twelve o'clock the Reform Party's bank manager rang. He had been happy to finance the by-election campaign whilst it looked as if victory were in sight. Given the scale of the defeat, however – and more particularly its circumstances – no bank manger could be expected to countenance the continuation of Reform Party's overdraft. Immediate settlement would be welcomed.

On Saturday Henry visited Crichton-Potter at the hospital. He was still under sedation and was not expected to recover for some days. On Sunday, Larry Boot-Heath was elected Mayor of Capri.

It was a new experience for George, being the toast of the BBC. Not only was he warmly congratulated by his Editor but he actually had to see the Director General to be personally commended. He emerged from the DG's office to find the Prime Minister on his phone positively bubbling over. 'A splendid performance, my boy. I've always said you were the finest journalist in the country.'

'No you haven't.' George was extremely wary of

accepting plaudits from politicians. He had always said that any journalist who was popular with ministers could not possibly be doing his job.

'Well, not always, perhaps,' the Prime Minister conceded. 'But I'm prepared to let bygones be bygones after your marvellous performance in catching this lunatic. You've helped us to uphold law and order, restore sanity and . . .'

'And win the by-election,' said George.

'There is that of course.'

The BBC's senior management, unlike George, were delighted by the Government's frame of mind. At the following Monday's meeting of the Corporation's Board of Management, the Director General was in expansive mood about its likely effects. 'We can't do anything wrong as far as the Government are concerned. And it couldn't have come at a better time.' His colleagues entirely agreed. 'Just when we needed it,' said the Managing Director of BBC Radio. 'Just as our negotiations reach their climax,' said the Managing Director of BBC Television. 'This,' declared the Director General, 'should put thirty or forty pounds on the increase in the BBC's licence fee.' They had reckoned without Hercules Fortescue.

BBC Television's Light Entertainment Department is on the fifth floor of the Television Centre at White City. Stepping out of the lift, you may bump into Sue Lawley chatting to Frankie Howerd or Bob Monkhouse passing the time of day with Michael Crawford.

In 1986, you might also have bumped into Hercules Fortescue, television producer extraordinaire. Hercules was hugely enjoying his new role and looking forward keenly to the first edition of his new series, the wickedly satirical *The End*, which was due to be transmitted the following Saturday. Of course, being Hercules, he had stuck rigorously to the brief which the Controller of BBC1 had given him.

'I want this show to be epoch-making,' the Controller had told him. 'I want it to break new ground. I want it to be a no-holds-barred sort of show to give the lie to all this talk about satire being dead.'

Fortescue took these instructions to heart. He was aided in his endeavours by the controllers of Radios 2 and 4, who also wanted the show to be epoch-making. That was why, ever since first rehearsals had begun, they had been covertly supplying Fortescue with a list of jokes which, if broadcast, would undoubtedly break new ground. They had given the jokes a more than even chance of being broadcast by sending their contributions on paper headed 'From the Controller of BBC1'. They had not actually forged his signature, merely ending their suggestions, 'a friend', but Fortescue took the point.

Some of his subordinates, on the other hand, did not. During rehearsals in the final week, the young Assistant Producer came up to Fortescue with a horrified look on his face. 'Have you seen this script?' he shrieked.

'I am the Producer, dear boy,' said Hercules patronizingly. 'Of course I have seen the script.'

'Well, what are we going to do about it?'

'We are going to perform it,' said Fortescue loftily.

'But . . . for pity's sake, man, look at the first joke. It says: "Why will the Prime Minister never get piles?" and then it says: "I don't know, why will the Prime Minister never get piles?" and then it says: "Because he's a perfect arsehole".'

'Yes?'

'You can't transmit that!'

'My dear young man,' said Fortescue, drawing languidly on his cigar and adopting the role of The Elder Statesman of Broadcasting, 'If you intend to progress in this Corporation, you really must learn to take a relaxed view.'

'Bloody hell,' said the Assistant Producer.

Three days before the first – and last – edition of *The End* was broadcast, the Director General decided that, for once, everything in the BBC garden was hunky-dory. The following Monday he would see the Government, to be told, off the record, what increase was being granted in the BBC's licence fee. He packed his golf clubs and fishing rod and told his personal assistant that he was taking a short holiday. 'I shan't be contactable by phone, so no doubt something catastrophic will happen and all hell will break loose,' he said with a carefree chuckle.

CHAPTER
12

The immediate problem was money. Motions of no confidence at Party Conference were bad enough but, unless Henry found enough cash to keep the bank manager quiet, there would not be a Party Conference because there would not be a party. Trust them to catch the Bank Manager Murderer just when we need him, thought Henry. Not that bumping one off would make any difference; any bank manager would have said the same. The Reform Party was heavily in debt, possessed virtually no assets save its tumbledown headquarters in Berwick Street, and appeared to have absolutely no prospect of the sort of success which would bring the money rolling in. Fundraising was one of the few talents Geoffrey Crichton-Potter possessed but even he, partially recovered from his collapse, found every door closed. As a rule, whenever a crisis of this sort occurred, Crichton-Potter wandered into the City, bought lunch for a few influential friends and touched them for ten grand each at an opportune moment over the brandy. This time he could not even persuade potential benefactors to accept the lunch invitations. The City of London has views about people who murder bank managers and stockbrokers, and the Reform Party suffered heavily from guilt by association. The party had always been proud of its classlessness. 'We are not tied,' it was wont to claim, 'to big business or the unions. In the Reform Party you will find individuals from every walk of life and every sector of society.' Over the past week that boast had been more than vindicated. This was all very well, but in most people's eyes securing a 'democratic base' for one's party did not entail the view that the voice of the homicidal maniac had a right to be heard.

'It's so bloody unfair,' complained Crichton-Potter. 'I mean, of course we didn't realize the man was a killer. It's hardly our fault that he chose to join our party instead of one of the others. As far as I can gather it could have been anyone. Going canvassing just happened to suit his purpose. If only he'd joined the Tories instead, we'd have won the seat by a landslide.'

'Yes,' said Henry. 'Mind you, you told me not to win the seat by a landslide.'

'I didn't tell you to lose it by one, did I?'

'Well, you can hardly blame this one on me, can you?'

'Look, dear boy, let's not quarrel about it. I'm not blaming you. The fact is, the pair of us are in the you-know-what together. We've got to put our heads together – well, at any rate, you put your head together and I'll . . . I'll contribute what I can.'

'Can you contribute any money?' asked Henry. 'If you can't the entire party's sunk.'

'Well, I'll . . . I'll go to my club and think about it,' said Crichton-Potter brightly.

'And leave me here to sort out the mess.'

'No,' protested Crichton-Potter, 'it's just that I'm sure you'll think much better in solitude.'

He ambled into Soho and hailed a taxi to take him to the Garrick. It was a bit naughty, he realized, going to his club at a time like this. The extravagance of taking a taxi was even naughtier but there are times when a man must have his comforts.

Crichton-Potter was not the only one in Berwick Street thinking of naughtiness that morning. Lord Gate's experience with Madam Sin had been kept a closely guarded secret. He had however mentioned it to his closest friend at the House of Lords, Lord Tone. In the case of Lord Gate, being walloped by a large and powerful woman had been a considerable shock to his system and an even greater one to his backside. Lord Tone on the other hand found the idea stimulating, and men of his age are not easily stimulated. Lord Tone found himself unable to get the idea out of his mind, not surprisingly given the resemblance of his mind to a small wooden box in which something once lodged is virtually impossible to remove. Lord Tone made Lord Gate look like Wittgenstein. Whatever his intellectual limitations, however, he was at least sexually more adventurous, and what to Lord Gate recalled the image of a raging fire suggested to Lord Tone a warm and exciting glow. He obtained from his friend the address in Berwick Street.

Back at the office, his daughter sat in Reform Party Headquarters, performing the onerous task of typing endless financial appeals and the much less onerous one of opening those that were returned. Laetitia had the distinction of being the only person connected with the Reform Party who was genuinely glad to see Henry back in London. The trouble was that every time she tried to speak to him he appeared to be in the grip of an intensely strong emotion. During the Talbotting campaign, Henry had been able to forget about sex. He had had too many other worries on his mind. Back in London, however, two things conspired to disturb his hormones. The first was that the loudly in-love couple in the flat above Henry's appeared to be attempting the world copulation record with a total disregard for the tormented insomnia they caused in the flat below. The second was Laetitia.

It had the makings of a classic tragedy. Henry wanted Laetitia – oh boy, did he want Laetitia – but he was too shy and nervous to say so. Laetitia wanted Henry. But why did the wretched boy gurgle at her instead of producing coherent speech? Laetitia remembered Madam Sin's advice – take the upper hand, dominate them, it's what they want – but that only seemed to make matters worse. She still longed for the romantic dinner she had been planning since before the by-election but decided that the roundabout approach was the only hope.

'You're looking very tired, Henry,' she told him. 'Are

167

you getting enough to eat?'

Stop thinking about her breasts, Henry told himself. Take your mind off the subject. Think about this bank statement. Don't think about sex. You'll only say something silly.

'Getting enough?' he gurgled helplessly.

'Don't you get hungry?'

'Starving,' he moaned dementedly. I told you not to think about it. I know they're wonderful. I know they're rounded and perfectly shaped and . . . Henry adjusted position. He held his legs together and pressed both hands into his lap. Control yourself.

'You look awfully careworn,' cooed Laetitia maternally. 'It's like that in a political party, isn't it? As soon as you think you've got everything under control, something's bound to pop up.'

In Reform Party HQ sat Gil Slack, Chair of the Young Reformers. He was still resentfully recovering from his profoundly traumatic experience in Talbotting. That, however, was as nothing compared with the trauma he was about to experience. He rose, irritatedly, to answer the door.

Lord Tone had to admit that he was a little disappointed. Clearly, Lord Gate's imagination had inflated this woman to about five times her actual size. Still, not to worry. 'I expect you remember my friend, Lord Gate,' he said a little shyly now that the moment of truth had arrived.

'I'm afraid I don't,' said Gil.

'No, well, not to worry. It's fifteen pounds, isn't it?'

'Is it?'

'I'm sure that's what he said.' Lord Tone entered and thrust three five-pound notes into Gil's hand.

Gil's ability to catch watermelons with his nose had not improved since the by-election selection meeting. His ability to catch geriatric buttocks as they headed nakedly in his general direction was non-existent. Confronted with the warmly welcome visitors, he had fled. Confronted with Lord Tone, he fainted.

The sound of him slumping to the floor brought Henry and Laetitia from their office to see what was going on. Laetitia was furious at being interrupted just on the point of convincing Henry that what he needed was a large but quietly romantic dinner. At first she did not recognize Lord Tone. Even her own father was not immediately identifiable from that angle. After a few seconds, however, Lord Tone, intelligently sensing that all was not well, stood up. A moment later his daughter fell down.

'Please don't worry, Lord Tone,' said Henry. 'I'm sure we can settle this matter amicably.' He returned to his office and rang Crichton-Potter. 'I think you ought to get over here,' he said, 'our financial affairs have just taken something of a turn for the better.'

You'll find them in every history of broadcasting: 1922; 1927; 1936; 1955; 1986. The first is the year of the first transmission by the British Broadcasting Company; in '27 it became the British Broadcasting Corporation; 1936 saw the birth of BBC Television; In 1955, its commercial competitor went on the air.

And 1986. Those who possess video recorders still treasure every second. Those without still curse, for the BBC has done everything in its power to destroy all record of the occasion. It came in a year when the great and the good had been much given to reflecting on the Fourth Age of Broadcasting (the previous three being those of Radio, Television and Colour Television). They spoke of cable, of direct broadcasting by satellite and of pay-as-you-view, and they were all wrong. The Fourth Age of Broadcasting began – and ended – with Hercules Fortescue. In a sense it was like the assassination of Kennedy. In future years everyone in the country could remember precisely what he had been doing that Saturday night. Coming home from a party, coming home from the pub, dozing in front of *Match of the Day*, actually being on the point of going to bed. But no one who saw the beginning went to bed before the end.

169

Perceptive broadcasting critics would have known something was up from the atmosphere in the studio. Little things – like the way the Studio Director replaced the conventional 'Good luck, studio!' with a plaintive rendering of 'Abide with me'. Like the sight of the Assistant Producer weeping quietly behind the set. That this would be no conventional programme became apparent to even the dimmest members of the studio audience when Hercules Fortescue insisted on acting as his own warm-up man. All day he had been taking a particularly relaxed view. Fortescue had a theory that your importance at the BBC was measured by the length of your cigar. To that end, he had spent all day sporting a Jimmy Saville special which was so long that every time Fortescue turned round he walloped somebody. In addition, he found an outrageous pair of spectacles which Elton John had left in the loo. The frames spelled the word 'Boom', a sentiment with which, under the circumstances, it was difficult to disagree. He was very good with the performers; there was no denying that. It is of course the Producer's job to calm down his actors and tell them the show was going to be a success. For most producers this routine was merely a method of hiding their own imminent incontinence. In Fortescue's case it was genuine. 'My darling,' he would say, 'you will be wonderful. Everything will be wonderful.'

The warm-up was not wonderful. If you wanted a Producer who would take a completed script and alter not a word, then Fortescue was your man. Faced with a live audience, however, he tended to revert to his previous incarnation, since Personnel jokes were the only jokes he knew. It may be of course that what Editor ZTCG said to EIEIO about Staff Instruction No. 4064 knocked 'em cold in Broadcasting House. It left the studio audience somewhat baffled.

Nothing like as baffled, though, as the show itself left them. Years later in his cell in the Tower of London, or wherever he wound up, Jim Wilkes, ex-Controller of

BBC1, would rehearse the continuity announcement between wailing and gnashing his teeth. 'And now on One, a new style of entertainment for Saturday nights. We think you'll find it amusing. Whatever happens in the next half hour we can promise you that this show will be *The End*.' The ghastly music – 'Waltzing Matilda' on a jew's harp to be precise – and the cheeky chappie host: 'Good evening. And, in a packed programme tonight, we tell which government minister's been having it off with small children. Satanism at the All England Tennis Club. We reveal the secrets of their private hell. But to begin with: why will the Prime Minister never get piles?'

At first the audience laughter was of the nervous variety, as if they were not sure how to react. They had come expecting satire, so they were quite prepared for irreverence. What they got was certainly irreverent but it was not satire. It was straight personal abuse. Some members of the audience also had a vague notion that the BBC was required, by its charter, not to be politically partisan. Yet, in thirty career-shattering minutes, there was scarcely a mention of the opposition parties. True, there was a reference to Crichton-Potter – 'the only man in British politics with a silk shirt, a silk tie and the mental capacity of a silkworm' – but that aside, the jokes were relentlessly directed at the governing party.

Then followed a sketch, ostensibly about the National Health Service, in which cabinet ministers were depicted as urine samples being analysed by a medical expert. Then another in which the Chancellor of the Exchequer was portrayed as a tattooed skinhead mugging old ladies. Finally the song, set, in order to cause maximum offence, to the tune of 'Land and Hope and Glory':

> Land of bloated Tories
> Set Conservatives free
> Hang the lefties and liberals
> From the highest tree.

171

Wider still and wider
May our pockets get
God, who made us wealthy,
Make us wealthier yet.

'And that,' said the continuity announcer, ashen-voiced, 'was *The End*.'

The BBC's Complaints and Correspondence Department, unlike the Prime Minister, got piles. Piles and piles and piles. The head of that hapless department rang the most senior person he could find and shrieked at him, 'Who is this bloody Fortescue lunatic? We've had a thousand letters in this morning! A thousand! In one morning! And I'm short of staff! There's been a man from the newsroom due here on attachment for weeks and weeks! What! Oh, I don't know. It was being arranged by some personnel officer called . . . Here, hang on a minute.'

Some did not even bother writing letters but merely returned their television licences. Others went further, loading their televisions into their cars and dumping the sets at the doors of Broadcasting House. Of the letter writers a tiny percentage praised the show as the funniest thing since Monty Python. A significant number were genuinely outraged and demanded the heads of everyone concerned. The majority purported to be outraged, whilst secretly longing for next week's edition. Sadly, they longed in vain.

One viewer was particularly appalled. The programme did not offend his taste, however. It was impossible to offend George Cragge's taste. But it did beget an eerie feeling that someone was trying to tell him something. No one else would have associated the phrasing of the programme's introduction with a set of telephone calls. George did. Of course, it might be pure coincidence.

But George found it scarcely possible to write off as coincidence the sketch about Mr Justice Frimlington.

Twenty-five years earlier, 'Hanger' Frimlington had sent to the gallows a young man who had subsequently been shown to be wholly innocent of the murder for which he was executed. Certainly the judge's robust summing up was thought to have influenced the jury. Certainly, the judge had never shown the slightest sign of the remorse which he so regularly urged on those brought before him. On the other hand, it was twenty-five years ago. In addition, it was hardly a fit subject for humour. Since none of the other subjects on *The End* had had their comic possibilities tested out either, it fitted admirably in with the rest of the show. The sketch began with the words 'Here is the noose' and went on to depict Frimlington not as a judge, but as the umpire of a tennis match, one of whose contestants wore a black executioner's hood while the other was obliged to play blindfolded. Despite this handicap the latter was quite clearly winning the points – clearly, that is, to everyone except the umpire. When the ball dropped in, Umpire Frimlington overruled until, at length, he called 'Game, set and match'.

'But,' protested the blindfolded player, 'that ball was in court.'

'Well, let that be a lesson to you, laddie,' said the umpire. 'Never appear in court before Frimlington.'

Most viewers had no idea who Frimlington was. Indeed, the sketch was widely believed to have something to do with tennis ('I remember when I was covering Wimbledon for the *Surgical Appliance Makers Gazette*' was one anonymous comment).

But to George Cragge, it signified something else. On Monday morning George was due to appear as a principal witness in the trial of Andrew James for the Bank Manager Murders. His credibility at the BBC depended on it. Frank Jefferson's promotion depended on it. Justice itself depended on it. And the justice in question was Mr Justice Frimlington.

Yes, it might all be coincidence. It might also be the maniac telling George that an innocent man had been

173

arrested and that the true murderer's real design had yet to come to fruition.

In Scotland, the fishing had been good and the golfing better. The Director General returned from his holiday on Monday morning refreshed and reinvigorated. He was a little puzzled by having to step over television sets on his way into Broadcasting House but he did not allow that to dampen his mood. 'Good morning,' he breezed to his personal assistant. 'Good morning, good morning, good morning.' His PA took a deep breath, deciding there was no way of breaking it to him gently.

'Um, DG, the Government would like to see you.'

'I know, I'm seeing them at three about the licence fee.'

'Actually, they want to see you sooner than that.'

'Oh. All right then. When do they want me?'

'As soon as you've seen the Board of Governors.'

'What?' So much for the effects of the fishing and the golf.

'The Board's meeting in emergency session at this moment. They said you were to go straight in as soon as you arrived only . . . well, I think you'd better see this first.' She handed him the video tape of *The End*.

The Director General did not manage to sit through the entire thirty minutes of *The End*. The first ten were enough. It was not as though the Prime Minister's alleged immunity from haemorrhoids was the only reference to cabinet ministers. There were an awful lot of jokes about cabinet ministers. They ranged widely over their mental capacity, their sexual proclivities and their parenthood. The Director General emerged from his inner office pale, shaking and numb with shock. He had to be led by the hand along to the boardroom next door to his office. Facing the governors he could scarcely summon the intellectual energy to gibber. From the boardroom he had to be led by the hand to his car waiting to take him to Whitehall and to oblivion.

When he had gone the Governors continued their

calculations of exactly how many resignations the situation required. In particular, ought they themselves to resign? They rather fancied not. After all, the Vice-Chairman pointed out, they were guardians of the public interest, not programme makers. The public interest clearly demanded unequivocal expressions of outrage from its representatives and these they were happy to supply. Their shock at the programme was in most cases genuine; most of them owed their appointments to the Government. Nor did the inevitable resignation of the Director General cause them any acute distress. As the Chairman put it, to general murmurs of assent, 'I never liked the bugger anyway.'

The suicidal mood in the Director General's office on the third floor contrasted sharply with the exuberance of two men on the fourth. As he stepped from his office, the Controller of Radio 2, like the politician he was, affected a worried frown. Once inside the Controller of Radio 4's office, however, he burst into helpless fits of giggling.

'Success, old boy?' he said when he had regained his composure.

'Success,' chortled CR4.

'I say, old boy – I rather think we'd better not pop a champagne cork in this building today, what? Might not sound too good.'

'No,' CR4 agreed. 'But I'm sure we'll think of somewhere.'

'What's the most expensive restaurant in London?'

'Oh, Le Gavroche, I should think.'

CHAPTER 13

'"The resignations of the Director General, the Managing Director of BBC Television and the Controller of BBC1 are necessary; indeed, had they not been voluntary, the country would have demanded them. But by themselves, they are not enough. The disgraceful scenes we witnessed on our television screens last Saturday night testified not only to a fundamental malaise in British broadcasting but to a more widespread moral turpitude which has traditionally accompanied extended periods of Conservative government."'

'It sounds fine, dear boy,' said Crichton-Potter. 'What does turpitude mean?'

'Oh, for pity's sake.'

'Well, I don't know. I just speak the stuff.'

'Then, may I suggest' – it had been a hard morning and Henry was exhausted – 'that you just read this and stop worrying about what it means.'

'Yes, I think that'll be the best thing. Well, I must be off to my club. By the way, have you had any ideas about what I'm going to say at Party Conference?'

'None,' said Henry. 'I mean, whatever you want, really. "It wasn't my fault, honest." "I didn't know he was a murderer." Or, "I did know he was a murderer and I thought he might bump off a few Tory voters." I mean, whatever. I don't know.'

'I like being Leader of the Reform Party,' said Crichton-Potter plaintively. 'I like going on television and giving my views – well, all right, your views – about things. What'll happen if we lose this vote? I mean, I might have to . . . I could have to . . .'

'Work for a living?' suggested Henry.

'Exactly,' said Crichton-Potter. 'Ye gods, what a

thought. You'll come up with something, Henry. You always do.'

Henry sighed wearily. 'As things stand,' he said, 'you've got just one thing going for you.'

'Which is?'

'Who else would want a crazy job like being Leader of the Reform Party?'

'Oh, come on, cheer up. What are you doing for the rest of the day?'

Crichton-Potter had intended the remark to lift Henry's spirits. Instead he had touched a raw nerve. 'I'm going out to lunch,' said Henry gloomily.

'Oh, splendid.'

'With Laetitia.'

'Oh.'

'Yes, quite. Well, what else could I do? She had a terrible shock, poor woman. I thought I'd better do something to help her get over it. I mean, how would you feel if you saw your father with his b . . . well, you know what I mean.'

'Yes. Still, didn't do us any harm, did it? Got us over our immediate financial problems.'

'Er, actually, I was meaning to talk to you about that. Have you got the cheque?'

'Certainly. I should run round and pay it straight in, if I were you.'

'Well, yes, except that . . .'

'Look, what on earth is the matter? You've been in a funny mood all day. What is it?'

'Well, Laetitia has been through a highly traumatic experience.'

'Yes.'

'And doing something to take her out of it does come under the heading of staff relations, doesn't it?'

'I suppose so. Why do you ask?'

'Because I'm not taking her to a fast food joint.'

'Oh, I see. Very wise of you. Good hot Indian curry. That is the stuff.'

'Not curry, actually.'

177

'Henry, where are you taking her?'

'Um . . . somewhere a bit expensive actually.'

'Henry, where are you taking her?'

'Le . . . Le . . . Le Gavroche.'

'Good God.'

'I know.'

'My dear boy.'

'Exactly.'

Crichton-Potter looked at the miserable specimen before him. He roared with laughter.

'You see, the thing is,' mumbled Henry, 'I can't really afford it.'

'Of course you can't really afford it. Nobody can really afford it. Oh, Henry, how splendid. Oh, don't look so worried. I'm sure Lord Tone can afford it. Pay the cheque into the bank and draw out whatever you want.'

'Seriously?'

'Yes, of course. We've just had a windfall, haven't we? Go on. Enjoy yourself.'

It is a matter for debate whether one truly enjoys oneself at Le Gavroche. Dinner at Le Gavroche is a once-in-a-bankruptcy experience. The place is situated in Upper Brook Street in Mayfair in what used to be a gentlemen's club. As you enter, you are immediately aware that unlike most restaurants where the staff treat the customers with deference, in Le Gavroche it is the other way around. If you make a bloomer when choosing the wine you are likely to be told, 'Oh no sir, that would be quite unsuitable.' If you feel a little warm and decide to dine in your shirt sleeves, you will be told courteously but firmly, 'I am afraid sir must keep his jacket on.' Le Gavroche is famous and knows that it is famous. It does not in the least object if when dining there, its patrons are filled with a sense of their own insignificance.

Such an inferiority complex however had never afflicted the Controller of Radio 2. Within seconds of his arrival, the ambience had blended perfectly with his mood. The champagne glasses clinked. 'To the salvation of BBC Radio,' said CR2.

'BBC Radio,' said CR4.

'Well,' said CR2 over the *Creme de Cresson*, 'I never thought it would be so easy.'

'Are you absolutely sure we're in the clear?'

'Completely. There's nothing on paper. Only two people know we had anything to do with it. One's Jim Wilkes and he wasn't even allowed to appeal. He was told to get out of the building in thirty seconds flat and never come back.'

'I bet he's not exactly in love with us.'

'No. But so what? Even if he did write to the Chairman, no one would take any notice of him.'

'I suppose you're right.'

'And the only other person who can implicate us is Fortescue.'

'I can't see him being much of a problem. What'll happen to him?'

'Disciplinary interview, I understand. They'll probably retire him early on grounds of insanity.'

'In that case I think we might have another bottle of champagne, don't you?'

'Yes, but we mustn't get too drunk. After all we still have Phase Two to discuss.'

'Phase Two? Haven't we done enough already?'

'Certainly not. We've removed the Director General. That was part of the master plan. But now we have to, shall we say, assist, in the selection of his successor.'

'But surely,' said CR4, 'his successor's bound to be the Managing Director of BBC Radio. He's the only one who emerges unscathed.'

'But does he really emerge unscathed? I mean, from our point of view? Look at it this way. We had to eliminate the DG because he couldn't protect the interests of BBC Radio, right?'

'Right.'

'Well, would that problem ever have arisen if we'd had a strong and effective MDR? Don't you think you could have done the job better yourself?'

'Of course I think I could have done the job better myself. Don't we all? But . . .'

'Would you like the job?'

'What?'

'How, for example, would you like to be Managing Director of BBC Radio and Deputy Director General?'

'We can't possibly achieve that. Who in his right mind would make me Deputy DG?'

'I would,' said CR2 simply. 'You don't seriously suppose I plotted the elimination of the DG for nothing, do you? My dear Controller, you are looking at the next Director General of the BBC. Now listen . . .'

'Henry, you're not listening to me.' The conspiring Controllers had been so engrossed in drinking champagne and plotting ways to drink a good deal more of it that they had not noticed the young couple at the table next to them. Normally, they would at least have noticed Laetitia who was, to put it mildly, physically striking. She had by this time entirely regained her composure. It had been Henry's intention to dominate the lunch. Even Laetitia, he thought, would be subdued after her father's performance at Party Headquarters. Laetitia, however, was not in the habit of being subdued. She knew exactly what she wanted out of the lunch and was determined to get it. Part of Henry wanted precisely the same thing but the terror which invariably afflicted him in the presence of an attractive woman had struck again. Every time Laetitia tried to steer the conversation round to sex, Henry steered it away again.

He was happy enough dealing with questions about his past life. The question about how he had become a speechwriter was not easy but it was at least easier than the one Laetitia wanted to ask. 'Politics is the only thing I've ever really been interested in,' he told her. 'When I left university with no obvious prospects – it was 1977, remember, and people were just discovering that there was such a thing as graduate unemployment – I vaguely thought I wanted to be an MP. But I reckoned that you shouldn't do that until you'd made some money. So for my first job I went into chartered accountancy.'

'I can't see you in chartered accountancy.'

'Neither could they. I got fired after three months. They gave me what they called a probationer's report. I've still got it somewhere. It says: "This man will never make a chartered accountant."'

'And did you?'

'Did I what?'

'Make a chartered accountant?'

'Anyway,' said Henry hurriedly, 'after that, I got a job in advertising. That was quite fun to start with but it got boring quite quickly writing slogans about knickers. Or rather . . .'

Whilst Henry was thinking about how to extricate himself from knickers, he caught a few snatches of the conversation at the next table. What the hell was all this about eliminating the DG? Laetitia was quite right; he was not listening – not to her, at any rate. He was listening, astounded, to the admission by two BBC Controllers that they had arranged the demise of the top man in British broadcasting. Henry did not need telling that information was power. And this information could prove vital in the battle to save the career of Geoffrey Crichton-Potter.

'No, no,' said CR2 over his second large brandy, 'I'm not suggesting that we work the same wheeze twice. Anyway we can't discredit MDR without discrediting Radio as a whole. What we've got to do is to appeal over his head.'

'How do we do that?'

'By going straight to the people who choose the Director General – the Board of Governors. We have to persuade them that the time has come for a younger man, someone not associated with the present Board of Management at all.'

'But we hardly know any of the Governors. How on earth are we going to persuade them . . . are you listening to me?'

181

'Shortly after that,' said Henry, 'this job as Political Assistant came up and, well, I've been playing Jeeves to Crichton-Potter's Wooster ever since in the hope that, one day, it might lead to a seat in Parliament.'

'I'm sure it will, Henry,' said Laetitia. 'You're so good at it. Look at the way you've managed to hush up this business with my father.'

'Oh, that was nothing,' said Henry. 'It would not exactly have helped the party if it had come out that Lord Tone had been caught in a sexually compromising position in the middle of Party HQ, would it?'

The controller of Radio 4 was quite right. CR2 was not listening. He was listening to the conversation at the next table.

Lord Tone was a Governor of the BBC.

'All right, I'll support you on industrial democracy if you'll support me on the Polisario Liberation Front,' said Gil.

'OK, I think I can persuade my membership to go along with that.' Eric Swann was Chairman of the Trade Union Reform Delegation at the Annual Conference of the Reform Party, now just a week away. His 'membership' consisted, at a generous estimate, of twenty-two. The Reform Party's trade union membership was neither large nor representative. Eric Swann, however, was both large and in a sense representative of trade union leaders. His self-importance grew as his actual importance diminished. He spoke the language of trade unionism with gruesome fluency, his conduct at Reform Party Conferences calling to mind the old question: To your mother you're a captain and to your father you're a captain, but to a captain are you a captain?

'What line are you taking on the Crichton-Potter motion?' asked Gil. In reality, that was the only question about Party Conference that really interested anyone. The Reform Party's democratic structure meant that the motions for debate were chosen by an elected conference committee from those submitted by individual constituencies. This raised several problems. First, it meant that the motions submitted were largely illiterate. Second, it meant that motions had to be sent in well in advance of the conference itself, thereby robbing them of newsworthiness. There were slots for emergency motions but these were brief compared with the time allocated to motions written months earlier. The third problem was that, in order to be fair to the different constituencies, the committee was faced with the task of compositing – that is, of making one policy motion out of several on the same subject. The resulting motions were always unreadably long; one celebrated motion on housing could have been published in several volumes had anyone been foolish enough to publish it. The chief difficulty, however, was to avoid boredom. The motions submitted had a depressing tendency to agree with each other and to restate what had been Reform policy for years. Consequently, not even the Party's activists could summon much enthusiasm for the actual debates, whose results were totally predictable. Reform Party politics thus gave the lie to those who contended that politics are about policy and not personality, for it was the issue of personality, in this case the future of Crichton-Potter's leadership, which set the adrenaline pumping in a way that, strange to relate, local government finance did not.

Even though the party's opinion poll rating had sunk to five per cent, an all-time low, Crichton-Potter still had his supporters. In most cases these were ordinary party workers who had either met him at a party function and thought what a nice chap he was or, more probably, had Seen Him on Television. This section of opinion would vote for Crichton-Potter because it had heard of him. Television had recognized his existence and so, therefore, did they.

Normally, this group in the party was enough but the signs were that, on this occasion, it would not be. The Reform Party MPs wanted a change and they, after all, were the ones who had to face the voters. The Reform

Party's local councillors wanted a change for they too saw elections looming. Far larger was the group of Reform Party activists who, whilst holding no elected position, dreamed of winning one day. That in many cases they had dreamed that way for years did not alter the fact that, for them, Crichton-Potter's genial image had been an asset and was now a liability. Add to these the ideologues who had never liked Crichton-Potter anyway and who wanted the party to be led by a radical firebrand and there was a clear majority in favour of the motion that 'This Party has no confidence in the leadership of Geoffrey Crichton-Potter.'

The Chairman of the Young Reformers was predictably one of these. For the first time since becoming involved in Reform Party politics, Gil saw a chance of turning it into the revolutionary vanguard he wanted it to be. The occasion offered a unique chance for his distinctive rhetorical talents and he intended to make the speech of the debate, even if it meant cultivating the support of one as boring as Swann.

In Le Gavroche, Henry, too, was anxious to escape. As well as the physical frustration induced by Laetitia's presence, he was suffering professional frustration. He had no intention of engaging the two Controllers in conversation in the middle of a restaurant but he was frantic to get back to Party HQ and communicate with Crichton-Potter. Laetitia was frantic to take him back to her flat, a prospect which filled his sexually repressed nature with terror. He ordered brandy upon brandy in an attempt to avoid the ghastly moment. Indeed even the champagne-swilling radio supremos had left before Henry and Laetitia did. In the Controller of Radio 2's eye was a twinkle of mischievous triumph. He was already planning the conversation he would have with Lord Tone.

Realizing that more brandy would render him incapable of talking to Crichton-Potter or anyone else, Henry eventually leapt to his feet in a jerky and inelegant fashion. 'Right, let's go,' he barked.

'To my place in Hampstead,' breathed Laetitia huskily.

'To Party HQ in Berwick Street,' Henry told the taxi driver.

'New End Square in Hampstead,' Laetitia told the hapless taxi driver.

'Berwick Street in Soho,' said Henry to the irritated taxi driver.

'New End Square.'

'Berwick Street,' said Henry firmly.

'But Henry . . .'

'I've got work to do.'

'But Henry.'

'The Leader's future is at stake.'

'But Henry.'

'*Work.*'

'Oh, piss,' said the daughter of the Fourth Earl of Tone.

On the opening morning of Andrew James' trial, the phone rang at George Cragge's house in Talbotting. The star prosecution witness had been suffering severe qualms about his role in the affair. The phone call confirmed them.

'George, you've got it all wrong.'

George's breathing quickened. 'I know I have. Look . . .'

'I don't want innocent people to suffer, George. Only guilty people. Like bank managers. And stockbrokers. And . . . but that would be telling.'

'Look, will you give yourself up?'

'Of course I won't. Not until we've finished – I mean . . .'

'What do you mean "we"?'

But the voice was gone.

Throughout his taxi ride to the Old Bailey George's brain was in a whirl. He did not believe that the calls were a hoax. And the caller had said 'we'. So there were two of them. At least. He had to have time. Slowly, he decided his strategy.

'Frank,' he told the detective outside No. 1 Court, 'I want to report this trial.'

'You can't report a trial in which you're one of the main prosecution witnesses, you silly bugger.'

'But this is going to be one of the trials of the century. I'm the best bloody crime reporter in the country.'

'George.'

'It's true, Frank, and you know it is. I've got to report this case.'

'And I tell you you can't. The BBC will have to send somebody else. You've got to stay outside the court until your turn comes.'

'Bollocks,' said George.

'Now look . . .'

'Oh, all right.'

George paced up and down outside No. 1 Court at the Old Bailey. It was a flaming cheek. Here was the man who had reported the Moors Murderers' trial, the Cambridge Rapist trial, the Nilsen case, the Yorkshire Ripper; here was a man who had stood shoulder to shoulder with the SAS at the Iranian Embassy; the man who wandered through dead bodies at Harrods reporting the foul work of the IRA. And they would not let him inside the nation's principal criminal court. It was enough to drive a man to . . . well, at any rate to look at his watch and notice that it was almost eleven o'clock in the morning. Just round the corner George could have the pick of the Fleet Street pubs. He was bound to meet somebody he knew in Fleet Street; he'd worked there for years after all. In any case George was feeling let down. After Andrew James' arrest, he had been the toast of the BBC. It was a fat lot of use, however, being personally congratulated by a Director General who promptly got fired. It was enough to make a man look at his watch and realise it was five past eleven. Moreover, ever since watching *The End*, George had been faced with an acute moral dilemma. So George did what he always did when faced with an acute moral dilemma; he looked for the nearest pub.

CHAPTER
14

The identity of the new Director General was not a matter of major concern to George. Like most BBC employees, he regarded senior management changes as a spectator sport whose impact on his life was negligible. On the other hand, George shared the widespread view that the new top man would be the current Managing Director of BBC Radio and the prospect did not please him. MDR's frequently expressed view that radio suffered from a surfeit of news was in itself enough to make any journalist shudder. More personally, there had been the time when George had hijacked the Managing Director's car. It had been a perfectly reasonable thing to do. A report had come in of an armed robbery in Bayswater. George had rushed out of Broadcasting House to find a car outside complete with a chauffeur. Naturally, he had jumped in and given the necessary directions. Equally naturally, MDR had sauntered out of the building carrying his golf clubs and looking forward to the weekend. The ensuing conversation had been brief.

'What are you doing in my car?'

'Going to Bayswater.'

'I'm the Managing Director.'

'Bollocks, blossom.'

It was enough to make a man realize that ten minutes of valuable drinking time had already been wasted.

Inside Court No 1, the Attorney General, Sir Haviland Perrywit, rose imperiously. 'Ladies and gentlemen of the jury. These last few years we have, you may think, witnessed a variety of grim killings indeed. There have been murders of politicians. There have been murders of prostitutes. There have even,' he paused for effect, 'been murders of policemen. A sobering tally.'

'But you may well think that a killer who chooses the ordinary innocent bank manager strikes at our very way of life.'

'My bank manager keeps striking at mine,' growled Defence Counsel.

'Bank managers,' continued Sir Haviland, 'are symbols of quiet respectable English life. Like village inns, like country churches, like . . .'

'Garden gnomes,' suggested Defence Counsel to the evident amusement of at least one juror.

'Does Defence Counsel wish to make a submission at this stage?' rumbled the Bench.

'No, Your Lordship.'

'Then would he kindly reserve his observations until later.'

Denis Bradley, QC, had had tougher assignments then defending Andrew James but he had to admit that he could not remember when. He reckoned he had two things going for him: the nature of the evidence, which was purely circumstantial; and the nature of Sir Haviland Perrywit who suffered from a singular incapacity to distinguish the majesty of the law from the majesty of himself. His other failing, to judge from the climax of his opening remarks, was that he sounded as if he were heavily addicted to alliteration.

'This heinous roll-call of roguery,' he boomed. 'This monstrous melée of murder,' he thundered. 'This odious orgy of execution will be laid firmly, incontrovertibly and beyond doubt' – he paused to thrust a stubby finger at Andrew James – 'at the door of the defendant.'

'And one for yourself,' said George Cragge, in the bar of the Tipperary.

Frank Jefferson was a good witness, there was no denying it. He was composed, factual and free from affectation. He was the kind of policeman who makes a tremendous impact on a jury because he is so patently honest. Denis Bradley decided to confine himself to a few simple questions.

'Chief Inspector, had you ever seen my client before apprehending him in Talbotting?'

'No, sir.'

'But you had a precise physical description of the man you were looking for?'

'Well, no sir, but . . .'

'We know that notes were found on the bodies of the various victims, each typed on a particular typewriter. Has this typewriter been found in the defendant's bedsitter?'

'No, sir.'

'Has any conclusive evidence been found?'

'No, sir.'

'A number of different weapons were used in the murders. Have any of these been found in the defendant's home?'

'No, sir.'

'Thank you, Chief Inspector.'

Sir Haviland Perrywit thought of re-examining the police officer but decided against it. He rose to announce his second witness.

'Call George Cragge.'

'Call George Cragge.'

'Call George Cragge.'

'They'll be calling last orders before we know it,' said George Cragge, in the bar of the Tipperary.

It is not known whether, when W.S. Gilbert wrote:

> It knows no kind of fault or flaw
> And I my Lords embody the law

he had Mr Justice Frimlington in mind, but he might well have done. A small waspish man with large ears, he was known to the Old Bailey hacks as Mr Spock, partly because of physical resemblance and partly because he shared with the *Star Trek* hero a belief that emotions were fit only for the lower orders – notably the friends and relatives of those on the receiving end of his brutal sentencing policy. He had a good brain, no heart and a passion for Egg McMuffin and Large Fries. He also had a robustly intolerant attitude towards witnesses who did not turn up.

'*Solvendum ambulando*, Sir Haviland?'

'My Lord?'

'Shall we find some way of getting around this problem? Where is Mr Cragge?'

'I don't know, my Lord.'

'Then you had better find another witness.'

'But Mr Cragge's evidence is vital, my Lord.'

'Then kindly produce him, Sir Haviland. Is this the Mr Cragge from the Wireless Corporation?'

'Yes, my lord.'

'Ah,' said the judge. '*Bibendum sibi semper est.*'

'My Lord?'

'The bugger's never sober,' translated Denis Bradley, who was beginning to enjoy the turn the case was taking.

'My Lord.' Sir Haviland was sweating with embarrassment. 'I fear I must ask for an adjournment.'

'I fear I must refuse. Sir Haviland, you have five minutes to produce your witness. After that the trial will proceed without him.'

In the Tipperary, George was proceeding quite happily without the trial. 'And the hangman said, "Hanging's money for old rope." And fell through the trap door,' he declared cheerily. 'Ah, those were the days. It's taken all the fun out of covering murder trials, the abolition of capital punishment.'

The events of the morning had convinced Frank Jefferson that there were some witnesses who needed to be hanged, whatever one did to the criminals. He knew where George would be. At least, he knew in general but not in particular. He was not in the George. He was not in the Bell. He was not in the Devereux. The look on Jefferson's face as he trudged from pub to pub seemed to say, 'If you're not brainless and legless before I find you, you will be afterwards.'

In court, Denis Bradley rose. He had no intention of letting Sir Haviland off this one. 'My Lord,' he said, 'may I point out that this trial is being conducted at considerable public expense, that the jury have come here perhaps at great inconvenience to themselves . . .'

'All right, all right, Mr Bradley,' said the judge, 'I'm perfectly well aware of the inconvenience. Sir Haviland, you will call your next witness.'

'My Lord, I really cannot understand it.'

'I can,' said the judge, who had a surer grasp of the psychology of the crime reporter than many of his Old Bailey colleagues. 'We will now proceed.'

The doors crashed open. 'This town ain't big enough for the both of us, judge, honey,' said Big George Cragge. He swaggered up to the bench and made as if to draw his imaginary revolvers. Jefferson assisted him with excessive vigour into the witness box.

George did not exactly take the oath but he did not exactly affirm either. First he attempted 'Peter Piper' and when that did not work, he had a shot at 'She stood at the door of Burgess's fish sauce shop welcoming in'. That was not a howling success either but it was clear that it was all the court was going to get from George in the way of a commitment to the truth, whole and nothing but.

'*Hic dies vere mihi festus*,' observed the judge drily.

'I shouldn't wonder,' George agreed.

'Horace,' said the judge.

'Horace who?'

'*Et in Arcadia ego*, my Lord,' concurred Sir Haviland.

'Bollocks,' said George.

Sir Haviland began his questions. It was not a cross-examination; it was a livid examination.

'You are Mr George Cragge?'

'Has anybody ever told you what a complete prat you look with that thing on your head?'

'You are employed,' said Sir Haviland, through gritted teeth, 'by the British Broadcasting Corporation?'

'He was yesterday,' grinned Denis Bradley. 'I

191

wouldn't give much for his chances tomorrow.'

'Kindly answer the question,' snapped the judge. 'Are you employed by the British Broadcasting Corporation?'

'I'm very glad you asked me that one, Horace,' said George. 'I am indeed employed by the BBC. And of all the bastard employers . . .'

'Mr Cragge,' Sir Haviland rushed on gamely. 'Were you at home on the night of October second?'

'What's it to you?'

'I beg your pardon?'

'I wasn't out with your wife, if that's what you're worried about. Even I'm not that desperate. Have you seen his wife, Horace?' asked George, turning to the judge. 'She plays in the second row for Hull Kingston Rovers.'

'Mr Cragge!' Sir Haviland bawled. 'Were you involved in the arrest of a young man claiming to represent the Reform Party?'

'Can't remember,' said George. 'Anyway, what's all this Mr Cragge stuff? I remember you at the Law Society Dinner dancing on the table.'

'Mr Cragge.'

'The phantom clog dancer of Claridge's, we used to call him,' George explained helpfully to the jury.

'Mr Cragge, will you kindly confine yourself to answering the question?'

'Bollocks,' said George.

'Were you called on by a political canvasser?'

'Very possibly. I expect I was too pissed to notice.'

'Do you know I have the power to fine you for contempt?' demanded the judge.

'You hum it, I'll play it.'

'Mr Cragge.' Sir Haviland decided to abandon his prepared questions about the telephone calls and to come to the nub of George's evidence. 'Would you kindly look at the defendant and tell the court whether you positively identify him as the young man who called on you that evening?'

George looked at the judge. Then he looked at Sir Haviland. Finally, his bloodshot eyes came to rest on his ex-friend, Frank Jefferson, at whom he stared with quizzical solemnity.

'Never seen him before in my life,' he declared defiantly. Whilst the jury pondered the significance of this remark George mounted the ledge of the witness box and stood with his back to the court.

'Back flip and turn,' he announced. 'Difficulty, six point eight.'

'The question is,' said the Chairman of the BBC's Board of Governors, 'do we go for somebody outside the Corporation? Is that the best way to restore confidence after the . . . er . . .'

'The deluge,' said the Vice-Chairman.

'Quite. Now that all discussion of the licence fee has been deferred, our first priority must be to find someone who will restore our standing with the Government. Someone who can convince them we're not a bunch of subversives after their blood.'

'Well, we could go for someone from the commercial sector,' suggested one Governor.

'Or somebody not connected with broadcasting at all,' suggested another.

'I don't think we need go as far as that,' put in a third. 'But what I would say is that we should look for a candidate in no way connected with the recent débâcle. Now what that means, surely, is that we can't choose anyone from the current Board of Management.'

'I quite agree,' said the Vice-Chairman.

'Oh, absolutely,' said the Chairman. 'They're all tarred with the same brush. But what do you suggest?'

'It seems to me,' said Lord Tone, 'that not only do we need to get away from the existing Board of Management. We also have to go outside the Television Service. After all, Radio hasn't been involved in our recent troubles.'

'Quite so.'

'Indeed, it could be argued that Radio has been most unfortunately compromised by its association with television.'

'It certainly could.'

'So what I propose is this: why not go for somebody from Radio Directorate of proven competence – not the Managing Director, he's on Board of Management – but one of the controllers.'

'You know, that could be the answer. Did you have anyone in mind?'

'I was thinking of Controller, Radio Two. He's got the track record and the right sort of image. I think he would make an admirable DG.'

'I think that would be a very good idea. In fact, if I may say so, it's the best idea' – what the Chairman meant was the only idea – 'you've had in your entire time as a Governor.'

Lord Tone smiled modestly. So it should be. CR2 had made him rehearse it often enough.

In the boardroom, it was CR2's morning; in his office it was not. In the first place, he had so little to do that he had been reduced to listening to his own network, which always put him in a bad mood. In the second, he was telephoned by the Political Assistant to Geoffrey Crichton-Potter, MP, phoning from the Reform Party Conference in Brighton.

'Good morning,' said Henry affably. 'Did you enjoy your lunch in Le Gavroche?'

'I beg your pardon?'

'Splendid place, Le Gavroche. Good food, fine wine, excellent conversation.'

'What?'

'Especially your conversation. Fascinating, all that stuff about the Director General getting fired.'

'Oh. Ah.'

'And how you helped to bring it about.'

'Ah. Oh.'

'It'll go down a treat when the Leader of my party

tells everyone about it in his speech.'

'What do you want?' CR2 sighed. He could recognize a political bastard when he saw one. He had done every day of his life.

'That's much more like it. I mean, I don't want to cause you any trouble, dear boy. I just want your help. We've got a little problem. I think you might be of some help to us.'

'Very well,' said CR2 huskily.

'Splendid. I'll phone you later with the details.'

Never before had CR2 understood people like George Cragge who needed a drink at ten in the morning. He did now.

But George was not in his office. If he felt like a drink, he was not getting one. He was getting his Editor instead.

'You pillock. You tit. You damn idiot.'

'I said I was sorry.'

'Sorry. They're only going to acquit the bastard thanks to you.'

'But surely they've got a watertight case.'

'Tight, yes. Water, no.'

'Well, all right, so I had a few.'

'A few what? Crates? You've done it this time, mate. There's nothing I can do to help. You're for the high jump. There'll be no talk of attachments this time, baby. It'll be the chop.'

'But . . .'

'There's no point in butting. You're finished. This thing you're doing tonight – the annual dinner of the Crime Reporters, or whatever.'

'What about it?'

'You may regard it as your last assignment for the BBC. How can I employ a crime reporter who's been responsible for the acquittal of a mass murderer?'

'And now,' said the fun-loving presenter on cuddly Radio 2, 'here is Billy Joel to sing "An Innocent Man".'

CHAPTER
15

The Reform Party's annual seaside knees-up was every political journalist's favourite conference. The Trades Unions Congress was all right but there was something frankly unedifying about trade unionists en masse. The Labour Conference was ghastly. Not only did Labour activists hate the media – at the previous year's conference Bamber Sampson had been physically attacked – but they were passionate, unyieldingly humourless and in many cases teetotal. The Tory Conference resembled a cross between a garden party and a convention of the Soviet Communist Party. Its delegates, or representatives as they called themselves, were, unlike their Labour counterparts, utterly uninterested in politics. They came to worship their leader and, as any political reporter will tell you, there are few more terrifying sights than that of a Tory ovating.

The Reform Party Conference, on the other hand, was fun. Partly this was because the party was impotent. The socialists argued bitterly about whether Labour Conference motions had been betrayed by Labour Governments. For Reform activists this question did not arise and delegates were therefore free to adopt policy motions which were whacky, whimsical or stark staring bonkers. The whole conference had a zany feel. In the evenings the delegates would rush from one fringe meeting to the next, from the Radical Alternatives to Sex discussion to the Legalize Cannabis rally, only to find that the guest speaker had been unavoidably detained.

Not that the party was free from bores and lunatics; there were plenty, many of them like Boot-Heath concealing under their professed abhorrence of cruelty to animals an unwholesome desire to be cruel to their fellow human beings. But in general it was almost impossible to treat Reform politicians with total seriousness and, to their credit, they did not do so themselves. The debates, the caucusing and canvassing and furtive whispering seemed like a good-natured parody of the political process.

In addition, the party's alcoholic capacity was second only to that of the Licensed Victuallers. Everyone looked forward to the Reform Conference – the journalists, the activists, the MPs and the Leader.

Except this year. This year Crichton-Potter had slunk into Brighton with a doleful expression and a grim sense of foreboding. In his suite at the Grand Hotel, he donned his jacket, morosely eyeing Bamber Sampson on his television and doing his sums. According to one straw poll, declared the ace reporter gleefully, of the 1010 delegates attending, 650 would support the motion of no confidence. 'My prediction is that Mr Crichton-Potter is going to lose this vote by a mile,' he smirked.

'You bastard,' muttered Crichton-Potter.

Henry came in. He hated Party Conferences. The activists who attended regarded him as an apparatchik whose purpose in life was to thwart their democratic will. They were of course perfectly right.

'Five minutes to midnight,' he remarked glumly.

'No, it isn't. It's twenty to five.'

Henry raised his eyes to the ceiling. 'The *Today* programme's doing a profile of you in the morning. I'm told it will be highly favourable.'

'How on earth did you manage that.'

'Well,' said Henry, 'never mind how I managed it. Let's just say I swung it. It should help, anyway.'

'Will it be enough?'

'No. But I'm getting Lord Tone to chair the debate.'

'But the man's an imbecile.'

'I know.'

'But he'll be a hopeless chairman.'

'Precisely. With him in the chair the debate will be

such a shambles that the entire motion may get discredited. Anyway, Lord Tone has good reason to be friendly to us.'

'So?'

'So he will exercise a fitting discretion in his selection of speakers. In short, none of your opponents who can string two words together has a chance of being called.'

'Will that be enough?'

'No. Unfortunately all of your parliamentary colleagues have declined to speak.'

'Why is that unfortunate?'

'Because they're such a useless bunch of morons that in comparison with them even . . . well, what I mean is . . .'

'Yes, thank you, Henry. I see what you mean.'

'Well, anyway,' said Henry, changing the subject rapidly, 'there's always the speech.'

'What on earth am I going to say?'

'I haven't actually decided yet.'

'This is the most important speech of my life.'

'And of mine,' said Henry. 'I think I may have to work on it all night. Tell you what. I'll dictate it on to cassette. Have one of the copy typists drop by early in the morning and she can type it straight off the tape.'

'Fine. You obviously won't be needing me this evening, will you?'

'How do you mean, I won't be needing you? I assume you'll be going round trying to drum up support.'

'Well, not exactly.'

'What are you doing then?'

'Well, I thought . . . I mean, if I'm going to lose tomorrow, I may as well enjoy myself tonight, what?' That had always been Crichton-Potter's philosophy of life and he saw no reason to change it.

'Oh, really,' protested Henry.

'But it's a dinner at the Mansion House.'

'Hell's bells.'

'The food will be splendid.'

'Bugger the food.'

'The wine will be superb.'

'Sod the wine.'

'The Governor of the Bank of England will be there.'

'Oh, give him my regards.'

'In fact everyone will be there. I'd be letting the side down if I didn't go.'

'Letting the side down? Damn it, man, wouldn't you rather stay here and fight for your political life?'

'Frankly,' said Crichton-Potter, 'no.'

If Geoffrey Crichton-Potter looked forward to the Governor of the Bank of England's Dinner, the Economics Correspondent of the BBC did not. His fellow guests would insist on talking about economics and that, as far as Max Parker was concerned, was incompatible with a civilized human existence. The dinner was an annual ordeal which his editor obliged him to endure on the grounds that it was important for the BBC's relations with the financial community. That was true, but what he did not seem to grasp was that such relations would have been better served by Parker's absence. It was not in Max's nature to remain silent for an entire evening but he had managed it on this occasion every year since the 'gaffe of 72' when he had entirely misunderstood an invitation from the German Finance Minister to give his impression of the e.m.u. Every time this event came around, Max was desperate to find an excuse not to go. In the small bar of the BBC he found George Cragge.

George had walked out of more jobs than he cared to remember but he had never before been fired. His first reaction had been shame. His second had been depression; he was a crime reporter, after all, and what else could he do? By the time he bumped into Max, however, these had given way to rage. How dare they fire the best crime correspondent in the country? How dare they? Full of resentment and Jameson's, George Cragge vowed revenge.

'They aren't going to forget me in a hurry,' he fumed.

199

'I'm sure they aren't,' said Max soothingly.

'I'm the best bloody journalist in the country.'

'Of course you are.'

'I'm the best fucking journalist in the world.'

'Very possibly.'

'Am I going out with a whimper?'

'I imagine not.'

'You imagine bloody right, mate. I am going out with a bloody great bang.'

'Good for you.'

'Except,' said George, becoming depressed again, 'how can I? I've got to go to the Crime Reporters Dinner. How can I tell them I've been fired? I'm the President of the thing. How can I admit I've been sacked?'

'You think you've got troubles,' said Max, 'I'm going to the Governor of the Bank of England's Dinner.'

'Sod the Governor of the Bank of England.'

'Quite so.'

'I want to misbehave. I wanna do something outrageous. How can I do that in front of my mates?'

'How can I do anything else when the Chancellor of the Exchequer asks me about exchange rates?'

'I wanna show . . . what did you say?'

'The Chancellor. And very possibly the Prime Minister. And a bunch of economics professors.'

'A sort of pillocks' convention.'

'I couldn't have put it better myself.'

George looked at his old sparring partner with a mischievous grin. 'Max, old son. Wouldn't it solve both our problems if I went . . . and if you . . .'

'But what would the Editor say?'

'Oh, lots and lots. He'll talk about it for years by the time I've finished.'

Max thought about facing his Editor. Then he thought about macroeconomic management and Third World debt. Then he bought two more whiskies and winked at his friend. 'You're on, mate.'

*

200

'A man more sinned against than sinning.' No, that wouldn't do it. 'Of one who loved not wisely but too well.' No, that certainly wouldn't do. Henry paced his hotel room with growing despair. Which other politicians had made comparable cock-ups? No, that wouldn't prove fruitful, they all had. Well, which other politicians had had to give major speeches after such cock-ups? Henry thought of Macmillan after the Profumo affair. 'I know that I have acted honourably; I believe that I have acted justly; and I hope that when it has heard my account, the House will consider that I have acted with proper diligence and prudence.' Well, that might offer some ideas. Nobody could doubt that Crichton-Potter had acted honourably; he was, thought Henry, too stupid to do anything else. Nor was his sense of justice in question. The problem arose with that last bit. How much prudence was appropriate for a small political party starved of funds and workers when somebody showed up bearing not only cash but a desire to become a member? Certainly one asked for some general endorsement of party principles but did prudence compel one to add, 'Oh, and by the way, are you a mass murderer?'

The other problem was that the outcome of the trial was as yet unknown. That one of the prosecution's principal witnesses had given evidence whilst somewhat non-compos had opened the possibility of an acquittal. If that happened it would look very bad if Crichton-Potter's speech appeared to assume Andrew James' guilt. Yet an assertion that the matter was sub-judice was technically correct but scarcely likely to swing votes.

Perhaps, thought Henry, he had better concentrate on Crichton-Potter's record. List his achievements and allow them to speak for themselves. Henry's mind ranged over the party's electoral standing, its finances and the size of its membership. He pondered the intellectual coherence of its policies and the cogency of its arguments. Perhaps he had better not concentrate on Crichton-Potter's record. He picked up his cassette recorder and put it down. He paced the room, stepped outside and paced the corridor. He stepped back into the room and paced that again. He poured himself a drink, thinking that might help, and, thinking it might not, poured it back into the bottle. It was going to be a long, hard night.

At the Mansion House, the official residence of the Governor of the Bank of England in the City of London, George Cragge looked, at eight thirty p.m., as if he had already had a hard night. In spite of his appearance, however – he was an aggressive shade of puce – he felt marvellous. If heads had turned at the announcement, 'Mr George Cragge', he had not noticed.

'Which one of these geezers is the Governor, then?' he demanded.

'Sir Carstairs, sir,' said the Master of Ceremonies imperturbably, 'is over there.'

'Baldy, over there?'

'That is Sir Carstairs, sir,' said the MC, a little less imperturbably.

'Funny-looking bugger, isn't he?' said George, and sauntered up to him.

'Hello, Gov, sunbeam.'

Sir Carstairs D'eath was indeed funny-looking. He was completely bald, he wore a monocle and he had inherited the family nose – a prize specimen, even by the standards of the D'eaths' noble conks. He saw no reason to doubt that he was the most important man in England and, very possibly, in the world. You could sum up Sir Carstairs from the briefest of glances. 'There,' you would say, 'is a man who is not used to being called "sunbeam".'

'I can't believe I have had,' he allowed an icy pause, 'the pleasure.'

'Haven't you?' asked George, staring at the Governor's wife. 'Well, somebody has, to judge from the twinkle in her eye.' He gave Lady Carstairs a vigorous slap on the back. 'No, seriously,' he said, 'I'm George.

202

Max couldn't come. But don't worry about that now. I expect you're busy. We'll sink a few sherbets later. Oh,' added George, handing the Governor his coat, 'you couldn't do something with that, could you?'

The Most Important Man in England looked as if there were something he would dearly love to do with it but George was off exploring the room. The dinner was a small, select affair. About twenty-five people stood around, in threes and fours, discussing the great economic questions of the day. In the middle of the room was a magnificent fish tank in which swam small but brilliantly coloured fish. George Cragge was delighted by the fish tank. The fish tank seemed to suggest infinite possibilities to George Cragge.

In the meantime, however, George saw a fellow guest to whom he thought he might owe an apology. Other people might have thought so too.

'Sir Haviland and Lady Perrywit,' said the MC.

Sir Haviland had scarcely stepped across the threshold when he spotted one of the least successful prosecution witnesses in legal history.

''Ere, Avelock, sunbeam,' it bawled.

'What is that man doing here?' Sir Haviland hissed.

'Hello, old son,' said George. 'I've come to say I'm sorry.'

'Sorry? When you've singlehandedly destroyed the case against the most dangerous and subversive . . .'

'Oh, yeah, yeah, yeah,' said George. 'No, I wanted to apologize for being so rude. Look.' George put his arm around the Attorney General. 'I'm sorry I called you a cunt, you cunt. OK?'

'Caviare, madam?' And very good caviare it was too, both red and black. George advised against it, however.

'I don't think I would if I were you,' he told Perrywit.

'Are you addressing my wife?' asked the Attorney General. He was trying to remember the law concerning duels at dawn. He could not remember anything which specifically forbade them.

'I shouldn't let her touch that stuff if I were you,' said

George. 'It'll set her farting like Red Rum after Oats Vindaloo.'

If George were not exactly top of the popularity ratings at the Mansion House, he was at least in somebody's good books. Crime reporters en masse are not an edifying sight but they have one redeeming feature; they do not talk about economics. Instead the conversation at their annual dinner in one of Soho's sleazier restaurants was of editors long deceased, of editors still living, of drunken editors and illiterate editors. Max Parker was in his element. For the fifth or sixth time, he toasted George Cragge and continued his anecdote, 'If I've told Ronnie Biggs once I've told him a hundred times . . .' The alcohol was abundant, the guests were loud, and the food, although plain, was plentiful.

'This soup,' said George, 'is congealed wombat piss.'

'It is *Vichysoisse St Germain*, sir.'

'It's disgusting.'

'Well, really, sir.'

'There is nothing the matter with the soup whatever,' snapped Dominic D'eath, who was seated opposite George. 'The man's an idiot.' The Governor of the Bank of England's brother turned to Sir Haviland Perrywit beside him. 'How hopeful are you of securing a conviction, in view of the not inconsiderable hindrances which have been placed in your path?'

'Touch and go. I must admit, I had hoped your own identification would have been more positive.'

'I could not swear positively that the young man I saw at the House was the same one I saw in the dock. I could hardly lay claim to a certainty I do not possess.'

'No, no. I quite see that.'

The guest on George's other side was eating hungrily, like a condemned man. Geoffrey Crichton-Potter had decided that, if this was the last smart dinner to which he was ever invited, he might as well make the best of it. He gratefully accepted the offer, therefore, that, having finished his own Vichysoisse, he should take

George's as well. His neighbour was clearly in an ebullient mood and, to be fair to Crichton-Potter, he was mercifully free of the self-importance and snobbery which affected his fellow guests. He had decided early on that he rather liked George Cragge.

'Well,' said George matily, always glad to make a new friend, 'your party's in the shit, then?'

Crichton-Potter grinned ruefully. 'Yes. I'm rather afraid it is.'

'Will you win the vote tomorrow?'

'Shouldn't think so.'

'Still,' said George, 'bollocks, eh?'

Crichton-Potter smiled. That, he felt, was precisely the spirit and he raised his glass. 'Bollocks,' he concurred wholeheartedly.

Sometimes Henry's brain worked better when he was in bed and sometimes not. On this occasion not. On the bedside table the cassette recorder was running but as yet no speech had been written. Henry was torn between 'I ask no special favours of this conference' and 'I beg this conference on my bended knees'. Henry put his head in his hands. So sunk in despair was he that he did not notice his door open. What happened next was, he was sure, an illusion. What he thought he saw was Laetitia Tone stark naked. The mirage appeared to speak. Something about not being prepared to wait any longer. Clearly he was hallucinating. There is, however, something undeniably corporeal about a grab for the genitals.

George Cragge shifted in his chair. Crichton-Potter was all right, but apart from him George reckoned that pillocks' convention had been an understatement. George could feel it welling up inside him. He was going to do something. He did not know what but he knew he was going to do something.

It was the Beef Wellington that did it. 'There is,' said the Attorney General, 'something direct about Beef

Wellington; it possesses a forthright Englishness.' So did George Cragge and he marched – well, at any rate, managed a semi-dignified lurch – up to the Governor of the Bank of England. 'What do you mean serving toad-in-the-hole?' he demanded. 'Look, let's ditch this muck and send out to the Chinese.'

'This is insufferable,' said Lady D'eath.

'You're telling me, love,' said George. He picked up Sir Carstairs' dinner and stared at it distastefully. 'You don't want to eat that.'

'Give me back my dinner.'

'It's horrible.'

'Give me back my dinner.'

'Not bloody likely. Call that dinner?' In support of his opinion, George swung back and threw the Governor's Beef Wellington into the fish tank, where it was hungrily received.

Dominic D'eath rose to his feet, a look of venomous, almost demented, hatred on his face. 'Throw this man out. Throw him out! Sir Haviland, kindly assist me.'

But Sir Haviland was not listening. He rose from his seat with a grim look on his face and crossed to the fish tank. Five fish had tasted the Governor's dinner and five fish lay immobile at the bottom of the tank.

'This meat,' said Sir Haviland quietly, 'has been poisoned.'

Dominic D'eath was quick but George was quicker. A flying tackle brought the Bank Manager Murderer down two feet from the door. His attempts at resistance crumpled when Crichton-Potter sat on him, an experience that not even long years of imprisonment would erase from his mind, or for that matter his features.

The smirk on Frank Jefferson's face when he was summoned to the scene was a record-breaker, even by Frank's benign standards. No matter that his daughter had divorced the bassoon-player in favour of an alternative spoon-player from Islington. No matter that his son, Bakunin, had written home to say that he was

206

changing his name by deed poll to Slobadan Zivoyina-
vitch. His promotion was as secure as the prisoner.

'As I suspected from the first,' he purred.

'No you didn't,' George told him.

'Well, not actually from the first. As a matter of fact,'
he confessed to Crichton-Potter, 'I thought it was you.'

Crichton-Potter chortled. 'You can get a long way in
politics by pretending to be stupid,' he told them. 'But
I didn't do it that way. You see, I actually am stupid.'

'Then I thought it was your speechwriter.'

'Well he may have had the motive,' said Crichton-
Potter, 'but I keep him so busy I don't think he's ever
had the opportunity.'

'Then I thought it might be Madam Sin,' said
Jefferson.

'And I thought it was the Controller of Radio 2,' said
George.

'But you solved the mystery.'

'Well, I wouldn't put it like that exactly.'

'Yes you did. You spotted that the one-pound coins
suggested the Bank of England.'

'Did I?'

'Of course you did. Then you examined the first
letters of the surnames of the murder victims. And what
do they spell? Cain and Abel. You see, the significance
of "the mark of Cain", as it were, had nothing to do with
a prostitute in Soho. It had to do with the hatred of one
brother for another.'

'I never spotted any of that. I only met Dominic
D'eath for the first time tonight. I did spot one thing
about him you didn't, though,' George admitted.

'Which is what?'

'That he was a complete cunt.'

'There was that, of course. Well, see you in court. You
will turn up this time, won't you?'

Frank Jefferson returned to the Yard and the praise
of his superiors.

In Soho, the crime reporters were finishing their annual

dinner as they always did, by visiting the ladies of Soho. From the third floor of a house in Berwick Street came the cry: 'When I was Education Correspondent of the . . . ouch!'

In a hotel room in Brighton a young couple slept a deeply satisfied sleep. Beside them the cassette recorder waited patiently until the copy typist collected it at six a.m.

In Rome, Larry Boot-Heath became President of Italy.

And from the Mansion House emerged George Cragge and Geoffrey Crichton-Potter, arm in arm. They were halfway down the street before George suddenly stopped and reeled back to the dining room. Crichton-Potter had eaten too much to match George's pace. When he arrived, George was swinging from a chandelier over the fish tank. 'Triple somersault, double flip and turn,' he told his new friend. 'Difficulty: Two hundred and twenty-seven.'

Statement by Dominic D'eath of Eaton Square to
Chief Inspector Frank Jefferson given at
New Scotland Yard October 1986.

I have always hated my brother very deeply. I am more academically gifted than he and it is fair to say that he combines mediocre talents with a peculiarly obnoxious personality. In spite of my obvious superiority he has always obtained preferment. His accession to one of the most illustrious posts in England caused my fluid intention to murder him to solidify and take shape. The advantages of murdering a series of unremarkable bank managers were twofold. First, the public's lack of moral sense about such people would render the killer a kind of Robin Hood figure whom it would not be possible to pursue too vigorously. For my realization of the second advantage, I pay tribute to Miss Agatha Christie. Her book, *The*

ABC Murders, is based on the principle that if you wish to commit one murder, it is well to commit many, in order to foster the illusion that a homicidal maniac is at large. I therefore confess to all the crimes known as the Bank Manager Murders. I typed the letters found at the scenes of the crimes. The telephone calls to Mr Cragge were made, at my behest, by my girlfriend, Miss Kelly Sharpe, upon the deepness of whose voice you earlier remarked. She has acted in collusion with me and found it easy to impersonate a young man. It was her idea to plant scripts on an inexperienced BBC producer, in order to make it clear to George Cragge that Andrew James was not the killer. It was never my intention that an innocent young person should suffer for my crimes. My hope in helping the police was to throw them off the scent, not to suggest a false one. I attempted the murder of my brother whilst Andrew James was in custody in order to clear him. I apologise to him and pay tribute to Mr George Cragge for bringing me to justice.

Dominic D'eath

CHAPTER
16

In the New Conference Centre at Brighton, Geoffrey Crichton-Potter was grinning so widely in his place on the platform that some observers feared that the smile would meet behind his ears and cause his head to fall off. It had been a wonderful morning. First, the *Today* programme had presented a glowing profile of him, culminating in a wildly exaggerated account by George Cragge of Crichton-Potter's role in catching the murderer. Second, the capture destroyed the reason for the vote of no confidence. Third, the debate had opened with a speech by Gil Slack. Every time he had attacked Crichton-Potter he had been hissed and he had left the rostrum, the booing ringing in his ears, to find that his chair-ship of the Young Reformers was to face a vote of no confidence. Finally Crichton-Potter was happy because he had the speech in his hand. He hoped Henry had let rip.

Henry had.

The speech began quietly enough, aside from a reference to the lumpiness of hotel beds which the audience took to be lighthearted banter. After a few minutes, however, a change came over Crichton-Potter. His eyes grew wide, the sweat poured off him, his voice rose and fell in a strangely suggestive rhythm and the whole conference became aware that this was no ordinary conference address.

'I'm fed up with looking at it,' roared Crichton-Potter. 'I'm sick of thinking about it. I want to get my hands on it and I want it now. And I don't just want it once,' he thundered, silencing an incipient swell of applause. 'I want it again. And again. And again.

'I am going to ask once and once only: will you marry

me?'

'Yes,' roared the conference.

'Will you spend the rest of your life with me?'

'Yes,' roared the conference.

'That's lovely,' bellowed Crichton-Potter. 'That's wonderful. That's exactly where I want it. Not down there! Up there!'

It was not only the delegates who were rapturous. So were the papers. 'Potty Goes for Gold,' said the *Express*. 'Government or Bust for Reformers,' said the *Mirror*. 'Mr Crichton-Potter,' declared *The Times*, 'has set his party's sights on full participation in a coalition.'

Only the *Sun* sounded a dissenting note. 'What the hell was he talking about?' it demanded, suggesting that it had a somewhat shrewder idea than its colleagues. It was, however, a minority voice. 'A politician of potential Cabinet rank' said one commentator, and that was the majority view.

At the celebration dinner that night, to mark Henry's engagement to Laetitia, a double toast was drunk. 'To us,' said Henry to his fiancée, 'and,' he added with a wink to his political master, 'to us.'

George Cragge, Director General of the BBC, swigged his champagne out of the bottle.

'You are,' the Chairman told him, 'just the man to restore the Government's confidence in the Corporation.'

'Too right, mate,' George agreed. 'Hang on a minute, squire; a few executive actions to implement.' He picked up the phone and dialled Bamber Sampson. 'Bamber, me old son.'

'Hello.'

'What sort of journalist says, "I predict Crichton-Potter will lose this vote," eh?'

'Well . . .'

'I'll tell you what sort. A complete prat. You're sacked.'

Then he telephoned the Controller of Radio 2. 'My

mate Geoffrey Crichton-Potter says you've been up to some funny business.'

'Well . . .'

'It hasn't changed my opinion of you.'

'Oh, good.'

'Because I always thought you were a prat. You're sacked.'

Finally he telephoned Hercules Fortescue. 'I'm letting you off your disciplinary interview.'

'That's wonderful.'

'No it isn't. Staff Instruction Number One: you're sacked. Prat.'

'Right, your worship,' George told the chairman, 'now get this.'

Champagne had never really agreed with George; he was a beer and whisky man. For his fourth executive action, George Cragge, Director General and best crime reporter in the world, threw up over the Chairman of the BBC.

Mr Andrew James of Mysore Road, Battersea, London SW11 went home without a stain on his character. On the doormat were letters from several bank managers begging for his account. The coincidence of being in the vicinity of the first murder had given him the idea. The experience of the by-election and the law courts should provide the material for plenty more Number One hits. Some of it had been unpleasant, of course, but if one were to write socially relevant lyrics, one had to be where the action was. Because Andrew James knew that the way to deal with bank managers was not to get angry, but to get rich. And, in his capacity as Ma in Razzmatazz, the hottest property in rock, Andrew James reckoned that he was going to get very rich indeed.